She's
No Angel

S0-AGJ-072

Also by Janine A. Morris

DIVA DIARIES

She's No Angel

JANINE A. MORRIS

Dafina Books

KENSINGTON PUBLISHING CORP.
http://www.kensingtonbooks.com

DAFINA BOOKS are published by

Kensington Publishing Corp.
850 Third Avenue
New York, NY 10022

Copyright © 2007 by Janine A. Morris

ISBN-13: 978-0-7582-1306-8
ISBN-10: 0-7582-1306-9

First Kensington Trade Paperback Printing: October 2007
10 9 8 7 6 5 4 3 2 1

Printed in the United States of America

*I dedicate this book to
my twin brother, Jason Antwon Morris.
Rest in peace.*

Acknowledgments

I thanked pretty much everyone in my debut novel, *Diva Diaries*, but there are a few people I must acknowledge again, and some new people that I need to acknowledge as well.

Frank Iemetti . . . I have been blessed not only to know you but to call you a friend and mentor; you are one of the most real and humble people on this Earth. Frank, I can't thank you enough for being such a source of reality from my first day in radio until now. You have never forgotten about me, and I will never forget about you.

My baby and best friend, Ahmad E. Meggett ("My Air"). You make every day easier. Being able to share the days of this life with someone I truly love makes me feel like one of the luckiest women in the world. You're my friend before anything, and I love you . . . with every beat of my heart.

My family—Carolyn Morris, Julius Morris, Tashah Bigelow, Julius "Jewlz" Morris Jr., Alex Bigelow, Hamilton and Tylah Bigelow, and Leila Morris . . . Don't know what I'd do without you. Mommy,—you're my idol . . . I just hope I never fall short of the strength you have.

My second family—Ma and Dad Meggett—I couldn't be more thankful to know you and I hope your son and I end up to be just like the two of you. Rashard and Leslie—Congrats on the wedding and many, many years of happiness. Rashida, Kai and the twins, many blessings. Thanks for all the love, I love you all . . . and I hope Ahmad and I have a relationship that resembles the one you share.

My buddies of the Fab 5 . . . Sytieya Mann, Derica Carty, Rene Hylton, Nicole Lytle, and our honoree member Mona Thompson . . . I love you all so much and they need to stop letting us loose out there. Friends are some of God's little treats and treasures, I'm happy we enjoy them. Ebony Esannason—we STILL got it going on, and always will . . . Can't tell you how much I love you girl. Alicia McFarlane and Kim Grant, when we graduate from law school we are going to be unstoppable. (Alicia—I truly hope you know that you have a blessed heart and you are a great friend to me and others, I'll always love you for being you.) Diandra Ortiz, Tenille Clyburn, April Debartolo, Dreena, Kimberly Pena, Vanessa Quinonez, Martha Cuellar, Tamanisha Miller, Nicole Bigelow, Darnell 'Snap' Childs, Sammy Martin, and Jessica aka Pookie. . . . old friends and new friends. what would life be without them. Craig "Speedy" Claxton (CB) ☺ and Ira "Bo" Miller: a decade and counting—nothing but love for you both. (Royal Toya in Maryland, thanks for the help.)

Selena James, my editor . . . Thanks for the patience and brainstorming. Karen Thomas, thanks for everything and for being real. Sarah Camilli, my agent—thanks for the advice and support this year. Candice Dow, for being not just a true friend but an author that I can call on for advice and strength when I need it most. Daaimah Poole, an inspirational author and friend, thanks for the motivation to hustle. Adeola Saul, my publicist—thanks for being my friend before business. Jessica McClean at Kensington, thanks for everything especially being the person to always keep it real, Gigi, my webmaster and friend—thanks for everything and for being beautiful in and out.

Michael Baisden, Fatman Scoop, DJ Clue, DJ Envy, Shaila, Kay Slay, Miss Info, Julie Jones, Flex, Donnell Rawlings: thanks for the support and love on and off the radio. Serena Kim and Benjamin Ingram-Meadows at *Vibe Magazine*, Alicia and Noni at *Jolie Magazine*, Datwon Thomas at *King Magazine* . . . Thanks for the support. Heather Covington, thanks as well for all the big ups.

Jeanine McClean at MBK Management, Helen Demoz at Def Jam, Cheryl Singleton at Warner Music, James Brown and Sherise Malachi at Sony, Jay Brown at Def Jam, Joe Riccitelli at Jive, Mike "Hollywood" Kyser at Warner Music, Karen Rait and Dave House at Interscope, Sean Pecas at Def Jam and the other real people in the music business . . . Thanks for keeping it balanced.

Mona Scott-Young, thanks for believing in me and my projects. I look forward to everything we have in the works, and I know Monami will make it a blockbuster success. Qianna Wallace and Spice Greene—thanks for working with me, it's been a blast. I hope this won't be the last.

All the book stores and book clubs I truly thank you for your time and support. Carol Mackey at *Black Expressions*, thanks for loving *Diva Diaries* and showing it and myself so much love and support. Last but not least to every person who picked up my debut novel *Diva Diaries* with the bright pink cover and took the time to sit inside my mind with me for over 400 pages of reading—(in the words of my hero Oprah), "I celebrate you."

Chapter 1

Charlene Tanner began to tense up at the sight of him kneeling down. Her eyes instinctively followed him as her lips curled up in a smile. Her heart was beating a million beats per minute, or at least it felt that way. Although he hadn't said a word Charlene seemed to know exactly what Isaac was about to do.

A cool wind blew through the trees, but Charlene was heating up inside. Her palms were sweaty and she was hoping it wasn't grossing him out. On the inside, she wanted to burst out and cry, but she also felt faint, like she was going to pass out. Charlene's mind was racing with a million thoughts, whereas Isaac Milton seemed to be focused on one thing. In her mind she wished that she could pause time, even if just for a moment, just enough time to gather her thoughts and actually enjoy the moment. Like most women, Charlene had imagined this moment in her life way too many times, but now that it was here she had no idea how to act or what to say.

She began to calm down some and focus on Isaac. As she looked into his eyes, she could tell that he wasn't down there just making noise, he was really pouring his soul into it. After she realized how sweet and romantic his speech was, she started to wonder how to react. She didn't know if she should just shout out, "Yes, yes . . . yes," like in the movies, or say "Of course" with a lot of excitement to switch it up. Or even better, say something really sweet, like "Gladly I will," in a soft tone. She tried to figure it out before he finished his speech, which all seemed like a blur because she was so anxious. Hearing his speech kind of tickled her, though. It wasn't humorous, it was just that she had always hoped that when she was proposed to, he (whoever he was) would find some unique way to tell her he loved her and that he wanted to marry her. Not that she'd thought about it often.

Despite her attempts to concentrate, all that had registered thus far was when he said, "I know you are the one for me . . . I look forward to raising kids with you and spending every night with you and waking up every morning with you." There was a lot more said, but for the most part it was all stuff she had heard before in some movie somewhere, or seen on a greeting card. Still, it sounded great just the same; especially with him on his knees and the shiny 2.5 karat diamond rock in his hand. She hadn't heard similar words from Isaac before, and that gave them even more meaning, hearing them from him for the first time. Isaac wasn't the emotional, sappy kind of guy. Even though their relationship had been going pretty well, she wouldn't have thought that he wanted her to be his wife.

Charlene felt like she was in the middle of a fairy tale, as if she was Cinderella putting on the shoe for the prince. Her heart was filled with joy and love for the man that was now half her height as she looked down at him. From the look in his eyes she felt like he meant every word. She wasn't sure if he noticed from the look in her eyes or not, but she was touched by everything he had to say. She hoped that he didn't change his mind.

Finally he was done. He could have only been speaking for

a few minutes, but it felt like forever. Charlene almost wished it didn't have to end; she wished she could have held on to the moment forever. Unfortunately, it did and it couldn't. It was showtime again. She was back on, back to reality. The last sentence out of his mouth was, "I couldn't live without you, and I would love if you can spend forever with me. Will you marry me?"

"Of course I will . . . of course," she replied in a soft tone.

Isaac removed the ring from the black velvet box and slowly placed it on her left ring finger. The ring was absolutely beautiful. He had made a great choice. How could she say no to such a piece of art even if she hadn't wanted Isaac? The center was a blinging flower-shaped diamond, and the sides were like petals, made of platinum gold with diamond-encrusted dewdrops. The band was simple and plain with an engraved stem going around it. Charlene loved flowers, so his personalization of the ring made it that much more special to her. Her eyes had welled up as soon as she spoke her response, and as he put the ring on her finger a tear rolled down her cheek. It was a joyful tear. She was happy, and still in shock that this was happening. She knew she would start crying, she was actually surprised she hadn't started sooner. As soon as he'd placed the ring on her finger, he looked up and noticed the tear. He stood up and he hugged her, and she felt an overwhelming rush of emotion. He held her tight and she held him just as tight in return.

Isaac and Charlene were engaged. She couldn't believe it. She still felt like there was so much that she wanted to say to him before accepting the proposal. She wanted to ask him if he was sure he wanted to be her husband; she wanted to ask him if he would feel the same love for her no matter what. It was too late, though, and besides, it wasn't the right time. She would just have to find out the answers to her questions over time. So she just enjoyed the moment as they stood there hugging one another. Tears continued to run down her face as he held her tight in his arms. She almost didn't want him to let her go, mainly because it felt so good but more because she didn't want the moment to end.

She tried to make sure there was nothing more she should say or do. She was thinking it over in her mind, to make sure that she had done everything as she should have. She didn't want to walk away and then later realize that there was something she had missed. She thought about stories she'd heard and movies she had watched, and nothing came to mind. She didn't want to come off as rude or unappreciative, so she was hoping that by saying "of course," hugging him and crying it was more than enough for Isaac. When she thought about it, she realized it didn't really matter, anyway. She couldn't make sure she put on a perfect performance, because it was his show. Regardless of how many times she played it over in her mind and tried to get it just right, Isaac was the director, actor, screenplay writer and producer of this show. Hell, he was even the casting director. She was just the actress he cast to play the role. She realized there was no perfect script for this, she was just happy that she had gotten the part. She was madly in love with Isaac. She had no doubts in her heart when she told him yes, and that was as perfect as it could get for her. He held her for a few seconds longer as he rubbed her back some and she squeezed her arms around his.

No one was around but Charlene and Isaac. They were standing by a pond, their pond, actually. The pond that they had come to on quite a few dates, and whenever they were in a rough patch they would go sit by it. Over time their essence filled the air there. As soon as they stepped out of the car, inhaling the moist air always refreshed them and rejuvenated their relationship with one breath. Charlene knew that he couldn't have chosen a better location.

He had let go and looked her in her eyes and glanced over her face. It was still soaked from her tears. Her eyes were still watery and her breathing was still a tad jittery. He began wiping her tears and drying her face with his bare hands. It helped some, and some it just smeared over her face. They both giggled at the mess they were making.

"Let's get out of here, so you can go tell everybody . . . I know you're dying to," he said playfully.

She giggled a bit. Although she wanted the moment to last some more, he was right. She couldn't wait to tell her mom. Besides, she knew if they stood there any longer, she wouldn't be able to look him in his eyes much more. She would be too afraid that he would be able to see through her. That he would see the guilt—the guilt from knowing that there was a discussion she had never had with him, although she had meant to. She had always hoped to have the discussion before this time came. However, for now she didn't want to think about that. She wanted to enjoy this moment as if she had.

Chapter 2

"Oh, my goodness!" Jasmine screamed into the phone as Charlene told her the news.

Jasmine was sitting on her couch curled up in her lavender cotton pajamas watching *The Office* when her phone rang. Two towns over, Charlene was still fully dressed sitting on Isaac's loveseat with her cell phone, smiling from ear to ear as she shared her breaking news story. Charlene would have died if she hadn't gotten Jasmine on the phone right away to tell her.

Jasmine was one of Charlene's closest friends, they'd known eath other since A. B. Gail Junior High School. They had been through a lot together, and they had celebrated and suffered a lot together. Jasmine was twenty-eight years old and she had been married for only a year to her high school sweetheart. Jasmine was one of Charlene's few childhood friends who had graduated from high school. Since high school Jasmine had been working at clerical jobs to make ends meet, and raising her baby girl, Serenity. Jasmine was also one of the few friends from Charlene's youth that she still kept in touch with. Jasmine, like Charlene, tried her best to live a better life than they had once had and to become a mature adult woman. They wanted to live a life for the future, and not remain stuck in their past. So, although they were at somewhat different stages in their lives, they always had that understanding and bond with one another. It was the bond of reform; they both knew where they had been and where they were trying to go—or, rather, what they were trying to leave behind.

Charlene and Jasmine had often discussed marriage in their friendship, but it was usually about Jasmine's, and about Charlene's belief that hers would never exist. So, without hesitation, Charlene had to call Jasmine to tell her that she was finally one step closer.

"I know, I know . . . It still feels like I'm dreaming," Charlene said back.

"How is the ring?" Jasmine asked.

"It's beautiful . . . looks like it's about two or three karats," Charlene said, holding out her hand to look at the rock Isaac had bestowed upon her.

"Uh-oh . . . Souky, souky now . . ." Jasmine said.

"Be quiet," Charlene replied, blushing. "The ring is designed like a flower with petals, it is the most gorgeous ring I have ever seen," Charlene said while still staring at her ring.

"Aww, that's nice. Especially since you love flowers," Jasmine added.

"Yeah, I know. I'm still kind of in shock."

"Charlene's getting married . . . go 'head, go 'head . . ." Jasmine started to sing some silly song.

They both laughed. Charlene would have loved to sit and talk about every detail of the night, but she had to rush Jasmine off the phone so she could tell her family and call one other friend to brag. It wasn't actually bragging, most of Charlene's friends were either married or engaged, but she had to let people know she was "validated" as well. Some of it was because at Charlene's age, when everyone is getting married and engaged, it messes with your self-esteem when your ring finger is still bare. However, some of it was from Charlene's own low self-esteem. She hadn't completely become comfortable and stable as the woman of worth she was trying to be. So Isaac hadn't only made her romantic dreams come true tonight, he helped make her whole. And Charlene was eager to spread the news. As soon as there was a moment of silence she told Jasmine she would call her back because she had to call her mother.

Charlene had kicked off her shoes and buried her feet into the couch in Isaac's living room. She looked over at the pewter picture frame that held an 8 x 10 picture of the two of them at Great Adventure. She looked over and smiled as she dialed her parents' house number. Most people would be surprised to find out that Charlene had any esteem issues. She was all of twenty-six years old, and full of youth and energy. She had the body of a runway model: tall and slender with long legs. She was light-skinned with a beautiful face that most people would say was made for television. High cheekbones with naturally rosy cheeks. She was gorgeous and she knew it, her looks got her by a lot in life. Yet with all her beauty, what made her feel like a true woman was sitting there on her hand, her left ring finger, to be exact. So, as she waited for one of her parents to answer, she sat there in Isaac's living room still glowing with joy.

Isaac was in the bathroom by then, but prior to that he was walking around the apartment doing his own thing. She had noticed him on the phone at one point, probably with his boy Surge, who he called Ser-Hey, telling him that he'd gone ahead and done it. But Charlene was too distracted to be nosy enough to overhear the conversation they were having. Usually Charlene played close attention to those kinds of things; she was always concerned with what his friends and other people said about her. She knew it was a level of paranoia, always being the subject of a rumor. She was always wondering if and what Isaac would find out.

Charlene's mom, Ann Tanner, answered on like the third ring, and Charlene could tell from her mother's voice that she already knew why she was calling. Initially Mrs. Tanner tried to sound normal just in case it hadn't happened yet. Then Charlene took her out of her misery, and told her that, yes, she was officially engaged. Between a mixture of tears and pure joy, she congratulated Charlene and told her how excited she was. Charlene also found out how and when Isaac had asked her parents for her hand in marriage. Charlene was happy that her mother was still alive to share this moment with her. It made her think about how happy Isaac's father would be to still be here to share it, too.

After she spoke with her mom, dad and sister she called her friend Tiffany, one of her cousins and another girlfriend. Charlene didn't have a lot of friends, most of them she had lost touch with over the last few years, but there were still a few people she was dying to tell. They all started asking her questions as if she had the wedding all planned out. Charlene had to explain this wasn't a save-the-date call, the proposal had only happened a couple hours ago. She realized then that most ladies don't brag so much and call everyone they know only moments after, so she decided to stop making calls.

As for the wedding, of course, like most women there were some decisions she'd already made. For instance, summer or fall wedding, short or long engagement, big or small wedding. These are things most girls think about and figure out when they play with their Barbie dolls as a little girl. Usually the color scheme is figured out as well, and some other basics, but not every detail of the wedding. Charlene answered the questions with a basic "I will let you know" response, along with whether she would be subjecting them to an ugly bridesmaid's dress.

Isaac had gone upstairs to watch television, Charlene assumed. As she held the phone in her hand she sat for a moment to reflect, digging her toes into his plush black and light gray carpet. She thought about the entire night as well as all the nights to come. She tried to imagine married life with Isaac and leaving the single life for good. She thought about moving out of her not-so-great place, and living in the beautiful and lavish condo that she was sitting in. She tried to think about it all, all the bright sides of the new life she would live. Soon her daydreaming brought her back to the present. She let out a little giggle when she thought about a question that Tiffany had just asked her: "So, are you going to invite Lacy?"

"I don't know, but I doubt it," Charlene replied.

"That's going to be an interesting situation . . . You may have to just suck it up."

"Yeah, I know, but we will have to figure it out. I just don't want any issues that day."

"Well, it all depends who is paying for it," Tiffany said, laughing.

"That's the truth," Charlene replied.

A few moments later, Charlene was hanging up the phone and laughing out loud. *That girl Tiffany, she ain't never lied,* Charlene thought to herself with a smile. Lacy was a friend of Isaac's that Charlene didn't approve of. She had no justification for her feelings other than her own jealousy, so she was kind of stuck dealing with their friendship. Although Charlene was sure it wasn't only in her head that Lacy wanted Isaac, she knew that there wasn't much to say without evidence. So for years she sat back and played a little game with Lacy, the one that females play when they communicate in a way that no one else is supposed to see. Tiffany's point made her think even more about all the drama that was bound to surface about the guest list, exes and friends that each of them would object to. Charlene wished she could expect otherwise, but she knew that jealousy and pettiness would definitely surface when it was time to work on the list. Charlene was hoping there wouldn't be too many skeletons surfacing along with it.

The longer Charlene thought about it, the more she wondered what she was thinking telling Isaac she would marry him. For a second Charlene thought to herself that she should run now, and give the ring back before her secrets exploded in her face. That was easier said than done, because Charlene knew that more than anything she wanted to live happily ever after with Isaac. Still, Charlene knew her life's track record, and she knew that whereever there's happiness for Charlene there lurks some amount of drama. If it wasn't the guest list it was going to be something else, so she had to brace herself for the ride.

Charlene had sat for about fifteen minutes thinking about all of that. The thought of the overall blend of guests for a quick second tickled Charlene. She started to think about just how funny this wedding was going to be. Her folks were so different from Isaac's she knew they would have quite an interesting wedding. His family members were extremely reserved and, aside from Charlene's parents, quite a few in her family were a tad more on the wild side. Charlene knew there would be some that would get along just fine; but there were a few jokes that definitely wouldn't get laughed at and a few strange looks that would be made. Charlene knew her wedding planning would be a handful and that she had her work cut out for her.

By the time she got off the phone and finished daydreaming about the wedding guests and made her way into the bedroom where Isaac was, he was already in his boxers, ready for bed. When she walked in the room, he looked up at her and smiled. *Damn, was he fine,* she thought to herself. She knew why she was the luckiest woman alive. He was brains and beauty . . . and body. He was brown skinned, 6'3", with a tight medium build. He had a chiseled chest with close to six-pack abs, more like a four-pack. He had a low caesar, which he kept bald most of the time. He had one deep dimple in his right cheek when he shared his beautiful white smile. His facial hair was minimal and well trimmed, and he had these juicy lips that she just loved. Man, did she feel lucky that he was her man, she thought as she crawled in the bed next to him. At first he just looked over at her and then glanced back at the television, but then he realized that it was a special night and he didn't want her to start complaining. So he turned over toward her again and started looking into her eyes.

"Did you tell the world?" he asked.

Laughing, she replied, "No, only half . . ." and then she thought about it and added, "Did you tell anybody?"

"Yeah, I told K.D., and I had already told most of my family before I asked."

"Well, don't you need to let them know I said yes?"

"Please, they know you said yes."

"Oh, really?" she asked. "And how do they know that?"

"Because it's me . . . And because who could turn down that ring?" he asked, laughing. He had better start laughing, because it was their engagement night and she didn't want any problems.

"What happened to the time when y'all would be scared and nervous that we would say yes?"

"I don't know, I never proposed before . . . I don't remember that time."

"Oh, you're real funny tonight, aren't you?"

Aware that their sweet night was capable of going sour real soon, he started to try to fix it up. He got closer to her and placed his arm around her waist.

"I'm only joking, baby. They knew you would say yes, because they knew what we have is real, and that I love you and deserve you as my wife and that we are going to have a beautiful life with about six snotty-nosed kids," he said, starting back up.

"Yeah, OK," she replied with a slight laugh.

Charlene didn't even want to think about kids right then and there. That stress was bound to seep up on her sooner than later, but she would rather it be later.

"Well, we can get started on some of them now," he said as he slipped his hand up her shirt to cup her breast.

She smirked. Maybe not for the sake of having the six snotty-nosed babies, but she couldn't say she wasn't all for partaking in some newly engaged sex.

Chapter 3

The engagement party was quite impressive. Especially for a girl that grew up in Mount Vernon, New York, with very little money. Who would've thought Charlene would grow up to be the well-rounded woman she was? A few years ago she graduated with her associate degree in management. Since then she had been working as an office manager for an advertising agency. She had a half-bedroom apartment on the border of Mount Vernon and New Rochelle, and she had just purchased a 1999 Altima. The past few years of Charlene's life had been prosperous and turning better, all starting when she made the conscious decision to improve her life. She had some regrets that she would have to live with forever. Still, she had already begun fixing what was within her power, and what was out of her control she tried not to stress over. In addition to all the other accomplishments, almost even more impressive to her was that she had managed to win the heart of Isaac.

Isaac was a twenty-nine-year-old, picture-perfect, finance manager for a Fortune 500 company. He had his master's in finance, and was considered to be one of the most promising executives in the field in New York. He was born and raised in Scarsdale, New York in a very nice suburban neighborhood.

Although it was basically a hop and a skip from Charlene's neighborhood, hers was definitely the other side of the tracks. His parents were both professionals. His father was an accountant and his mother was in banking. Isaac went straight to college from high school. He took up accounting in college, pledged a fraternity and started on his path to success.

After working a couple of years he purchased a two-bedroom condo in Palisades, New York, overlooking the river, which was the hometown of an even higher class of folks. Although Isaac was one of the few of his kind there, he fit right in, especially with his 2007 burgundy Mazzerati with the peanut colored leather interior parked out front. The inside of his condo looked just as good, if not better than any of his neighbors'. He had dark gray micro fiber furniture in the living room, with black and white photos all over the place. His dining area was colorful with hues of burgundy, blue and green. The kitchen was stainless steel, accented with black. He had walnut furniture in his second bedroom, and marble floors and tabletops in his home office. There was even a mini NASDAQ ticker in the office. Isaac wasn't one for sloppy seconds; he definitely enjoyed the finer things in life.

The women from around Charlene's way became envious of her as she started getting her life together and decided to go to college at age twenty-one. As trivial as it was, they would have smart remarks when they would see her dressed for her office job, wearing slacks and loafers or pumps. Sad part was that they weren't jealous because she had on nice clothes, but rather that she had a job to wear them to. Most of them did nothing all day, had a couple of kids and had no direction in life. Most of them had been her friends growing up, but Charlene didn't think they were still growing. They had made some smarter decisions than Charlene had, and some that weren't as smart. Charlene definitely almost got stuck in their same rut, but her not-so-smart decisions had become too much for her and she had to get out. Eventually she moved out of her parents' house, but that's when the girls really started to hate her and have a lot of negative stuff to say. It was the separation, it was the last step of growth beyond them and they couldn't take it. Their back turning only made it easier for her to exclude most of them from her life, and start a new one.

The last year that she lived at home with her parents before she got her own place was when Isaac started coming around. That had been interesting. The neighborhood girls were green-eyed and lurking without even trying to disguise it. They were trying to get all in his business, and trying get close enough to throw themselves at him. They were hoping to catch his eye long enough to get some. It was easy for them to see that Isaac wasn't just one of the around-the-way guys that they were used to. They could tell by his clean-cut look and stylish clothes that he was something special. For most of the girls clocking, the car and money made him even more special. What was bothering them the most though, was that they were all wondering how Charlene did it, how she got a guy like him. Most of them assumed that it probably had a lot to do with Charlene's looks. She was definitely considered one of the physically advantaged. They were always jealous of her caramel-brown complexion, her beautiful head of shoulder-length dark brown hair, her hazel-colored almond-shaped eyes, her full lips that Angela Jolie would trade in for, and her body to die for. You would think she had a personal trainer. She was 5'6", 129 pounds, a 32C with JLo's junk in the trunk. She had the looks of a chick in a rap artist's video, but instead she was Isaac Milton's trophy girlfriend, and the girls would rather she not be the latter. Those were the signs that these girls weren't really her friends. Misery loved company, and miserable was all that she had been all those years. So with that reality, and her fear that they might one day get a chance to put the wrong information in Isaac's ear and ruin it all for her, she knew she had to move away—and quickly.

Regardless of her looks, for Charlene there were many more benefits that came with having Isaac in her life. She had someone to motivate her to be more, and he always knew what steps she needed to take to be successful at things. Whether it was how to write a better resume; get a better job, or make presentations at business meetings, he knew what to tell her to wear, do and say. He boosted her self-confidence and gave her hope in life. There was a time that she didn't think she would ever get a man to marry her, and he made her feel like she was living a whole new life. Charlene was elated that he saw some worth in her as well, and that they were celebrating their relationship.

The engagement celebration was held at Charlene's aunt's house out in Huntington, Long Island. She had a beautiful, spacious six-bedroom house with amazing landscaping. A majority of the guests were outside sitting poolside and along the patio. Coworkers, family and friends were socializing with one another and enjoying the ambiance. Most of Charlene and Isaac's family and friends had come, bringing the number up to approximately one hundred. They had drink specials for the night that were Charlene and Isaac's favorites: Watermelon Martinis and Rémy Martin XO. For entertainment there was music from Aunt Abby's jukebox, card games, pool and swimming, with some couples games planned for later on. A photo album was in rotation filled with pictures of the couple, which was sparking a lot of conversations.

The affair was pretty much going as planned and there was a sense of real joy and happiness in the air. Of course, there was the occasional emotional scene, and some people got all excited at the sight of the ring. As Charlene had expected, her mother started hugging her and crying the second she stepped foot in the door. It was like Ann Tanner never had thought the day would come or something, but if so she wasn't the only person to doubt it. It could have been that she was happy that Isaac was finally going to make an honest woman out of her daughter, but whatever the reason it was the happiest Charlene had made her mother in a long time. Her dad reacted similarly, minus the crying. David Tanner, a more reserved and quiet older man, didn't often show many emotions.

Charlene was happy that Isaac had been smart enough to go to him to ask for her hand in marriage, otherwise the whole thing would have been null and void in his eyes. Her dad was definitely old-fashioned, as was her mother. A few aunts and uncles got emotional as well, but it was all joyful. Charlene's sister, Paige, on the other hand, was way too excited to cry. She just jumped up and down when Charlene and Isaac walked in. She hugged Isaac and repeated at least three times how thrilled she was. Charlene knew her sister was genuinely happy for her, but she also knew Paige, like everybody else, was in shock that Charlene had managed to snag herself such a good one.

Isaac walked around the party greeting the guests and taking in his congratulations and "lock down" jokes from the men. He worked the crowd like a pro, flashing his gorgeous smile and giving his clichéd, one-liner responses. At one point Charlene took a moment to watch him, and from the look on her face you could see that what she saw made her happy. She didn't see any looks of doubt. He seemed happy and positive about the engagement, and that made Charlene feel confident that he was as sure about this as she was. She had wondered once or twice since the proposal if he had been pressured by his father. However, seeing his demeanor at the party convinced her that the proposal was from his heart. Isaac seemed to be in a great mood, and so was Charlene—until Paige caught her alone for a minute in the kitchen.

Charlene was pouring herself a glass of her aunt's fresh-fruit punch. She looked up and could see Paige coming toward the kitchen entrance through the screen door. Charlene decided to drink her beverage in the kitchen and take a moment away from the crowd. Paige pulled back the screen door and stepped in, and then walked to the edge of the kitchen to glance inside the living room. Charlene watched her as she did all this, and continued sipping on her drink. Once Paige walked back to the kitchen, she stood next to Charlene.

"Did you tell him yet?" Paige asked.

"What?" Charlene asked.

"Did you tell him?" Paige repeated, giving her the "you know what I'm talking about" face.

"No," Charlene replied in somewhat of a snappy tone. "Why would you bring that up now?" she asked as she placed her drink in the sink and began to end her moment away.

"I'm just asking. You better hurry and tell him now, don't you think?"

"Paige, go somewhere with that right now . . . dang."

"Excuse me, I was just asking," Paige said with a slight attitude back.

Charlene had already begun opening the screen door by then and was walking out. Just like most older sisters, sometimes Paige really got on Charlene's nerves. Always thinking they know everything, or that because they're older they can do whatever they want. Paige's intentions were in the right place, but she definitely didn't consider the concept of bad timing. Paige was good for blurting something out in front of the wrong person, or bringing up something touchy at the most inopportune times. So it didn't surprise Charlene that Paige didn't consider that just maybe she didn't want to think about anything negative on the night of her engagement party. Most people would understand that she had waited for this for so long, she just wanted to enjoy it. Charlene couldn't blame Paige for wondering, though. Paige, being one of the only people who knew, was curious about what was on Charlene's mind, now that this time had come and she hadn't mentioned it to Isaac. Charlene honestly didn't even know what she was thinking herself.

As much as she tried to brush off Paige's question, she walked out of the kitchen with a different facial expression. Charlene had really tried not to think about any of the issues that she knew were going to arise eventually. The regular stuff, like the size of the guest list, was nothing compared to the real issues that she expected to occur as the engagement moved forward. Charlene figured the real drama was going to come from truths revealed, true colors being shown and of course her uptight mother losing her cool. It was to be expected with all weddings and relationships, but Charlene knew that hers was going to have some additional elements.

Speaking of the drama, as soon as she stepped outside into the backyard, there she was. Lacy was just coming in the gate holding a gift box in her hand.

Oh, great, Charlene thought to herself. All at once, the event had hit its downside for Charlene. First Paige's question, which had dampened her mood, and now having to be in pretend mode 'cause Lacy showed up. As she headed toward Lacy, Charlene noticed Isaac a few steps ahead of her, en route to greet Lacy. She walked up beside them as they were hugging, and chimed in.

"Don't mean to interrupt here, but just came over to say hello," Charlene said as Isaac and Lacy released their embrace.

"Hey, Charlene," Lacy said in an overly excited voice.

"Hey, miss," Charlene said back as they hugged hello.

"Here, this is for you guys," Lacy said as she handed Charlene the gift box in her hand.

"Oh, you didn't have to bring anything," Charlene said.

"No problem, it's just a token of my happiness for you guys . . . It's a bottle of wine."

Charlene wanted to say, *"No, you really didn't have to . . . hell, nobody else did."* Except Charlene was well aware that this was just one of Lacy's ploys; trying to be deemed good old, sweet Lacy. Charlene saw right through her.

To an outsider it would appear that Charlene and Lacy got along just fine, but there was a lot seething beneath the surface. Although Charlene had been pretending for a long time now that Lacy was a friend, she didn't trust Lacy—not one bit. Lacy knew both Charlene and Isaac, they had each met Lacy at different times prior to their relationship. In high school Charlene used to spend time with one of Lacy's brother's friends, and she and Lacy associated at some social events. Then, years later Isaac and Lacy met while freshman at Iona College. Obviously, Lacy was closer to Isaac, since they'd been friends for more than a decade, whereas Charlene and Lacy had barely gotten to know each other. However, since Charlene and Isaac had been dating, Lacy had grown closer to Charlene, except Charlene would never let her get but so close.

Although in her heart Charlene knew that Lacy would

snatch up Isaac the first chance she got, she couldn't blame Lacy. Most women did want him, especially the Lacy type, who saw Isaac as their ideal man. Isaac was every woman's ideal man, Charlene thought, but only a few deserved a man like him, and Lacy felt she was one of those few. Not that Charlene was prepared to admit it, but her fear was that Lacy or anyone else in their crowd would think that she wasn't one of them. Charlene figured that regardless of what Lacy thought of her, Lacy still considered herself the better woman for Isaac.

As time went on, Charlene and Lacy began to play this silent game with each other. Lacy was well aware that her relationship with Isaac made Charlene uncomfortable. She could tell from Charlene's facial expressions, demeanor and occasional comments. However, like most women Charlene didn't want to appear insecure so she didn't say anything, she just waited for Lacy to show her true intentions so she could point them out to Isaac. Lacy, aware that Charlene was biting her tongue, played it very carefully—always making sure that her actions came across as friendly—even though she knew that Charlene could tell they were not.

For example, Lacy would offer to take Isaac to the airport for his business trips, or pick him up from the airport. Lacy would claim she was doing it so Isaac wouldn't have to pay for airport parking and Charlene wouldn't have to go in late to work, but Charlene knew better. So although Charlene never could say it, her silent communication meant, *"I see what you're up to, but since it can't be proven, it would sound silly to say anything, but one of these days . . ."*

Charlene was hip to the game; she actually played it herself on both sides of the board quite a few times. The game is all about doing things that can seem innocent to the naive, but to the skilled and aware, it's obvious what those actions are. Making the game even more frustrating for Charlene was that she couldn't warn Isaac, who would see Lacy's acts as innocent and genuine, and so Charlene would seem deceitful, paranoid and jealous.

So Charlene was better off playing along and waiting for Lacy's actions to become more obvious or just downright blatant. It could take forever, but usually when you give someone an inch they take a mile, and that's what Charlene was waiting on. Especially now, with the engagement, she expected Lacy to pull some tricks from her sleeve. But Charlene wasn't too worried.

"Well, I'm going to put this inside and I'll be right back," Charlene said as she walked away from where Isaac and Lacy were standing.

As Charlene walked toward the kitchen, approaching from the side entrance of the house was someone else she hadn't been prepared to see. It was her brother's best friend, Torian, who had been her high school sweetheart. Charlene and Torian had never lost contact, but she didn't think he would come to the engagement party. Although it had been years since they had been together he always made her feel vulnerable. It wasn't because she was still attracted to him or had strong feelings for him, it was because of all that he knew about the real Charlene. Torian was probably the closest a guy had ever gotten to her. She assumed that was because he knew her brother, and because of that he didn't treat her like the rest of the guys did. At the time Charlene had wanted her relationship with Torian to last, but her ways had eventually caught up with her and became too much for him. Charlene was no angel back then, and Torian took all that he could stand before he ended it.

Isaac was able to tell that Charlene and Torian shared something he didn't see in their own relationship, and he had let her know that. So, although she was happy to see Torian, she knew that the saga definitely had just begun. With all the surprise guests in attendance, there would be numerous awkward moments throughout the night. She blamed Paige, her untimely question had jinxed the celebration.

Chapter 4

The birds were chirping on the tree branches outside, but in Charlene's head it sound like screaming. She struggled to open her eyes, surrendering to the morning's callings. She tried to place her hand over her eyes so the light wouldn't hurt them as much. The minute she began to shake off last night's dreams, she felt the pain of her mild hangover.

She looked over to the other side of the bed and Isaac wasn't there. She glanced around the room at the royal and sky blue with brown décor. She was nestled in his sky blue down comforter, and was still resting her head on his down brown and blue pillows. She happened to love the blue color in his room, because she always felt like she was in heaven in there. The room was just as well designed as the rest of the place. The interior designer that Isaac had hired when he moved in did an awesome job with the entire place, even the bathrooms. Isaac gave the designer the extra loot that was needed to go ahead and get a Jacuzzi and heated tiles installed in the upstairs bathroom. He even had the television sitting over the Jacuzzi, a nice-sized flat screen, too. Isaac's place could have been covered by one of those crib shows on MTV, it was that nice.

The engagement party had been quite an event, and between the drinks and the late night Charlene wanted to do nothing but lie around all afternoon. Charlene slowly staggered out of the bedroom and down the hall, and still there was no sign of Isaac. She walked past the flight of stairs and went into the bathroom and decided to freshen up. She brushed her teeth and wiped her face clean with a washcloth. Once she was done she popped two Excedrins that she got out of the medicine cabinet and washed them down with some tap water. After she took a morning pee, she wrapped up in the bedroom and headed back on her quest to see where Isaac was. With very little energy, she made her way down the stairs toward the living room where she heard the television. There he was with the remote in one hand, holding the phone to his ear with the other. He seemed startled when he saw her but remained calm. Of course, like most females, her innate detective skills emerged. She nonchalantly walked over by him to see how he would react and whether she could hear a voice through the phone. He kept his cool, but he also started talking, so there was no voice to hear on the other end. Charlene knew that men were hip to most of the female tricks, and they knew how to counter slick with slick. Still, she thought, as usual we can outsmart them. She pretended to be in the mood for some attention, and sat in his lap and planted a kiss on his cheek.

He ended his thought and threw her a "Good morning, baby."

That surprised her a bit. That's when she heard the voice through the phone; it was the voice of a male.

She said, "Good morning," back and stood up. She walked into the kitchen, thinking to herself, *Why do I always imagine some stuff up in my mind and half the time I end up looking stupid?* Charlene had to admit that she was good for jumping to conclusions with Isaac. She wasn't sure if it stemmed from her insecurity and her thinking that she wasn't worthy of Isaac, or her paranoia about her own secrets.

She started to get a glass of orange juice when she thought she should probably make their breakfast. She knew she had some domestic tweaking to do and she better get used to it. So, she pulled out some eggs, bacon and grits and began preparing breakfast. She put on the little radio in the kitchen and started dancing around to the R&B hits that were playing. An old Toni Braxton song had just gone off, and a classic Barry White started playing when Isaac came into the kitchen. He walked up to Charlene and stood directly behind her as she stirred the egg batter. He cupped her frame inside of his large frame and held her. He started to sing the words of the song into her ear as he swayed from side to side. She lit up as she hummed along and finished stirring the eggs. She wanted to stir until the song was over because she didn't want it to end, but she also didn't want to mess up the meal and the pan had already melted the butter.

Once she moved away to pour the raw eggs in the skillet, Isaac said, "I have to run out real quick, I'll be right back."

"Where you going?" she snapped.

"Have to run and get something for my father real quick."

"Babe, I'm making breakfast, it can't wait?"

"Oh, you're making that for both of us? I thought that was for you."

"Isaac . . . Yes, it's for both of us . . . You think I would just make myself breakfast without asking you first?"

"Umm . . . Yeah. You've done it before . . . Besides, I'll be right back. He needs his prescription picked up."

"Whatever, Isaac, just go, I'll see you when you get back."

He began singing the last few lines of the Barry White song to her, as he reached over and picked up a piece of the already-done bacon off the plate.

"Get out of here," she said.

"Babe, stop that. I'll be right back. I told my dad I'd get the medication first thing this morning."

"Whatever, just go. I'll see you when you get back."

Isaac walked out of the kitchen on that note. Charlene knew she shouldn't be so upset. It was his father's medication, and he was terminally ill. Isaac's father had been diagnosed with cancer and the doctor said he could live anywhere from a year to three years, but no guarantees. This was the weight on Isaac's heart that he tried not to speak about much. Phillip Milton was Isaac's hero, and the thought of his death was too much for Isaac to bear. Isaac was his only son, and so the only one to carry on the Milton name. This meant the world to both Isaac and his dad, and his illness had tainted their dreams tremendously, so if there was one touchy topic it was that. Besides, how evil could she be to complain about Isaac bringing him medicine?

Even though she was still annoyed that he wouldn't tell her he was leaving as soon as he saw her making breakfast, she had to ask herself if she was somewhat to blame. It wasn't like it was so far-fetched for her to not have been making some for him, too. Was she that selfish—enough that he really didn't even expect her to think of him? She knew she wasn't the most domestic partner. That was partly because growing up her mother was such a family woman, she did everything and Charlene never learned to do much on her own. She hadn't been in relationships where she needed to cater to anyone, and because she used to use her looks to get what she wanted she didn't have to do much for herself. Regardless, she was trying to be better than that and so was making breakfast for both of them, and she didn't appreciate her attempts being in vain. So, although she decided to not argue with him over it, she could feel she still had a slight attitude.

She finished up with the eggs and was looking for a bowl to place them in when Isaac walked back in the kitchen. He began taking out plates and silverware.

"What are you doing?"

"Setting the table," he replied.

"I thought you had to go."

"I called my father and he said it can definitely wait until after breakfast," he replied.

With a slight smirk on her face, she said, "Thank you, baby."

"Not a problem . . . It just better be good, that's all I know," he said, laughing.

They set the table and made up the plates together. Once they were done, they sat down to eat and chat. Isaac wasn't always a big talker, but he had his moments—like after business functions, if he was drinking, if there were people around, with his coworkers, and other scenarios like that. However, when it was just the two of them often he didn't talk much. This was one of those times, though, that he was in a talkative mood.

"So, did you have fun last night?" he asked.

"Sure, did you?"

"Yes, it was a good time. Good having everyone together."

"Well, just a taste of what the wedding will be like."

"I guess."

"Well, all those people won't get invited, and there will be others that we will have to invite," Charlene said.

"Like who? Who wouldn't we invite from last night?"

Charlene wondered if she should mention that she would love to exclude Lacy from the guest list, but she knew she hadn't come up with a good enough answer to the question he would undoubtedly ask immediately after. So, she decided not to go there as of just yet.

"I'm just saying, the guest list will look slightly different at our wedding."

"That's rude, to invite someone to our engagement party and not the wedding," Isaac replied.

"Not really, people know weddings cost a lot and everyone can't be invited."

"Well, we will discuss that at a later time, but I would think if anyone should be cut it should be those people that weren't invited to the engagement party before the people that were close enough to us to be there last night."

There Isaac went again—being logical. Sometimes Charlene hated Isaac's rational way of thinking; he was so in the box; so all about what's right and wrong.

"OK, Isaac, let's discuss that later. I'm sure by the time our parents add names and we sit down we will see a better picture than we do now."

"All right, whatever," Isaac replied.

Charlene changed the topic to something less touchy. She brought up one of the drunk and embarrassing guests at the engagement party, which instantly started them both cracking up laughing. Charlene wanted to enjoy the morning without any deep, thought-provoking conversations. Besides, Charlene knew her reasoning was based on jealousy and fear, and that would probably get her nowhere.

Chapter 5

The third door to the left was shut. Charlene was relieved to see that her boss hadn't made it in yet. Messing around with Isaac all weekend, Charlene just couldn't get herself together this morning. A few coworkers were fiddling at their desks trying to get their day started as Charlene walked past them to her desk. As soon as she plopped down in her chair she emptied her hands of the bags she had been carrying. One was her lunch for the day—she had packed some leftover lasagna from the engagement party, but she told herself that after today she would watch her diet so she would be the size she wanted to be for her wedding. She tucked her work bag under desk.

There was an Asian lady dressed all in brown at the coffee-maker waiting for her morning java, while two African American males stood close by discussing their club experiences from the weekend. Charlene waved and smiled hello to all of them from a distance, then immediately started to get ready for her workday. She logged on to her computer, and in the back of her mind she was hoping that when her boss arrived she would appear as if she had been on time and already settled at work. It must have been a lazy Monday, because one of her girlfriends at work was also running late. Charlene was keeping an eye out for her to see when she made it to her desk so they could talk about the engagement party and gossip.

By the time Charlene checked her messages and email she felt well into her day. Her boss had arrived and handed her some documents to revise, and she was already answering calls and updating documents. Considering she was at work, she was in a pretty uplifted mood. It was about 10 AM when Charlene's phone rang at work. Paige was calling to apologize for her question Saturday night. Charlene's cubicle was out in the open, surrounded by three other cubicles, and at least three more in hearing range. So she hated having personal conversations at work. Still, since two of her closest cubicle neighbors were away from their desk she figured she could have the conversation quietly and quickly.

"I'm sorry, Charlene, I really am," Paige said. "Besides, I know how you don't like talking about it," she continued.

"It's OK, Paige, I know you didn't mean anything by it. Sorry for snapping. I know I have to face it at some point. I just didn't want to think about it at my engagement party."

"I know, Leen . . . that's why I felt so bad since."

"Don't . . . I know you meant no harm."

"I didn't, really. Regardless, I'm here whenever you want to talk about it or handle it."

"Thanks, Sis. But it definitely won't be here at my job."

"I understand. How's his father doing, anyway? Is he still on chemo?"

"He is doing OK. There's no way to tell what's going on day to day. Especially with Isaac, he doesn't say too much about it."

"Well, that's good, I guess, as long as he is still stable, and Isaac doesn't have any bad news."

"Yeah, he is as stable as he can be, I guess."

"Well, I'm sure everything will work itself out. Just let me know when you're ready to talk and handle stuff, Charlene," Paige said.

"Paige . . . I will."

"I'm just saying, Charlene, you have to tell Isaac at some point, and it's in your best interest to get it looked into for yourself, anyway."

"I know. I will."

"Want me to make the appointment for you?"

"I have a list of doctors through my insurance; I'll make the appointment today."

"OK . . . That sounds more like it. Call me and let me know when, I'll go with you."

"OK. Thanks, Nosey," Charlene said back.

If Paige wasn't such a good sister, Charlene would have to wonder whether she wanted Charlene to tell him because it was best or so that her perfect world would get shaken up. Charlene knew that a lot of people who thought that she didn't deserve Isaac were waiting for something to break them up or open Isaac's eyes to what they saw. Charlene knew, though, that Paige wasn't one of those people. Not only had Paige always been a loving and caring big sister who kept Charlene's best interests at heart, she knew that Paige was right about this.

There were quite a few things she hadn't told Isaac about herself. She hadn't told him that she had been in a gang as a teenager for about six months. She hadn't told him that she had been arrested for shoplifting, had been left back in school and suspended for getting caught with a boy on the staircase. And she hadn't told him that she had pretty much been a stereotypical wayward teenage girl for quite a few years. She dreaded Isaac knowing any of that, and several other things she'd never happened to mention to him. Paige may have been right that Charlene really did need to go to the doctor and that Isaac was entitled to know about her condition, but Charlene dreaded telling him that secret more than she did any other.

Chapter 6

Outside it was still sunny and bright but inside Charlene's apartment it was gloomy and dark. It was about 6:20 PM when Charlene arrived home for the first time since the proposal over a week ago. It was stuffy and needed cleaning, and she was hoping to get to it before Isaac arrived. He was supposed to be stopping by to bring her some of the things she needed that she had left at his place. She didn't know if he was staying over her place or heading back to his own after he dropped off her things, but she didn't want the place to still be a mess when he got there. Funny thing was, after all the lovey-dovey nights they had spent together in engagement bliss, she actually hoped he wouldn't stay. She wanted a night to herself, some space. She had recently realized that having space and time away from the world was to be treasured. She needed time to clear her thoughts, and to just relax without having to keep up the role of the perfect new fiancé.

She opened some windows, lit some candles, picked up some clothes and rearranged some furniture that was out of place. Charlene's place was pretty simple for the most part. When you walked in the front door there was a small foyer with a chic little black table there. To the right of the front door was her kitchen, it was a fairly small kitchen but cute and clean. She had white appliances and black countertops. She kept some food items in this one-of-a-kind countertop basket she had ordered from the Home Shopping Network that she just loved. She had two potholders that read TOO CUTE TO COOK hanging right above her two cookbooks. Her living room was straight ahead from the kitchen door, also not very spacious but cute. Her color scheme was peach and tan in there, and the colors looked great together. She had a tan leather couch and a small coffee table. Off to the left was her bathroom and it wasn't anything fancy at all. Her bedroom was lavender and cream—pretty bright yet soft colors that Charlene felt made the room very cozy. They called the style of her apartment a half bedroom, rather than a studio, since the bedroom was somewhat separate—you had to turn out of the living room to be in the bed area.

Charlene hadn't hired anyone to decorate her place, so her apartment wasn't as fancy as Isaac's, but she thought it was still well designed and comfortable. Charlene had painted the rooms herself and she went shopping at Ikea and Target and decorated herself. Besides, she didn't have as much room as Isaac had to work with. Her bathroom, kitchen and bedroom all together could fit in Isaac's bedroom with still some room leftover to play.

She had straightened up most of the place when her house phone rang. She ran to answer it, and it was Isaac saying he would be there in about fifteen minutes. She hung up and continued her cleaning. She didn't care if it wasn't spotless; it wasn't as if she had just met Isaac and needed to impress him. She just didn't want it to be dirty and uncomfortable for him to chill in for a bit. So, she started doing the dishes that were in the sink and waited for his arrival.

She had finished with the dishes and had started folding

some "only partially dirty, not ready for the laundry bag yet" clothes when the doorbell rang. As soon as Charlene opened the door, Isaac gave a "Hello" and walked in and went straight into the living room area and sat on the couch. He had his keys and cell phone in one hand, and Charlene's little overnight bag in the other. He placed the bag down on the floor by the couch and immediately reached for the remote.

"No hug, no kiss, no conversation," Charlene said as she followed behind him.

"I'm sorry, Char, I had a rough day," he said as he stood up to give her the hug and kiss.

"What happened?"

"Nothing much. Work was just stressful and my dad wasn't feeling well today."

"Did he go to the doctor?"

"No, he has an appointment next week . . . It just bothers me to know he is in all that pain and I can't do anything about it."

Without saying a word, Charlene slowly rubbed Isaac's back as he spoke. She knew that finding out about his dad's illness had been a turning point in his life. She was actually surprised that he had proposed in the midst of all the gloominess with his father. He had mentioned before that he wanted his dad to be alive to witness his marriage and the birth of his children, which would mean more than anything to him. So, although he didn't come right out and say it, Charlene assumed that played a part in why he decided to go ahead and propose to her. Charlene could only pray that things would work out the way Isaac dreamed.

After a few moments of channel surfing, Charlene got up and brought Isaac a Heineken from the kitchen. He put down the remote after he had seen some of *The Contender*. As he watched the story about the two boxers striving to become professional, he seemed to be quite relaxed. Charlene was amazed that he ever managed to relax. Inside that man's mind was a blueprint of his whole life. Isaac was the type of guy that had it all figured out, and he didn't really know how to adapt when things went off course. That was another reason it made it so hard for Charlene to tell him about her secret. She knew there was a good chance he wouldn't take it too well. Besides, he had enough on his plate with his dad and all the changes at his job.

Charlene figured she would give him this time to unwind and get over his rough day, so she opened some mail and jotted down some numbers she had to call. Once she was done she decided to check her answering machine, and since she had been gone for a bit there were quite a few messages. The first message was from her cousin and the next from one of her girlfriends. Then, after a bill collector or two, came a message from Rich.

"Hey, babe, it's me, Rich . . . I just wanted to say hello and congratulations. I spoke to Kevin yesterday and he told me about the news. I'm still kind of shocked. When I think about you just a few years ago, I wouldn't of thought you would be getting married . . . And you just told me last month that it wasn't in the plans. Now look . . . Well, hey . . . Thought it would have been me . . . Heh, heh, well, give me a call back if you're still allowed to."

It all came out so fast. Charlene didn't know if she should jump to stop it, only to have Isaac want to hear it anyway and her look guilty or just remain calm and let it play out, fearful of what he might say. She chose the latter, and sure enough her heart had skipped a few beats for those fifteen seconds that Rich's voice filled her living room. Rich was a guy that Charlene used to mess with, actually, the last one she was with before Isaac. They had dealt on and off for a bit and they shared a lot of mutual friends, so since the breakup years ago they had always remained somewhat in contact.

As soon as Rich was done talking, Isaac stared directly into her face. Charlene knew that pretending not to see him would only make the situation worse, so she looked back at him.

"What was that?" he asked.

"I don't know . . . He just called to say congratulations to us . . . And he was just being silly, I guess," she replied.

"You guess? It sounds like you said some silly things too . . ."

Charlene had hoped that Isaac hadn't listened to it all, or at least that the volume from the television had made it harder to hear. Unfortunately, it seemed not; he must have tuned those contenders out and started getting ready for his own round one.

"Izzy . . . It was just small talk," she responded.

"First of all, what were you doing talking to him, and then you told him that we weren't in your plans?"

"We talk like once in a blue moon, nothing major . . . And it just so happened that the last time was about a month ago, but we don't usually talk like that."

"He thought it would have been him . . . What would make him think that?"

"He was playing, Isaac, obviously, if we were talking about if me and you were getting married last time we spoke; he knew that it was me and you."

"No, he didn't. Not if you told him it wasn't in the plans . . . Besides, since when is it appropriate to keep in touch with your last boyfriend? It's not, and I'm sure he knows that."

Rich had never really been her boyfriend, but that's what

she had told Isaac because it sounded better than the truth. Not that she wanted him to be jealous; she just knew that telling him that they were just messing around would have raised more questions and red flags.

"We don't talk like that," she said again.

"Yeah, just enough that he thought you and him still had a chance, and for him to feel comfortable enough leaving you that message on your house answering machine," Isaac said as he picked up his cell phone and keys off the coffee table.

"Isaac, don't make a big deal out of this, please. It was nothing. I promise."

"I'm not making a big deal out of it, I'm leaving you alone so you can return his call in privacy."

Isaac continued toward the door, and Charlene didn't know what to say to defuse the situation. Nothing she could say would make it look better, especially since she didn't know how to explain her prior conversations with Rich. Besides, she was well aware that Rich was the one man that made Isaac the most jealous. For one he was fine as all hell, and his personality was even attractive. To Isaac's knowledge he was the boyfriend that Charlene had had the longest relationship with, and he had still been in the picture when Isaac and she first met. She actually had messed around with Rich longer than she had any other guy, on and off for years, actually. Still, there was nothing going on between her and Rich at this point, so she was irritated by Isaac's reaction.

"Isaac . . . Let's just sit down and eat dinner."

"I'm not hungry . . . I will call you later."

At this point Isaac was by the door, and Charlene was close behind him.

"Isaac, I'm sorry I didn't tell you that I spoke to him . . . It really wasn't anything. I'm sorry."

"No need to apologize . . . Just make sure when you call

him back you let him know that I said thanks for the congrat-ulations on our engagement."

Charlene gave up. She wasn't having the best day, either after the conversation she had had with her sister earlier and now this. She told herself to forget it, she couldn't take any more. Isaac walked out the door without giving her a kiss good-bye or any acknowledgment, and Charlene closed the door behind him.

She went into the living room, turned off the television and went into her bedroom. She actually considered calling Rich back, even just to tell him what he had caused, but she figured maybe she should not, at least not yet. She immediately sprawled out on the bed. She didn't turn on the television, no radio; she just lay there in silence. It was only moments before tears began to roll down her face. She was already emotional from the memories that resurfaced when she was talking to her sister earlier. So Isaac walking out on her only added insult to injury. Isaac didn't know it, but his walking out so easily spoke volumes to her. It had been Charlene's fear all along, Isaac not willing to accept and love her despite her flaws. She was a tough girl who had been through a lot, and you would never know the turmoil she dealt with underneath because she was good at keeping a smile on her face. Still, as the tears rolled down her cheeks onto her lavender cotton comforter, her worry clouded her mind.

Charlene knew that it made no sense to be with a man this long and tell him so many lies, not expecting for them to catch up with her. The thing was, she wasn't expecting the relation-ship to last this long, or for her back to be against the wall like this. Charlene knew it didn't make sense to allow a man from her past to cause friction between her and her present man. Charlene never could sever ties with the men she dealt with, because she didn't trust that her current one would be there for the long haul and she wanted to have someone to fall back on. She wished that she could have faith in her relationships, especially this one, since she'd just agreed to stay in it forever. She knew she could only feel that confident if Isaac was still around after he found out her secret.

Chapter 7

Charlene stood in the doctor's office waiting for her name to be called. Paige sat beside her with a *Glamour* magazine in her hand. Charlene looked around the room at all the pregnant mothers, bellies protruding almost out to their knees, most who looked happy as a lark. A few of them did look miserable and irritable, their faces looking swollen and noses wide. A lot of them were with their husbands, that's what the matching rings told; some were with other females and a few alone. There were five doctors who practiced at this office and at least sixteen women waiting. The whole scene depressed Charlene. The sight of all these mothers there to ensure the health of their bundle of joy to come, and there was Charlene sitting in the waiting room of an ob-gyn to get a medical condition checked out and face her pain.

A few patients weren't pregnant, or at least they didn't appear to be, some looked young, as if they were there for birth control. Charlene wished that at that age she could have been on such a couch on her way to finding out about preventive methods. Instead, she was grown and was visiting an ob-gyn's office for the first time. She had been seen by one before, but that was in a hospital, and she never did go back for her follow-up appointments. So, for the first time, at the age of twenty-six, she was seeing an ob-gyn. Her older cousin Dakota had referred her to this one, in Yonkers, a Dr. Kim Ginyard.

The office was cozy and clean, and all the staff was very friendly. There were tons of pamphlets all over the office regarding female health issues and information. Charlene read most of their titles from a distance while she waited. She didn't want to look like a first-timer, or to show any of the fear she was feeling, so she tried to remain as calm as possible. Meanwhile, she was sweaty and had some pretty huge butterflies in her stomach.

Charlene hadn't planned what she was going to say. She didn't know how she was going to get the doctor to give her the information she needed without having to go into detail about everything. She debated with herself about confiding in her doctor, but the more she thought about having to discuss everything the more nervous she got. She was close to convincing herself to walk out of the office, to forget about all of this and go on with her life as she had. But with her sister sitting there, and her folder being next in the bin, she fought the urge. Moments later, she heard her name.

"Charlene Tanner," the nurse called.

Charlene stood up.

"The doctor will see you now."

"Can my sister come in with me?" Charlene asked in a low voice, hoping nobody else in the waiting room would overhear her immature request.

"Sure she can," the nurse replied with a smile on her face.

As Paige stood up and they walked toward the doorway where the nurse stood, Charlene wondered if the nurse found her request odd. She wondered if her fear was obvious and if she looked like a fool. Charlene wished that this visit could be regular, like it was for most women her age. She had dreaded this day for quite some time—not wanting to have a doctor between her legs, to be probed inside and to be told bad news. She didn't handle it well at all the first time, and she had never quite mustered up the strength to face it again.

She sat down inside the exam room. She saw the stirrups, and all the medical supplies on the table, and she started feeling on the verge of tears. She told herself over and over to be strong and relax, but the feelings kept wavering in and out. Eventually the voice of the nurse calmed her some. She started asking some basic questions like age, time of last period, medical history. Charlene answered all of her questions to the best of her ability, and then she got her height and weight taken. She was 5'6", 125 pounds; she had lost four pounds in the past couple of weeks and was happy to see it was still off. After the nurse jotted down her measurements, she left the room and told Charlene to change into the provided robe and that the doctor would be right in.

Charlene discreetly put on the robe that was practically made of paper. She was slightly exposed for a few quick moments, but Paige saw nothing she hadn't seen of hers while growing up with her. Paige could see in Charlene's eyes that she was nervous, so she began talking to her to calm her down some.

"So, have you decided on the wedding colors yet? . . . You're so indecisive; you'll probably change it twenty times."

"I'm still thinking light pink and mauve."

"That would be nice, but you need to make up your mind because it sounds like Isaac is trying to have a short engagement."

"I know . . . Isaac has a lot in mind . . . whether I have it in mind or not."

"You want a long engagement?"

"No. I just don't want to be rushed. Everything is on some timetable that's not mine."

"Most women would be excited their man can't wait to marry them."

Charlene wasn't up for a disagreement, and since she knew that Paige was trying to distract her from the nervous feeling sitting in her stomach, and she appreciated those efforts, she went along.

"If that was the reason . . . But his rush is simply because he wants his father to be around."

"There's nothing wrong with that, as long as it's you that he wants to be with."

"I guess. I just wish he would see what I want first . . . It's all about what his dad wants right now . . . the marriage and kids to follow. That's why I'm sitting here half naked . . . 'cause of his father being sick."

"That's not nice to say, Charlene," Paige said.

Before Charlene could respond, the doorknob turned and in came Dr. Ginyard.

"Hello, ladies, how are you doing this afternoon?"

"Fine," they both replied practically in unison.

"Great . . . I am assuming you are Charlene," the doctor said, seeing Charlene in the robe sitting on the table.

"I am," Charlene said with a smile, raising her hand slightly.

"OK . . . And this is your . . ." Dr. Ginyard said.

"My sister," Charlene replied.

"Nice to meet you," Dr. Ginyard said.

As the doctor looked through Charlene's file, she asked some other basic questions, like her age, and if she was sexually active and if she used birth control. For Charlene the visit was getting more and more uncomfortable as the moments went by, although not because Paige was sitting there hearing all her business. Charlene and Paige were close like that and there wasn't much Paige didn't know about her baby sister. It was because Charlene knew that soon the doctor was going to have to get down to what she was there for.

Dr. Ginyard asked Charlene to lie back and place her feet up in the stirrups; she was going to take a look. As soon as

Charlene began to lie back, Paige gave her a look of reassurance to let her know that she was there by her side. If anybody knew how Charlene was feeling at the time, it was Paige. For years Paige had tried to convince Charlene that she should get this over with, so she knew that this was harder for her than it appeared. As Dr. Ginyard got her instruments, she asked Charlene when she had last had a Pap smear. Charlene had thought the questions might be over and wasn't prepared for this one.

"Ummm . . . It's been a while," she stuttered.

"What's a while?" the doctor asked as she began to place the speculum inside of her.

Just as she finished asking the question and Charlene felt Dr. Ginyard begin to swab, her emotions got the best of her. Her voice cracked as she began to answer the question, and right behind it came a flood of tears down her face. Before Paige could calm her, it was too late. Charlene was already in the middle of a full-blown emotional attack. The doctor looked up over the robe to see what was wrong.

"What's wrong? Am I hurting you?" she asked frantically.

Charlene couldn't pull herself together to answer. Paige reached down and hugged her, and the doctor took that as a sign to stop. The room felt to Charlene as if everything had stopped and like it was filled with a whole lot of pain and confusion all at once. Paige could tell that Dr. Ginyard didn't know if she should get involved or just wait the moment out.

Finally she asked, "Do you ladies want a minute alone?"

"No, she will be fine. Can she get a cup of water, though?" Paige asked.

"Sure," Dr. Ginyard said as she exited, looking relieved to get out of there.

"Are you OK, Leen?" Paige asked

"Yes, I don't know what happened . . . I was handling it so well."

"Listen, Leen, she is a doctor. You don't have to feel uncomfortable around her. She can help you out. Besides, she sees many patients every day, she is not thinking about what she sees down there."

Dr. Ginyard walked back in with the cup of water and noticed that Charlene already looked a little better. The doctor had other patients to see, so she knew she had to continue on with their visit one way or the other.

"Is everything OK, Charlene?" the doctor asked.

After looking over at Paige, Charlene replied, "Well, yes and no."

"What does that mean, sweetie?" Dr. Ginyard asked.

Something about Dr. Ginyard's sincere and caring demeanor made it that much easier to just spit it out, and so she did.

"When I was only thirteen years old I got pregnant and I was unable to tell my parents about it, so my friend and I tried to abort the baby on our own . . ." Charlene began in a low and shaky voice. She was holding her head low, clearly ashamed by the story she was about to share for the first time. Everyone who knew about it was there when it happened, and rarely ever was it spoken of since.

The doctor looked at her as she spoke. Charlene hoped that the doctor didn't think she was being a drama queen. She figured that the doctor had seen and heard much worse, but to Charlene this had been the most traumatizing situation of her life.

"We didn't know what we were doing, so after poking the knitting needle around up there I began to bleed a lot . . . And eventually my friend called my mom and she rushed me to the hospital . . . They thought I was going to bleed to death. At the hospital, they removed the baby but they said I had perforated my uterus and my chances of giving birth were slim to none."

By the time Charlene finished telling the doctor the story,

her face was soaked by the tears that had fallen and so was Paige's. Paige knew the entire story, but hearing Charlene relive it out loud for the first time gave her goose bumps. Paige had been with their mother when she received the call. They rushed home and found Charlene in a pool of blood—that was something that would never leave Paige, just like it would never leave Charlene. It felt like it took months to completely get rid of the blood. Paige could remember that all Charlene's friend Tanai kept screaming was, "We killed her! We killed her!" It was the most horrific scene.

The doctor took a moment to respond, and then she asked, "Did your last doctor tell you the same thing?"

"This is the first time I have been to the doctor since the incident."

"Since you were thirteen?"

"Yes . . . I have been to a general doctor, but I haven't been examined down there since."

"Wow, Charlene . . . They didn't suggest counseling or any follow-up appointments?"

"They did, but I wasn't really willing to go through anything else at the time, the physical and emotional pain stuck around for quite some time, and besides, my mother just wanted us to put it behind us."

"At the risk of your health?"

"My mom is very religious, and she was very disappointed in my behavior so she said we just had to pray on it."

After realizing that there were several aspects to this issue the doctor realized that this was better suited for a licensed psychologist, so Dr. Ginyard decided to leave the family issues alone.

"Do you mind letting me examine you?" the doctor asked her.

Without answering, Charlene began to lie back down on

the table. The doctor put her gloves back on and began to slowly open Charlene's legs. Surprisingly, now that Charlene had told the doctor, it was a lot easier for her to lie there calmly. At first she was very squeamish when the speculum and swab entered her again, but she lay there and let the doctor do her work.

It was quick and painless in the end, and Charlene was actually happy that she was finally getting this done. The doctor said she wanted to look at an ultrasound as well to take a look at her uterus, so she sent her over to another room. Charlene did everything that the doctor asked, and Paige was right there by her side for it all.

Charlene never thought she would feel such a relief after reciting the tragic story of her childhood to someone, but she was actually happy that she had. She hoped she could feel the same relief after telling Isaac the story, along with the results from the doctor.

Chapter 8

Outside kids were playing and running around making all sorts of noises. There were four girls playing a mean game of double Dutch right outside Charlene's window. The ropes hit the ground and a girl in lime green jumped right in, her skinny legs jumping and bending fast as lightning. She'd probably been jumping for years.

A day had gone by and Charlene was still awaiting her test results as well as the right moment to have her talk with Isaac. He had already let go of the silly fight over Rich, somewhat. They had talked on the phone since then, but they hadn't seen each other in a few days. Even though it seemed like things were getting back to normal, she knew the timing wasn't right to cause issues again with this secret. Besides, she wanted to know what the doctor said first, because if the doctor had positive results from her checkup she would be telling him for nothing.

Charlene knew that most people would be more afraid about the results from the STD tests, but Charlene was more concerned with her chances of having a baby. She knew an STD could be cured, at least if it wasn't HIV; but not being able to have kids was permanent. Of course she was hoping that she was disease free—she definitely was a candidate for an STD, but it had been a while since she had put her self at risk and she hadn't seen any signs of anything yet. There were no bumps, rashes or coughs; so she figured that nothing had caught up with her. Besides, she mostly used protection with all her partners—just not with Isaac, but she wasn't worried about him.

Charlene finished using the bathroom and peeked outside the window at the girls jumping rope. It brought back memories, good and bad ones, from when she was their age. Charlene couldn't help but smile as she heard the girls singing along to their jump rope song. She almost wished that she could go out there and jump in for old times' sake, but she knew she would look like a fool. So she went on past the window and went back to sitting on her couch, and curled up with the remote and some potato chips.

She was watching *Bridezillas* on Lifetime, laughing at all the dramatic fiancés. She knew she was very capable of being just like those women, but she would never want to be on that show because she had too much to hide from too many people.

There was a lot of Charlene she had to hide from her mother while growing up and today as well. Charlene's mother was very strict and not very warm. She raised her children with an iron fist. She tried to keep a tight reign on them, and with Charlene's ways they had bumped heads throughout most of Charlene's youth. Although they had come a long way and their relationship had mended some, there was still an underlying distance and disdain between them. So as Charlene did better for herself she always felt like she was proving her mother wrong. Usually when Charlene was around her mother, she was never one hundred percent herself and tried to keep up the image that she was A-OK.

Then there were some of her friends who were always trying to pick her brain and get her to show weakness and embarrassment, so she always had to be fake with them. It was like people didn't want a girl like her to get a second chance. They wanted to believe she wasn't worthy of a good life just because she had made some bad decisions in her life. Isaac at least knew the real her—well, at least the Charlene she was today. She was always herself around him, and felt so comfortable. That was, unless her past came up, that was the part of Charlene she never really opened him to. It wasn't like she had lied about anything major; she'd just kept secrets from him along the way. She always considered them as the kinds of things to be told on a need-to-know basis, and most of them he didn't need to know. In Charlene's opinion, nothing he didn't know was really that relevant today, other than this one about children. However, her justification was that she wasn't sure if she was or wasn't capable and, boy, was she praying she was.

In any normal relationship child-bearing issues wouldn't seem so devastating, it would be something that most couples in love would try to overcome. However, with Isaac he had been looking forward to and planning on having kids for years, like *really* looking forward to it. He was the epitome of a family man, because that's all he wanted to be. Although he was a very successful businessman, for Isaac it was family first, career second. He took a lot of pride in being the last man in his family to carry on his family name. It meant even more to him now that his father was passing, it was probably his deepest desire to have his father alive to see his grandchild.

That's why Charlene felt so guilty for never telling Isaac about this, but she didn't know it would come to this. Charlene was used to messing with men that didn't want kids or didn't really care either way. Even more so, she wasn't used to doing much more than just messing with men. She wasn't the relationship type of gal prior to dating Isaac. She knew as their relationship grew that it was different from any other she had been in, but she didn't expect him to care this much about her or having a baby. Besides, Charlene always believed it was the mother's choice; it was the woman who made a big deal about those kinds of things. It was just her luck that she fell in love and was engaged to marry one of the few men that cared about having kids more than anything. It was like karma for all of her deceit.

It wasn't really deceit, though, she didn't live the lie, the situation was in her past and she was just trying to keep it there. She honestly hadn't prepared herself for down the line with Isaac; she only lived day to day with him. When they met a few years back, she never would have thought she would be marrying him. It was strange enough being in a real relationship, then it was lasting, and the craziest part was she was forced to show every part of herself. Charlene wasn't prepared for this, but she did wish that she had been. She loved Isaac and wanted their relationship to work more than anything. Yet, here she was facing all of the lies she had told him and the possibility of losing him.

The *Bridezillas* show was coming to an end, and Charlene started flicking through channels looking for another show to help mope her day away. She was slowing down in the movie channels area just as her house phone rang. She got up to answer, it was Paige.

"How's my baby sister doing?" Paige asked.

"I'm fine."

"What are you doing?"

"Just watching television."

"I was just thinking about you . . . making sure you're OK."

"I'm as OK as I'm going to be."

"Did you hear anything from the doctor's office?"

"No, I'm still waiting to hear from them."

"When did she say they will be ready again?"

"Top of the week."

"You nervous?"

"Slightly . . . I am more nervous about telling Isaac."

"I understand that part, baby girl."

"Between me and you, I have even had mixed emotions about what I want the results to be."

"What do you mean by that?" Paige asked, sounding surprised.

"I have been spending most of my life prepared not to have kids. Ever since the doctor told me that years ago . . . I have just been prepared for the worst."

"But shouldn't that mean if you find out you can, that would be good news?"

"I guess . . . because I know Isaac, and Mommy and Daddy . . . and you would be happy . . ." she said.

"You don't want kids, Leen?"

"Not really . . . I have already convinced myself of how great life could be without having kids. I had to find a way to cope, ya know?"

"Yeah, I do. Well, regardless of what the results are you will have a fulfilling life."

"The issue is if Isaac will have a fulfilling life."

"I really think you should talk to him, Charlene. Don't wait until after you get the results."

"I know . . . I plan on telling him."

For a few moments neither of them said anything else, then they made some more small talk and got off the phone. Paige didn't want to be the annoying angel on Charlene's shoulder, and Charlene wasn't in the mood to be annoyed. Still, Charlene knew Paige was coming from a good place.

Paige's talks were like therapy sometimes for Charlene, because Paige was the one person in her life that she could talk to about any and everything. Charlene had a couple of good friends, but none of them knew about this, except Tanai. And although the situation really affected their friendship they remained in touch through the years. When they were younger, their friendship was mainly confined to the school day, then once they got older they spoke over the phone from time to time. Still, no matter how many years they had been in each other's lives, their friendship had lost its heart. The two of them had lost their innocence together. Being faced with such a grown-up situation at such a young age had brought them closer in one sense, yet had torn them apart.

Charlene wasn't angry at Tanai, but her mother rarely allowed her to play with her after it happened. Ann Tanner, being as strict and religious as she was, was not only devastated by the news of Charlene being pregnant, but embarrassed. She was distraught over what the other church members might think. Charlene remembered feeling like her mother was more concerned about her getting pregnant than about the fact that she had almost died. As she got older, she resented her mother for not taking any blame, for not realizing that it was Charlene's fear of her mother and her mother's lack of acceptance of imperfection that made her resort to such extreme measures to begin with. Regardless of Charlene's view, her mother was stuck in her ways. So not only did Charlene feel guilty, she felt ashamed all these years and she never quite regained all of her self-confidence back from that. She always felt like she was her mother's biggest disappointment.

Charlene's dad, on the other hand, although also strict and religious, was more understanding. Paige and her dad always had a better relationship, but it still wasn't quite the kind where she could go to him about anything. He would discipline and scold her, but still for Charlene, his love was enough; just knowing that he accepted her meant the world to her. Sometimes she wondered if he would have stopped caring. But he continued to show Charlene his fatherly love from the moment it happened until the present; she never felt any difference in her relationship with him. He would even try to help her mother see things differently, to no avail. She was one stubborn woman, and she had her list of rights and wrongs and no one could tell her different. Paige was her trophy daughter, even though she was far from perfect. And after Paige survived her youth without getting pregnant or locked up, that made her the better woman in their mother's eyes. Paige and Charlene both knew that, and so did everyone else who knew the family.

Still, in Charlene's opinion, despite all of her struggles growing up, she definitely turned out to be quite a lady. She'd had her share of indiscretions, definitely so. But she hadn't fallen by the wayside. She kept her head above water and kept on going. Even when she felt that she was the black sheep of her family, or like she wasn't worthy of a man's true love, she still got up every day and completed life's tasks with the world never knowing her woes. There were many times when men made her feel low, when she was used and abused. There were times she would find herself practically living the life of a hooker, when she would sleep with men for money or gifts. Charlene would hear all the time what a beauty she was. Most men felt a sense of conquering when they got with her, but when they saw how easy she was, they would realize she wasn't a treasure after all. She was a scorned beauty.

It wasn't until one day, when she was twenty-two years old, that she decided she wanted a fresh start. She was tired of those lonely nights, and of pretending to herself. To start anew she denied her past, changed her ways, and handled her life and men differently. That's where her lies and deceit with Isaac came in to play. She never had planned on having to be the old Charlene again, so she never had prepared for the day when the old Charlene would make an appearance.

Chapter 9

The street was filled with parents and their kids, or maybe that's all Charlene seemed to notice. A small girl was walking alongside her mother and as she moved forward she danced. She was dancing to a tune inside her own head because no one else could hear it. She was about three years old, all of her hair was brushed into two pigtails and you could tell her mom, like a lot of black mothers, gave her the Vaseline face for moisturizer. The little girl was dressed in a beige jumper-style dress with some black Mary Jane shoes and was having herself a good old time making her way down Yonkers Avenue. Charlene was following right behind her on her way to the corner deli for a sandwich.

She had about thirty minutes left on her lunch break; she had stopped by Pay Half to buy a few shirts before she picked up her meal. Usually she stayed inside for lunch, checking her MySpace page, and more lately, checking wedding websites. However, today she wanted to go outside for a little bit, add a little excitement to her week. She was happy that she chose to, because the sight of this adorable little girl filled with so much joy immediately jumped right into Charlene and left her feeling just as joyous. The little girl caught Charlene's eye at one point and Charlene gave her a big smile, and the little girl smiled right back.

Unfortunately Charlene had to stop walking behind her dose of joy to go where she was headed to begin with. She went inside the deli and walked up to the counter. She was familiar with the clerk.

"Hey, sweetie," he said to her as soon as she approached.

"Hey, Jose," she said back.

"What can I get you today?"

"I'll take honey turkey on a roll, with cheese, lettuce—" she replied.

Before she could finish, there was an interruption. "And mayo with a little salt and pepper."

She looked over her shoulder, and there was Rich looking absolutely fine as hell, if she did say so herself. He was dressed in a cream Polo button-up, dark blue jeans and cream and tan Timberlands. He had a fresh cut, and his light complexion was just glowing. His light eyes were just piercing down at Charlene, and for a quick moment she was speechless. He gave her one of his electrifying grins as soon as she turned to see who the familiar voice belonged to.

"Hey, Rich," she said, grinning from ear to ear.

Before he could reply, Jose interrupted. "So, lettuce, cheese, mayo, salt and pepper?"

"Yes, Jose, I'm sorry," she said as she quickly turned to him and then back to Rich.

The gorgeous, just-caused-a-huge-argument-between-her-and-her-fiancé Rich. Looking in his face, she knew he was worth the trouble. Although Charlene had only been with Rich on and off, they were some of the most magical times in her life. Early on he didn't know much about her, but that didn't last long. Mount Vernon wasn't a big town, everybody knew somebody that knew everybody. So it wasn't long before somebody who knew everybody knew Rich. Rich slowly began treating Charlene different from the way other guys did. But after a while it went from great to Rich feeling like maybe they should "slow things down." That was pretty much when their relationship lost any potential, but Charlene took what she could get. Eventually it got worse, but they never stopped communicating. They had seen each other and spoken on the phone on occasion since then, but they hadn't been physical in some time. There was one time after she first got with Isaac, that she had had a run-in with Rich and she slipped up and slept with him. She just couldn't resist his smile and swagger. He had that magnetism they say Billie Dee Williams has. Charlene knew Rich definitely had something. Luckily, she felt so bad on that one occasion that she refrained from any other run-ins.

However, here she was running in to him again. The chances weren't that unlikely, because White Plains, where Rich lived, and Mount Vernon both had only so many businesses and things to do. It was just ironic that it was so soon after the answering machine incident.

"Where are you coming from?" she asked him.

"I was at a meeting on Central Avenue."

"Dressed like that?"

"It was just something informal, nothing big."

"Oh, OK. Well, I'm on my lunch break, about to head back in a few."

"How much longer you got?"

"About twenty-five minutes probably."

"OK, I'll drive you back."

Her initial thought was to say sure, but then she worried about what it would look like if someone saw them together. She knew that as a newly engaged woman, it wasn't going to look good for her to be seen on her lunch break sharing a car with a guy she used to share a bed with. Who would believe that they had just bumped into each other? Isaac especially wouldn't, not after he had *just* heard that message and found out that they had never broke contact completely.

"No, it's OK. I'll walk back, it's not that far," she spit out.

"It's at least eight blocks, and it is windy out there . . . It's nothing for me. I'm going back that way, anyway."

Charlene wasn't sure how she could turn down his offer, especially when it seemed so logical and she seemed so silly to say she'd rather walk back. She wasn't sure if Rich could read what the real reason was and didn't care, or if he really was sincere.

"OK, let me just grab a drink and we can go."

She walked to the coolers in the back of the deli, picked up a cold Lipton Green Tea and headed to the counter. She thought about the odds of her being seen with Rich, and she decided it would be almost impossible for it to get back to Isaac. It was less than a five-minute drive, it really wasn't that big of a deal. By the time she finished paying for her lunch, she hadn't thought of another excuse to turn down his offer, and so she headed out the door with him to his car.

A 2007 S-Class beeped and the lights blinked on and off. She looked over at Rich and he was the one aiming a remote at that beautiful car, parked a few feet from the store entrance. She had no idea he had gotten a new car, or that he had stepped it up quite so nicely. She was happy to see it, though, not just because it was a nice car but because it had very dark tints and now she wasn't as worried about being seen with him.

He pulled out and without saying a word began driving down the street. Charlene was happy to see Rich, and although nervous, she enjoyed being in his presence even if only for a moment. Rich was one of the good catches from around her way. He was one of the guys who made the girls in her old neighborhood jealous that she had him, too. He and everyone else knew he was fine, and he was always looking and acting like fresh money. Even if she did have a chance to get Rich to settle down with her, and hadn't wanted Isaac anymore, there was still that one issue: that with Rich came her past. And that wasn't a package deal she was willing to accept.

After a few moments down the road, he started talking about a mutual friend that had just got out of jail and how he was doing. She pretended to be very interested, even though she only cared slightly. It seemed that he didn't realize how detached she was from that world, or at least how she tried to be. She was constantly trying to mentally block out those days of her life when she had no control and very little class. So she sat there listening to Rich, and saying very little in return, waiting for the car to stop in front of her office building. Although Charlene knew that her life was better now than it had been in quite some time, she also knew that there were pros and cons to both lifestyles. She definitely knew that a life with no expectations and no secrets to bury was a lot easier than the life she was leading now. She couldn't deny that her old ways tempted her from time to time to live in the moment, and Rich with his fine self wasn't helping right now. Luckily, before she could act or think about any of the temptations, she was getting out of his car heading back to work.

The good-bye was simple and quick. His smile and wink were torturous.

Chapter 10

They had only been engaged a few weeks, and already there seemed to be this unspoken tension. Charlene had been distancing herself, fearing her guilt was written all over her face. She wasn't sure what his issue was exactly, but he seemed to have a chip on his shoulder since the answering machine message situation, and she thought it was going on too long. They were back in their usual routine, but he seemed to be a little less talkative, and less enthused about their new engagement.

After seeing Rich yesterday, and remembering what her life used to be, she knew that she should probably ensure that her present life was moving as smoothly as possible. Deep down she almost felt like that didn't matter until they were actually married—because deep down she wasn't truly convinced that she would make it down the aisle. She felt like even if they miraculously made it to that point, hers would be that one-in-a-million wedding where someone stood up and objected when the reverend asked the guests if they wanted to speak or forever hold their peace. Besides, she knew that nothing in life was guaranteed and it was still hard for her to believe she could actually have a perfectly happy life, so she expected the drama to always be right around the corner.

She was feeling a little concerned about her relationship with Isaac. Despite her fear of losing him, she damn sure wasn't ready to. Also, she knew if and when that day came she would go out fighting for him. The more she thought about it, the more she was convinced that she should make all the effort she could to make Isaac see that he was the man she wanted to spend the rest of her life with. He had proposed to her, so he had to know she loved him. Still, she was nervous that he didn't trust her 100 percent, although she knew deep in her heart that she hadn't earned all of his trust or love. More than anything she wanted somehow to get him to trust her and to know that she would never hurt him. Yet, on the other hand, she had this secret that would hurt him if he found out. How was she to convince him of her love when she was afraid he would find out the secret stuff about her one day and then wouldn't trust her again? She decided that she should go ahead and tell him before he found out, but that she should present it as something she was completely regretful of and apologetic about and not throw it in with a discussion about their other issues.

Isaac was supposed to come over to her place, just for a visit. They had both finally made copies of their apartment keys to exchange, and he was going to help lift and stack her bins of summer clothes in the back of her closet. He said he would be by around 7:30 PM, so she left work exactly on time and headed straight home.

Once she arrived at her place, she got comfortable and began preparing dinner for herself and Isaac. The last time he was over things didn't go so well, so she wanted this time to be better. She was safe and cleared her answering machine, and straightened up the living room area and the bedroom. She was sifting through the mail when her doorbell rang. She placed the mail back down on the end table and went to the door. She was dressed in a cropped white wife beater, exposing her great abs and pierced belly button, and some light gray spandex. Her hair was in a curly ponytail and she still had on traces of the make-up she had applied before work. She looked casual yet very sexy, her favorite look. As soon as she opened the door, she greeted him with one of her angelic smiles. Isaac returned the look of endearment and stepped inside her apartment. He gently kissed her on the forehead as she leaned in for it with her eyes closed. They both then proceeded to the living room.

Once settled he began to look for the remote.

"What are you making?" he asked.

"Just some baked chicken and rice," she replied.

"Can I have a glass of water?"

"Sure," she answered as she headed back to the kitchen.

She couldn't put her finger on it, but she felt something. A wall of some sort between them, and not the one that she had built from day one. It was a new one, and she didn't quite know where it came from. She would have assumed it was about the message on her answering machine, but it had been over a week, and he didn't act as if he was still upset about it. She knew she was going to have to make an extra effort tonight to get things back to normal. She had walked on enough eggshells hiding her past and trying to be perfect; she didn't need the extra stress.

She came back in the living room with a tall glass of water and sat it down in front of him. By then he had already located the remote and had started channel surfing. She sat next to him for a second, looking for a way to break the ice. She took her legs and slowly wrapped them around his waist, and sat on him, facing him. As she seductively cuddled her body closer to his, he lifted his arm to make some distance.

"What's wrong?" she asked.

"I was watching something, and now you're in my way."

Offended by the rejection, Charlene quickly removed herself from his lap.

"Not like that, I'm just saying."

"What are you saying? I try to have your undivided attention and I can't have it for a second?"

"I just got here, I had a long day at work, can I just relax for a second?" Isaac asked.

Charlene thought about his response, and she knew he had a point. Besides, if they started having sex, the food would burn, so she took it as a good thing. Still, Charlene didn't take rejection well, especially when it came to denying her sex. She was used to using that to get what she wanted, so when a man turned it down it made her feel powerless. This situation was no different. If Isaac had looked in her face he would have seen the sad look in her eyes, but he kept his eyes on the television.

Charlene decided to try another route to break the ice.

"So, how was work, baby?" she asked.

"It was good, closed a few accounts today," he replied.

"That's good. That should have put you in a good mood."

"Yeah, I'm good."

"Glad to hear that . . . You haven't been acting yourself lately."

That comment seemed to catch more of his attention.

"Yes I have. What are you talking about?"

"I don't know, you just seemed a little closed off."

"No . . . I have been myself," he said matter of factly.

"OK, maybe it has been in my head . . . Well, happy to hear you're good," she said as she rose up to go back into the kitchen.

Just as she stepped away he responded, "Isn't that the pot calling the kettle black?"

She stopped midstride and turned around.

"What does that mean?" she asked.

"Me being closed off . . . That's your thing," he said.

Definitely not the conversation she wanted to have, but she

was also interested to know what he meant. She didn't know that Isaac had a real sense of that.

"What do you mean? I'm not closed off."

"Yeah, you are. You are always keeping something in."

"I have no idea what you're talking about. I am very open and talkative . . . too talkative at times, you say."

"That is true, it just seems you are selective about how open you are and what exactly you want to talk about."

Charlene was starting to lose her footing. She wasn't prepared for this direct reality check. She thought she would be getting Isaac to share what was on his mind, and it turned out he was trying to get inside of hers. She didn't want to appear nervous or uneasy, so she tried to remain as calm as possible.

"Whatever you want to know, just ask," Charlene said bravely.

"What is the extent of the relationship you still have with Rich?" Isaac blurted out as if he had been just waiting to ask that question.

Damn, she thought to herself. She wasn't really expecting him to ask a question, and she definitely wasn't prepared to answer any questions. Besides, whenever anything or anyone from her life before Isaac came up she became a little uneasy, but she was especially uneasy only a day after she saw Rich. She knew it was one more secret she was going to have to keep, because this surely wasn't when she wanted to tell him that she spent a little bit of time with him recently.

"The extent? . . . We have spoken a few times over the past few years but that's the extent of it," she finally replied.

"That's the extent of it? . . . How often have y'all spoken?"

"Maybe every few months, just for a few moments, he will call me to say hello."

"Just to say hello? It's always just to say hello?"

"Pretty much . . . to say hello or catch up."

"How did you end up telling him that marriage was not in me and your plans, then?"

Trying not to show how much this conversation was making her uncomfortable, she made a conscious effort not to hesitate as she answered his questions.

"He just happened to ask me last time we spoke. I told him that it wasn't in the plans. Not that I wouldn't marry you . . . I had no idea at that time you were going to pop the question."

"Why would he ask you that, though? . . . Or was that to catch up?" Isaac asked, slightly sarcastic.

"Yeah, basically. He just asked how I was and how we were and stuff."

"OK, whatever . . ." Isaac said, showing his dislike for what he was hearing. "So it's always been on the phone, you haven't spent any time with him?"

Charlene could feel the extra perspiration forming on her body. Still, she didn't take long to answer.

"No, it's always just on the phone," she replied.

She had gotten so used to keeping things from Isaac she found herself hiding things that weren't even necessary to hide. She didn't know if her innocent ride from Rich was one of them, but as usual she took the safe route to protect her image and chose to leave out that information. Other than yesterday, she had only seen Rich a few times since she had been with Isaac, nothing she thought was worth mentioning now.

"Well, just so we are clear, I don't know how much I like you talking on the phone with your ex-boyfriend who happened to be your first," Isaac said.

"It's really not that often," she answered.

"I really don't care. When I'm sitting here with you and have to hear a message from him saying our marriage should have been for you two, I realize there's something you're not telling me—"

"It's not—" Charlene tried to interrupt.

"SO . . . I am telling you, I don't want you keeping in touch with him."

The room fell silent for a second, and then Charlene responded.

"I respect your feelings. I just want you to know it's nothing like that. He knows I am engaged and happily involved."

"Well then, he should understand that it's time to let go."

Charlene was done with the conversation. Isaac had spoken, and there was no need to try to defend Rich. She knew that she would just dig a deeper hole if she continued, and possibly have to answer more questions that she wasn't prepared to answer.

Regardless of how much progress Charlene had made with getting comfortable with her life, she always felt a sense of tension when her past surfaced or was questioned. She never knew when anything that she had ever twisted the truth about would come to bite her in the behind. It had gotten to the point that she forgot the truth sometimes, and she lived the lies that she had told. The thing was, she never saw them as such major lies, nothing other than what most people leave unsaid about their past. Charlene wondered what woman still confesses to the world about her wild youth, the number of partners she slept with, a reputation she had in her neighborhood . . . those types of things. Charlene knew she was doing what most women would. It wasn't as if she was telling complete lies to Isaac, he knew all the things about her that he needed to know, in her opinion—her real age, where she grew up, her parents, her plans for the future. As far as she was concerned as long as he knew the person she was today, yesterday was irrelevant. Besides, everyone deserves a second chance.

Chapter 11

It was 10:15 on Tuesday morning when the doctor called her office phone. She saw the number in the caller ID and took a deep breath before she answered.

"Hello?"

"Hello, can I speak to Charlene?" the other voice answered.

"Speaking."

"Hello, I'm calling from Dr. Ginyard's office. The doctor would like to speak with you, can you hold for her for a moment?"

"Sure," Charlene said.

"OK, please hold," the nurse said.

As Charlene waited on the other end of the phone she felt her heart beating a hundred times a minute. The irony was she was more nervous about what the doctor might say about the condition of her uterus and her chance at motherhood, than she was about the results from her Pap smear, and the STD and HIV tests. Considering she hadn't been tested since she was barely a teenager, for all she knew she could be dying in less than six months. Somehow she felt more confident about those tests, she hadn't had any symptoms and she wasn't that unsafe. However, she was worried about the findings from her sonogram. Most likely because she could still remember that doctor years ago telling her mother that kids were very unlikely in her future. Charlene remembered so vividly how the doctor spoke like she wasn't even sitting there, or as if she was too young to care or comprehend. That doctor couldn't have been more wrong. Not only did Charlene comprehend, she cared; she had been caring deep down ever since.

Charlene was so nervous as she waited for the doctor to pick up the phone and give her report. She was sitting at her desk doodling in her notepad, drawing a star and outlining it over and over, until it began to look messy. She knew that what the doctor was about to tell her would be crucial to the success of her upcoming marriage, and she hadn't quite mustered the courage to hear what she felt she already knew. The hold music was starting to annoy Charlene. She asked herself, *Why did they call me if the doctor wasn't available yet?*

Charlene began to think about what she would do next after she hung up from this call. Would she call Isaac and tell him, just get it over with now that she knew for sure—as if that's what she was waiting for, or something? Would she call Paige and cry her eyes out, or would she go back to work as if nothing had happened? She wasn't quite sure how she would react, but while she thought about it she did convince herself that she wasn't ready to tell Isaac about her pregnancy issue after all. She didn't know why she let Paige get in her head, anyway. She told herself it wouldn't do anything but make it worse. She figured if the doctor confirmed that she was unable to have kids, then she would tell Isaac what he needed to know. There really was no purpose in telling him the story, it would only make things worse than they already were. It would only cause more doubt and suspicion between them. She had come this far maintaining the stories she had told. There was no need to go back now. At least that's what she decided as she sat there waiting on the doctor to come to the phone.

After a few more moments of listening to the Kenny G hold music, a voice came through the phone.

"Hello?"

"Yes, hello," Charlene replied.

"Hi, this is Dr. Ginyard. How are you?"

"I'm fine."

"Good, sorry to keep you on hold so long."

"No problem," Charlene said, lying as if she wasn't pissed off just a few seconds earlier.

"Well, I wanted to discuss your test results with you," the doctor replied.

Charlene could feel the tightness building in her body. Her stomach suddenly filled with these colorful little butterflies, and her breath fell short. She didn't respond right away, and Dr. Ginyard took that as a sign to continue.

"Well, Charlene, from our visit you disclosed some information to me that caused me to look into your situation further. You seem to be aware of the risks you are facing due to the improper abortion you had. However, I don't know if you understand exactly what shape your body is in. So I want to help you completely understand what happened. Is that OK with you?"

"Sure," Charlene replied in a tone that echoed just how unsure she really was.

"OK. First let me ask, have you been practicing safe sex since you left my office?"

Charlene hesitated. She hated being asked such personal questions, and even more she hated telling the truth to such personal questions. Still, she knew if there was one person who needed the truth to help her, it was her doctor.

"Not really . . . Me and my fiancé had used the pull-out method for the most part, like I told you, but lately we don't even do that."

"Why is that? Are you guys trying to get pregnant?"

"Well, yes and no. He wants children, and although ideally it would be after we are married, he wants them as soon as possible because his father is really sick."

"And you?"

"Well, I haven't worried about it either way, because I figured I couldn't get pregnant, anyway."

"Why do you figure that?"

"First off because that's what the doctor said after the abortion, second, I haven't been pregnant since, and . . . Let's just say it wasn't 'cause of the protection or lack of sex I was having."

"OK . . . Charlene, let me explain. That doctor didn't say you could not get pregnant. I pulled your file from the hospital you went to."

Just hearing her speak on that time in the hospital gave Charlene a slight chill. She thought back to that day for just a moment, and quickly she became even more uncomfortable.

"OK," she replied.

"What that doctor said was that you may not be able to get pregnant when you get older, and that you lowered your chances severely."

"I'm not a hundred percent sure, but I know she said I did something to myself, and that my chances of having children were very unlikely."

"Now, that's correct, and you did do something. You ruptured your ovaries. However, your sonogram shows that you are capable of getting pregnant. It's just that it won't be as easy for you, your chances are very slim, but it's possible."

"Really?" Charlene asked with a hint of excitement in her voice.

"Sure you can. But . . . It's unlikely you will get pregnant on your own, and you must know that you are at great risk if you were to carry a child to full term."

"What does that mean? Charlene asked.

She could hear in the doctor's voice, that that was the piece of information that she wanted to tell Charlene herself. The test results could have been delivered by any one of her staff. This, however, seemed to be the real bad news.

"It means that if you did manage to get pregnant, which would more than likely be the result of medications and regulating your cycle, you still are at a severe health risk. You have to remember you have a history of uterine damage so it can cause some serious health issues for you."

Charlene didn't reply. She was still trying to take it all in.

"There's always bed rest and other ways to monitor progress, but you definitely have to factor those risks into the decision to have children."

"I understand," Charlene said.

"Otherwise, you're completely healthy. No STDs and no other problems."

"Great," Charlene said. "Thanks for the call."

"No problem. You take care, and make sure you're back in my office in six months for a checkup."

"I will do. Thanks again."

Once she was off the phone, she couldn't even put the phone down before the tears began to fill her eyes. She held her hand up to her face to stop them, with the phone still in hand. Her heart felt heavy and her spirit was completely low. She had tried to keep up the happy face and pretend life was as it should be, but reality just kept surfacing and smacking her in the face. She didn't know why she was upset, as if she didn't expect bad news, but hearing it seemed to hit her in her heart. Before she went to the doctor she knew that the visit would dig up these feelings, but for some reason she still felt defeated.

It was like she was reliving the pain all over again. The pain that had started her life on the wild path that it took. The pain from the abortion, emotionally and physically. The pain from the boy she thought she loved who had abandoned her when she told him she was pregnant; the pain from the inability to confide in anyone but Tanai, and then losing her, too, because of it; the pain from murdering the child inside of her that she thought she wanted, because it would love her uncondition-ally; and the pain from her mother being ashamed of her.

In addition to all that built-up pain she felt new pain. A pain from knowing that she now may not have the chance to be a mother, that she had aborted the one child she could have had to love her for who she was. A pain from knowing that her mother's embarrassment was justified, because even she was embarrassed of herself. A pain from knowing that she was so ashamed of the life she'd led, she was running from herself. A pain from knowing that she was living a lie. She felt pain knowing that she was with a man that had no idea who she really had been all those years, and she had no idea how to begin to be real with him because she had been phony for so long.

The worst pain of all was knowing that this secret that she kept inside was now going to hurt her in a new way. Isaac wanted kids so badly, how was she going to break the news to him that she couldn't do that for him? She had known for quite some time that he was eager to have kids for the sake of his father and himself. She also knew that he had names picked out and everything; he was one of the great future fathers. She didn't like discussing it with him in too much depth because she always knew there was this possibility. She knew that it was likely, but she always hoped that things would be different. That the doctor would say that her uterus had healed and she was just fine. That's what she always dreamed would happen the day she finally faced the situation. Instead the nightmare was a reality, and she had to tell Isaac that it was very unlikely his future wife would bear children for him. The more she thought about telling him and his likely reaction, the more she figured she was better off telling him after she said "I do."

Chapter 12

Before she took into consideration that she might change her mind and not tell Isaac the whole truth, she had mentioned to him that she was going to the doctor. She noticed that when she told him he had seemed very surprised, yet happy that she was going. He actually had noticed that she hadn't been to the doctor since he'd met her, and was wondering when she would go. He also wanted her to go because he knew for a woman it was important to get checked out. So as soon as she told him, he expressed his concern about the results. It was obvious that he was only thinking of the basics, like breast cancer and any diseases, but she wondered if problems with bearing children had crossed his mind. He had been very clear that he wanted to have children sooner than he had planned, but he hadn't sat down and spoken with Charlene seriously about it.

She spoke to Isaac and saw him the same day she spoke to the doctor, and the following. Although she considered mentioning the doctor's call, she was afraid that she may not be able to hide that she was withholding information. Charlene had become pretty good at withholding info and bending the truth, but she was aware of her weakness and the intricacies of this facet of her life that always left her a little vulnerable. So as a result she didn't bring it up. Not that it mattered, because she knew eventually Isaac would ask her about it. Especially since he showed so much concern about the appointment. Sure enough, a day or two later he had asked how the appointment went. Still not ready to discuss it, she told him she had to wait a few days for the results. But she knew it was only a matter of time before he asked what ever happened with the results.

She had been at his place for less than twenty minutes when he brought it up. She came in his apartment walking quickly, she had been holding her pee in the entire way over. She rushed into the bathroom to go, and she sat in there for a couple of extra minutes. She was just relaxing, meditating, mentally preparing to spend the rest of her night with Isaac. She finished up in the bathroom, came out and headed straight to the kitchen. She looked around the sparkling clean kitchen for a snack. The stainless steel appliances were glistening they were so shiny, as usual impressing her how clean Isaac kept his place. She finally grabbed some Oreo cookies and a glass of milk and headed back into the living room. Isaac was in the living room already, he had been in there since she first keyed in. She had quickly thrown him a hello as she was rushing to the downstairs bathroom. He was working on some files from work, and she sat about three feet away from him in front of the television with her snack.

As soon as she nestled in the couch, he blurted out, "So, what did the doctor ever say about your results?"

Charlene tensed up. Her body language showed she was uneasy. She was as unprepared to answer that question as she would be if he had asked whether she found his best friend attractive—a friend who just happened to be drop-dead gorgeous.

"Nothing much," she said with a slight crack in her voice before she straightened it up. "She said everything was OK for the most part," she continued.

"For the most part?"

"Well, she said I don't have any diseases to worry about, and my breasts are healthy." She bit into one of her Oreo cookies.

"So then everything was A-OK?"

Charlene could hear like ten voices in her head. An angel and a devil, her sister and her mother, and every other inner demon that she dealt with. She didn't know how to tell him that the doctor had also told her that she may never be able to have kids, when she knew that was the last thing he would want to hear. So, despite the temptation for once to tell him the truth even though it wasn't good, she decided to take the easy route.

"Yeah, A-OK," she said.

Isaac had been looking in her face the entire time as if he could see right through her. He watched her as she reached for replies to his questions, and when she was done he turned back to his work.

Charlene sat there watching the television program that was on, eating her milk-dipped cookies, trying to remain as calm as possible. She realized after a few moments that she was always being interrogated, and also that she was rarely telling the truth. She knew that this wasn't a healthy relationship with Isaac, but she had gotten so deep in it she didn't know how to get back out. Sometimes she wished that he would pry more, and finally catch her in her lies so she wouldn't have to sustain them anymore, but he never did. She did wonder, though, if he, too, knew what was really going on. She didn't know if it was her guilt or what, but she always felt like he was able to see that she was lying and that he wanted to see just how many lies she would tell before he jumped out and said, *"Aha! I got you."*

She worried that maybe the concept of karma was true, or that the cliché "what's done in the dark comes to light" was true. She knew that she had a locked closet full of skeletons and she was so afraid he would find the key to it one day. It was truly her worst nightmare.

Chapter 13

It was like God was sending her a message that he wanted her to finally bring some sort of closure to this part of her life. It was a major step for Charlene to even talk about it openly with Paige again for the first time in a long while, let alone go to the doctor and discuss it. It was like she was having a confession with a priest. All of this digging up of truths and emotions was starting to break Charlene down.

Just when she thought that maybe she could move on from this nightmare that was starting to begin again, her friend Tanai called her. It had been so long since she'd spoken to Tanai that when she saw the name on the caller ID, she literally did a triple blink to make sure she was seeing it right.

Charlene hesitated about whether to answer the phone, but then quickly decided that if there was anybody that might know what to do right now, it would be Tanai. She answered the phone and initially there was some awkwardness, but before long they had made plans to hang out for a bit and Tanai was on her way over to Charlene's place. For some reason Charlene cared about what Tanai thought about her, at least somewhat. So even though she didn't change her clothes, she combed her hair and applied some light makeup. Tanai didn't live very far away, and she arrived in no time. Charlene didn't know why she cared, but she assumed it was because of all the unspoken feelings between them. They had gone from knowing each other's every secret, to hiding behind a façade that they were doing just fine. And Charlene definitely wasn't prepared to lower the curtains just yet.

As soon as Charlene opened the door, she felt a gush of emotion. Just seeing Tanai again felt really nice, and she immediately reached out to hug her. Tanai was just as excited to see Charlene, and she held on tight for the few moments they hugged.

"Come on in," Charlene said, pointing toward the couches.

Tanai looked almost exactly the same. She was dressed in some True Religion jeans, a brown fitted shirt and some cowboy boots. She was about 5'7", 135 pounds. She was dark skinned, with long black and copper hair. She had slanted eyes, a narrow, pointy nose and full lips. Tanai still was as she had been— absolutely beautiful. She had a nice shape and a pretty face, and the boys adored her. When they were younger, they used to get so much attention they didn't know how to act.

When they first sat on the couch, they began making small talk. They discussed how Tanai had got lost on her way over and how she found her way. Then after the small talk subsided it was like they both needed to get stuff off their chest. Charlene had thought about whether she would bring up what had been going on if Tanai didn't mention anything serious first, and she hadn't come to a decision. She decided to just go with the flow, but she didn't have to wonder long because Tanai wanted to talk seriously, too.

"I really want to talk about the past ten years of our lives, Leeney," Tanai said.

It came out of nowhere. Tanai had interjected all the phony small talk to work up to saying something of substance. At first Charlene didn't know what to say, but then she replied.

"What about?"

"Just all the things that we never did talk about, and how things are between us now."

"I would like that, too," Charlene said, although sounding unsure.

"Listen, Charlene, I know that it's not easy to talk about. I also know that something that bonded us shouldn't be the cause of our separation as well," Tanai said.

"You're right," Charlene said.

"I never thought we would be able to actually sit down and talk about it," Tanai said.

This whole conversation was kind of throwing Charlene off, but it was also kind of refreshing to hear the honesty.

"Me, either, trust me. It's just one of those things I was hoping I could leave tucked away forever," she opened up and said.

"I know, Charlene; I wish I could take it back, too. I have had nightmares about it, up to even a year or so ago."

"Well then, you can imagine how it haunts me," Charlene said.

"Yeah, I know having an abortion is emotional enough, but to have it as painful and memorable as that, I can imagine," Tanai said.

Charlene didn't respond right away. It was still hard for her to speak about it.

Then she said, "It definitely hasn't been easy."

"Now they give counseling. God knows we both needed it after that, but back then they just sent you home."

"If my mom would have let me go anyway, but she wanted to put that behind us as quickly and quietly as possible," Charlene responded.

"I know, your mom was no joke. I just wished she didn't take it out on me. I needed you at that time, and I think you needed me."

"I did. Especially since you were the only person I could talk to."

"It was like double the punishment," Tanai said, sounding as if she was still angry at Charlene's mother.

"Sure was . . . I had to cope with it somehow on my own, and I think I was just trying to deny it ever happened."

"I know, I think I tried to forget it myself."

"That's what I did, I lied to myself. When I wasn't having nightmares, I tried to forget it as much as I could."

"I'm just happy that you survived it and you're healthy and happy today," Tanai said, truly sounding sincere, like she had been wanting to tell Charlene that for years.

"Well, I just hope that I am able to have kids and I can put this all behind me."

Charlene was deep in thought just staring down at the floor. On the couch next to her, Tanai had her head dropped, fiddling with her hands. There was an uncomfortable silence until Tanai interrupted it.

"I don't know if I have ever told you this, Charlene . . . But I am truly sorry."

There was silence again. Charlene didn't look in her direction, she kept her head low, staring into her lap. Slowly a tear rolled down her cheek and she sniffled. She tried to contain her emotion as she replied.

"Thanks, it's OK . . . It wasn't your fault," she said real low, trying to keep back her tears.

Tanai, also attempting to contain her emotions, continued the conversation despite the obvious—that it might be more than either of them could handle.

"I should have never suggested doing that, and I shouldn't have continued to encourage you . . . I will forever live with that guilt."

"You were just trying to be my friend, and at that time you were all I had."

Tanai got up and went to sit closer to Charlene and held her. By this time both of their faces were soaked with tears and they had both felt a load lift from off their shoulders. After all these years, they finally were able to speak on that dreadful day. Charlene didn't know that Tanai felt the way she did, and she didn't know that all these years it weighed heavily on her heart as well. It felt kind of good, knowing that she hadn't been alone all those years after all. It felt good for them both to finally just let all their balled-up emotions and thoughts exit their souls. In that moment, all the distance that the painful memories had wedged between them was taken away. Just that fast they had become closer than they ever had been. All that pain finally brought them both some joy, even if only for a moment.

Chapter 14

Charlene spent the next few days in her apartment, just relaxing and trying to clear her head. She ran a few errands out on White Plains Road, went to the grocery store and to a few knickknack stores. She picked up some things she would need so she could settle down inside without having to go out for anything. Usually she kept on the move, trying to ignore all the issues and drama surrounding her. This time she decided to take it slow. She had taken a few days off work to get a grasp of things in her mind, and in her life.

"Slow Down," by India Arie was playing out of her stereo as Charlene whisked around her apartment cleaning. She felt better than she had for the past few days. Her sit-down with Tanai left her feeling like everything would be just fine. Although Charlene grew up in the church, attending with her parents, she didn't consider herself very religious. She knew the Lord, and knew he was her sheperd; but she felt like with all the sins she had committed in her life she didn't know if she could claim spirituality. Still, she knew that although she was no angel, God was watching over her, and sending Tanai over was his way of telling her just that.

She was wearing a lime green tube top with black and

lime boy shorts and flip-flops. Her toes and nails were mani-
cured with a peach-colored nail polish, her hair was up in a bun
and she had a white cleansing mask on her face. She hummed
the words to the song seeping through her speakers.

"You're 'bout to wreck your future
Running from your past
You need to slow down baby . . ."

Charlene knew that that music truly spoke to the soul, because if this song wasn't the most appropriate song for her she
didn't know what was.

She was dusting and throwing things away, and feeling
mighty good about herself. The words of the song was making
her feel how things could be much better. As she bounced and
bopped around the apartment, her phone rang. She stopped
and walked toward the phone, and when she checked the
caller ID it was Rich. She looked at it for a few seconds and
put the cordless back down. She definitely wasn't in the mood
for any drama right now. Regardless of why he was calling, it
wasn't anything she wanted to deal with. For once she had
erased everybody, including Isaac, out of her thoughts and was
feeling happy as Charlene. As Tanai had said, just thankful to be
alive and healthy.

Charlene tried to go back to her bouncing and bopping
and singing but she felt a slight distraction. The song finally
went off, and the next song by India was coming on. Charlene
walked over to see if he had left a message, he didn't. She couldn't
help but be curious as to what that call was about, and also
thankful that Isaac wasn't over. She decided to go ahead and
give Isaac a call. She hadn't spoken to him all day, and she figured she should have a small conversation with him to make
sure she wouldn't get tempted to call Rich back.

She dialed Isaac's cell phone and waited for him to answer. She began to walk over to the stereo to turn it down when she heard a voice. It didn't sound like Isaac's, it sounded like a female's, but she wasn't sure because the music was still turned up.

"Hello," Charlene said as she lowered the volume.

"Hello," the female voice said back.

Charlene recognized the voice, it was Lacy. *Here goes the drama,* she thought to herself.

She almost wished that Isaac knew how she felt about Lacy, so that he would have known better than to let her answer his phone. It was hard for Charlene to admit to Isaac that she had some jealous feelings about Lacy, but Lacy pretending to like her backfired time and time again. It wasn't that Charlene was insecure, because despite anything Lacy did, Charlene was well aware that the problem was in her own mind. Charlene never once felt unattractive, she knew she was a beautiful woman. There were many other reasons why Lacy made her jealous, but it wasn't something Charlene could easily admit to. She believed that Lacy was only a friend to Isaac, but Lacy reminded Charlene of everything that she was not. Lacy reminded Charlene of everything that she pretended to be. Lacy made Charlene fear that if Isaac found out who she really was, that he might think Lacy was a better fiancé for him. She realized that that had something to do with her own insecurity about her self-worth. It was her own fault that she didn't know whether Isaac truly loved her for her, she knew she never gave him the chance to know the true her.

It didn't help that Lacy was beautiful as well, tall and slim just like Charlene. She was a few shades darker than Charlene, but had a beautiful complexion with pretty light brown eyes. She had long dark hair and a beautiful Colgate smile. She looked like a cover girl model, actually, and she had the lifestyle to match. Charlene was equally as beautiful if not more, so she didn't feel threatened by Lacy's looks. However, she did know that Lacy wouldn't be a downgrade if Isaac was to end up with her. Unlike Charlene, Lacy grew up in a good neighborhood, and went to good schools and led a pretty good life. She probably didn't have many indiscretions in her past, and had a childhood that she could tell stories about. She and Isaac had more in common than Charlene and Isaac did, and that was what bothered Charlene the most. Isaac was well aware that she was from the other side of the tracks and that she'd had it rougher than he did growing up, and he still loved her anyway; but she assumed that he was impressed by Lacy's upbringing.

When Charlene called Isaac's phone and Lacy picked up, she couldn't help but pause. She didn't mean to be obvious, but her displeasure was heard loud and clear through her silence.

"Charlene, you there?" Lacy repeated.

"Yeah, I'm here," Charlene finally said.

"Hey, girl. What's up with you?"

"I'm fine, how are you?" Charlene replied, still obviously caught off guard and clearly trying to gather her thoughts.

What part of the game was this? Charlene was asking herself as she tried to continue this phony conversation with Lacy.

"I'm good. Isaac just ran to the bathroom and he left his phone by me. When I saw it was you, I just wanted to see how you were and if that ring is making your finger tired yet." Lacy said before she let out a loud chuckle.

If only Lacy could see Charlene's face through the phone.

Trying to remain polite, Charlene gave her a phony chuckle back, and said, "No, not yet."

"Well, I'm sure it will soon, that is quite a rock."

What the hell is she all in my rock for? Wishing it was on her finger, probably, Charlene said to herself as she got herself more upset.

"Yeah, it is a beauty . . . You know Isaac."

"I sure do," Lacy replied.

She sure does? Charlene repeated to herself. Lacy knew what she was doing. She made remarks and responses that on the surface seemed so innocent and funny but had an underlying smirk to them. It was her way of being slick. Lacy knew that there was no way Charlene could be a hundred percent comfortable with her answering her man's phone, regardless of how cool they were. So, she knew what was going through Charlene's mind, or at least she had an idea. So, little smart remarks like "I sure do know your man," weren't exactly rubbing Charlene the right way. Unfortunately, even if Charlene wanted to make a big deal out of it, she couldn't because she would seem like the catty, jealous girlfriend.

"Yeah, that's my Isaac . . . Is he out of the bathroom yet?" Charlene asked, trying to gain control of the conversation.

"Here he is, actually, hold on, girl," Lacy said as she handed off the phone to Isaac.

After a few seconds, Isaac got on the phone.

"Hello?"

"Hey, Izzy," Charlene said, trying to sound calm.

"Hey, babe," he said, actually sounding excited to hear her voice.

"What you doing?"

"I'm just heading out to the office, about to get out of here," he replied.

"What are you doing tonight?"

"Probably just some work at home . . . Why? Whatsup?"

"Come do the work over here," she said back.

Charlene hadn't been calling to ask that, but after hearing he was with Lacy she wanted to state her claim for some reason.

"Babe, I don't know if I can."

"Why not?"

"I have to drop Lacy off at home and then get like ten reports done by tomorrow. You know I can barely get work done around you. You are distracting."

"Distracting?" Charlene was getting upset, knowing that Lacy was probably listening to the whole conversation.

"I meant that in a good way, baby. I'm going to want to sit and cuddle with my fiancé over getting work done."

Charlene wasn't sure why Isaac was being so sweet, but she was happy that he was. That was more what Charlene wanted to hear, or rather wanted Lacy to hear.

"I promise I won't distract you," she said.

"OK. I'll try to make it, babe. Let me see what time it is when I'm done."

Charlene accepted that answer, because she knew that that was probably all that she was going to get from him at this point. She wanted to tell him to drop off Lacy right now, and once she knew he was alone, she would tell him to stay home and do his work. She wasn't in the mood to keep all the guilt and fear she was feeling disguised, anyway. She did know, however, that if she didn't request his presence he might hang out with Lacy all night, and she didn't like the thought of that, either. Usually she was a trooper about it. Showing how secure she was, or pretending to be at least; and trying to show them both that she was confident in her relationship with Isaac. She didn't know if they could see through it or not, but the truth was that it bothered her extremely, and she wished that one day Lacy would find someone of her own, and go away. She hoped that happened before she had to finally show her weakness and get rid of Lacy her damn self.

Chapter 15

It couldn't have been more than a week that went by before it seemed as though she could barely face herself in the mirror. The more sweet and romantic Isaac was, the more that the guilt from not being up front with him was driving her crazy. She knew he deserved to know the life he would be signing up for if he married her, but she was afraid she would lose him if he knew. She wondered if he loved her enough to give up having a child. She knew no man would find that an easy decision to make, especially Isaac, who took so much pride in carrying on his sick father's name. She couldn't help but wonder if it was a punishment for all her sins and deceit.

She had discussed it with her sister and Jasmine, and they both understood her dilemma but didn't quite agree with the way she was handling it. They didn't know how long she was planning on trying to keep the truth from him. They agreed that for most guys it probably wasn't as big of a deal. However, since it was Isaac, one of the few men in this day and age that actually yearned for children, that changed the whole situation. It wasn't like if she never brought it up, he would never notice he wasn't having kids.

Charlene knew that they were right, she was just unsure

about how to face him with it. She knew that it would crush Isaac, and she wasn't sure if he would work things out with her. He might want to go find a woman that he could definitely have his kids with. The sense of urgency was even more severe since his father was sick, and waiting around while trying to impregnate Charlene would probably not be something he would be too happy about. Charlene knew in her heart that Isaac loved her. However, if she told him the truth about why it was almost impossible for her to bear children, he would probably be just as upset realizing that she had told him some lies.

And Charlene knew that not only were Paige and Jasmine right, it was only a matter of time before Isaac would ask her to go get checked out if he started to realize his sperm weren't successful. So she realized that she was better off telling him now than later, since it wouldn't be at such a sensitive time.

It was about 8:00 PM on a Saturday night and she was waiting on Isaac to come over to her house. She had planned on going by his place, but her car was acting up some and she didn't want to drive it any more than she had to until she got it fixed.

Isaac arrived at about 8:30, and as usual he headed straight for the couch. He was dressed in a navy blue Sean John sweatsuit and white Air Force 1 sneakers. Charlene liked it when Isaac dressed like that, especially since it didn't happen that often. It was a little nippy in her apartment so she grabbed a blanket from the linen closet and joined him on the couch. He went straight to one of his favorite television shows *My Wife and Kids*, and got engulfed in the story. He looked so happy, Charlene thought to herself. He really had the perfect life, at least for the most part. She started to feel guilty that the worst part of his life right now, besides his father being sick, was that he had a fiancé that he didn't really know. She used to be able to convince herself that the past is the past, and as long as he knew her today that's all that mattered. However, she realized after a while that he didn't know her today, either. He only knew a part of her, and the image of her. He couldn't possibly really know her, without knowing her past, because her past was so much of who she was today.

Charlene sat there trying to muster up the courage to tell Isaac the truth, or at least some of it. After his show was over he started flicking through the channels, and Charlene thought it was a good time to strike up a conversation while he wasn't focused on anything.

"So, how was your day, babe?" she asked.

"It was good. Business went well; I was home at a decent time. It was a good day . . . How was yours?"

"My day was cool, too."

He didn't reply. His attention got caught up in the channel that he had landed on, and he seemed to be checking out the program. Before he got too interested in it and she lost him completely, she continued.

"I have something to tell you, baby, and it's really not good news," she said in an obviously nervous tone.

Isaac instantly looked over at her, right in her eyes. It was like he was searching for the truth before she could even say what it was.

"What does it have to do with?" he asked.

"Me and you," she said.

"Something to do with Rich?"

"NO!" Charlene said pretty loud. "What would make you say that?"

"Just asking," he said.

"What do you think, that I am cheating on you with Rich or something?"

"I didn't say that. Now, what is it?" he asked, sounding frustrated.

"Well then, why was that the first thing out of your mouth?" she asked, sounding equally frustrated.

"No reason, just a guess . . . Now, what is it?"

Realizing there was no reason to harp on the topic and draw more attention to it, she went ahead and continued.

"Something Dr. Ginyard told me," she said.

Isaac paused for a second, as if he was trying to imagine all the things that could come next.

"What did she tell you?" he finally asked.

After a moment of hesitation, she replied. "She said that I will more than likely have a hard time getting pregnant."

"What's that mean?"

"Just that . . . I may not get pregnant easy; we may have to work at it."

"I don't understand, why is that?"

"She just said that I may not be that fertile, that I may have to work at it for a while."

Isaac was looking down for a second as he listened to her news. Then he looked over at her and put his arm on her leg.

"That's fine, baby, then we will just work at it."

Charlene didn't know how to react. She was surprised that he wasn't upset, and touched that he reached out to console her.

"Thanks, baby," she said.

"You don't have to thank me. Millions of couples don't get pregnant right away. It's normal to take some tries," he said.

"Yeah, I guess you're right."

"Yeah, like they do on TV, they track when you ovulate and stuff," he said, slightly giggling.

Trying to act normal, she giggled back. "Yeah," she said.

"We will be fine," he said, lightly rubbing her leg.

Charlene realized that her light version of the truth hadn't helped much because Isaac didn't seem to get it. Then again, how could he? She hadn't really told him. He is thinking that it would be the same difficulty that any of his friends would have if they were trying. He didn't know that he would probably never be successful. Charlene felt uncomfortable knowing that if she left the conversation where it was, it would have been a meaningless conversation because he still wouldn't know the whole truth and she wouldn't know how he would react if he did.

"I guess you're right, we just have to work at it . . . But how would you feel if it didn't work?"

"Don't even say that, Charlene, we will be fine."

"I know, I'm just asking. What if . . . What if it turns out that we can't?"

"I don't even want to think about that, or talk about that. We shouldn't jinx that. You are young and healthy, and so am I. We will have no problem having our babies."

His words just pierced Charlene's heart. How was she going to tell this man just the opposite, that she wasn't healthy and that they would have nothing but problems having them?

Charlene remained quiet. She took a moment to let it all sink in. She tried to figure out what if anything she could say to make it more clear without putting her foot in her mouth. Before she could think of another comment to make, Isaac interrupted.

"You OK, baby?"

"I'm fine. I just know how bad you want to have kids and I am worried."

"Don't be . . . This is everyday stuff, you'll see. If anything, I'll go with you to the doctor next time, and we will ask questions."

Although it was very sweet of him, that was the last thing that Charlene wanted. She realized then that she had done all that she could for now. Her attempt at being honest may not have been the most effective, but it was a start.

"Let's go try right now," Isaac said slightly playfully as he started to rub her leg again.

Charlene started to giggle some, realizing that this conversation was pretty much done. Isaac continued on to start their efforts, and Charlene went along with it.

"You ready to make our baby?" Isaac asked as he slowly kissed her neck.

Charlene didn't know what to say, but she also knew confession time was over even if her conscience did try to convince her otherwise.

"Yes, I am," she whispered back at him as she fell deeper and deeper into his caress.

He slowly kissed her from her neck down to her chest. Once he reached a point where her scoop-neck shirt began to cover her bare skin, and he couldn't kiss any lower, he began to remove it. He lifted her shirt over her head and continued where he left off. He kissed lower, kiss by kiss until he reached the split in her chest. He started with her right breast, as he slowly and softly kissed all around her breast and nipple. Once he made her right nipple hard, and he had given it his undivided attention, he moved on to the left. He slowly and softly kissed and sucked on her left breast, while he softly caressed her right breast with his free hand. After he had succeeded at making both of her nipples nice and hard, and he could tell her body was yearning for more, he continued down his trail. Charlene just lay back allowing him to do his magic. That's one thing that Charlene never had a complaint about, was Isaac's foreplay. He always knew how to get her body nice and moist.

He had started to slowly lower her pants as he continued to kiss and nibble at her upper body. Once he had slightly lowered her pants, he ran his lips along her waistline slowly and gently. He didn't use his tongue, just his soft lips. The feel of his soft, plump lips lightly rubbing against her pelvic border was driving her wild. He continued to slowly pull down her pants, and with his assistance she wiggled out the rest of the way. The entire time he kept his mouth on her body, and once her pants were off he made his way past her panties. By this point Charlene was absolutely craving him. She was wet and overly excited. He had taken his time and remained so gentle that she was even squirming on the inside. After he had begun tongue kissing her lower set of lips, she just lay back and enjoyed every second of it. As she lay there, she started to fill with joy that she had a man that loved her so much and she felt lucky that he was so good in bed. What more could she ask for? She knew a man with his talents was hard to come by. Most men didn't know when and how to take it slow, but Isaac was definitely a pro.

Just as she drifted off into lust and happiness, he stopped and began undressing. It seemed he couldn't take any more of her moaning and wiggling, he wanted to join in. Usually he was a trooper, and always finished what he started but it seemed he had another goal in mind tonight. He climbed on top of her and entered her with one aggressive push. From the start it went from soft and slow to hard and fast. No complaints from Charlene, 'cause she was surely loving this, too. Especially since Isaac's package wasn't slacking by any means, so she loved a good pumping from her man. Everything was just great, she was moaning, he was biting his bottom lip, they were both in pure ecstasy. It was only a matter of minutes before Charlene was going to orgasm and begin her jerking movements. Sure enough after a few more pumps, she felt that wonderful feeling go through her body, and she tensed up, enjoying the moment. As her body convulsed with pleasure, she squeezed Isaac's back. He continued thrusting in and out of her, so he could then join her, now that mission number one was complete.

Charlene just lay there in bliss awaiting his nut. The best part of it all was that Charlene had actually forgotten what had started all of this in the first place. The whole conversation just slipped her mind really quickly. That was, until Isaac finally spoke again. Just as he began to tense up and hold himself inside of her with one stiff motion, he spoke into her ear.

"With your pussy, I can do this all day . . . We will make a baby in no time."

Charlene didn't respond. Isaac pushed himself as far inside of her as he could, as he, too, enjoyed the pleasure he had just given Charlene. That quickly, he drew her out of her trance and back to reality. If only he knew that they could do that all day, every day, but a baby would not come in no time.

Chapter 16

Charlene was at the office, multitasking—talking on the phone and doing some data entry on the computer. The office was pretty quiet and calm and Charlene had spent most of the day online looking up information about damaged uteri. She surprised her own self that she was able to just face it head on and deal with this part of her life. It was as if just talking about it, and having it come up more in the past month than it had her entire life, had helped her grow up overnight. She realized that as rough as this had been for her, it was probably time for her to try her best to address this issue the best way she could. She had spent years burying it as deeply as possible, and still it had surfaced.

Charlene had started to fool herself. She started to believe her own "new life." She liked it better being the Charlene she had become and it was hard for her to go back to that old place. So although she knew that it was a bit childish to create a new identity, it was the answer for her if she was to have any chance at a normal life. Her plan was to leave out some information about her life, and to pretend to most people to be somewhat of a Goody Two-shoes. It was only a matter of time until she had played the part so well she landed herself Isaac and a lot of new friends who thought better of her than anyone ever had.

What woman wouldn't want a fresh start if she could have one? No judgments, no smart comments, no guys asking in front of everybody for one more jump in the sack, no girls trying to beat you up, no drama. Living life day to day like none of that had ever happened, Charlene became addicted to her new life and persona and she didn't think she should feel guilty about that. It had been a few years since she had first made her changes, or, as she liked to call it "the none of their business creed," and life had been fine until now.

Still, Charlene wasn't going to let this ruin everything; she wanted to see if there was a way she could make it right. Maybe there was something she could tell Isaac so that he would never one day have to wonder why it wasn't as easy to have children as he was expecting.

"You told him?" Paige asked.

"Yeah . . . Well, kinda," Charlene replied.

"What's 'yeah, well, kinda?'"

"I told him the doctor said that it may be difficult for me to get pregnant, but I told him it was because of my fertility, I didn't tell him the whole truth."

"OK, I guess as long as he knows the important part."

"Yeah, except I don't think he got the important part, either."

"What do you mean?" Paige asked.

"He seems to think this is a normal case, and if we just try or have sex often enough we will still be having a baby as soon as we want one."

"But the doctor said it's almost impossible, like a one-in-a-million chance, right?"

"Yeah, basically."

"So, he doesn't know that part?"

"No, he doesn't. He also doesn't know that if I did miraculously get pregnant it would be a high risk."

"Charlene! So what did you tell him?"

"I sort of told him that it won't be 1, 2, 3 to have a baby . . . He at least knows that if it's not happening, he knows why . . . I didn't lie . . . I just left some facts out and downplayed the truth, but the result is the same."

"If you say so, Leen," Paige said, tired of arguing about it.

After Paige was done giving Charlene her opinions and views, they had hung up, and now Charlene was back to doing only her office work. A few coworkers stopped by to make small talk and drop off work to her. She sat at her desk for the remainder of the day working diligently and listening to Bugsy on 98.7 KISS FM. As she let him talk her troubles away with laughs she welcomed the end of the workday. The day had worked her emotions more than anything, and she was ready to head home.

Some days she would stop by at a coworker's desk at the end of the day, just so they could walk out of work together and say good-bye. But she wasn't in the mood for that today, she just packed up her things and walked out, and went straight to her car. After the great sex she'd had the night before, she should have been in a better mood, but between Paige's comments and her own guilty conscience, it was hard to be happy with her situation.

She got in her car and headed down I-95, toward her house. There was some congestion on the streets, and she began to get annoyed the longer it took her to get from one block to the next. She picked up her cell phone, and tried to call Jasmine, hoping it would pass some of the time away.

"Hey, girl," Jasmine said as she answered the phone.

"Hey, J, what you doing?"

"Nothing much, you?"

"I'm driving home, mixed in with all these nondriving fools."

Laughing, Jasmine replied, "I know, I just got home myself."

"Well, you take the train, at least you don't have to deal with this nonsense."

"At least you don't have to deal with people all in your personal space," Jasmine replied.

"Yeah, I guess. They both suck."

"That's the truth."

"So what you doing for the rest of the day?"

"I'm about to head to the mall, actually, I have to pick up a navy blue skirt. Tomorrow we are having a party for the volunteers, and the party planners have to wear navy blue," Jasmine said.

"Which mall are you going to?"

"Cross County."

"I'll meet you there, I'm a few exits away. I would love to look at some things to clear my mind."

"OK, I'll be there in about fifteen minutes."

"See you there," Charlene said.

She continued down the road in a better mood, knowing that she was about to shop. Her day was looking up already, it was better than going home to her empty apartment and just dwelling on things she couldn't control. She was happy that she'd called Jasmine, and even happier that she was free.

Charlene got off at the exit and drove into the mall parking lot. She picked up her Nine West bag and stepped out of her car. She locked up and began to walk toward the main entrance to the mall. She picked up her cell phone to get an ETA on Jasmine. As she dialed the phone number, she noticed a group of girls walking toward her. She paid them no attention while she waited for Jasmine to answer. As the phone rang, she could hear the girls getting closer.

"Hey, I just parked," Jasmine said as she answered the phone.

"Ok, I'm right in front of Macy's," Charlene replied.

Right as Charlene was finishing her sentence, she heard a familiar voice say, "Yup, that's that bitch."

Charlene was hesitant to look over at the girls, because she had a feeling that she was the bitch they were talking about.

"That's her, we should beat her ass," one of the girls said.

Jasmine had already told her she was on her way, but Charlene was too busy focusing on what the girls were saying to respond.

"Charlene?" Jasmine said.

"Yeah, I'm here waiting on you," Charlene replied, trying to remain calm.

"She trying to act like she don't hear us. If I go over there and knock her in the head, she'll hear me," the familiar voice said again.

Charlene finally looked over in the girls' direction, and sure enough they were all standing there looking straight at her. There were only three of them, two of them Charlene knew. It was Takesha and Shareena with some other brown-skinned girl Charlene had never seen before. Takesha and Shareena were from Charlene's old way, and years back there was some beef between them that it appeared they felt was unfinished business. So it didn't take long for Charlene to realize what this was all about. Once she made eye contact, the street in her wouldn't let her just turn away, but she wasn't up for the drama. She looked directly in Takesha's face, because she knew that hers was the familiar voice popping all the junk.

"What you looking at?" Takesha asked as soon as Charlene looked in her face.

"Whatever," Charlene said, rolling her eyes.

"You must not think that I will beat you down right here," Takesha said, with her backup singers instigating, saying, "Must not."

"Yeah, I must not," Charlene said back.

Charlene knew deep in her heart that she didn't want to fight these girls. Mainly because she was too damn old to be fighting, not to mention she knew she wouldn't win up against three girls; and it had already crossed her mind how the hell she would explain it to Isaac. Besides, Charlene was dressed in a black button-up sweater, khaki slacks and black pumps. Except for Takesha's weave ponytail, the girls all looked street-fight ready in their sweats and sneakers. However, it wasn't hard to tell that Charlene didn't have the upper hand. Charlene hoped and prayed that the girls had also lost some of their street edge as they had aged, because she knew that if it had been some years ago Takesha and Shareena wouldn't have even wasted time talking.

The funny thing was, Charlene used to be right along with them, fighting and bullying chicks. It was ironic that these were the same girls threatening to jump on her. They hadn't moved since her comment, but they were still making smart comments. If Charlene hadn't said that she would meet Jasmine right at that spot she would've walked away to prevent things from escalating. However, she knew that the girls would think she was scared, and although she kind of was, the Mount Vernon in her couldn't let her go out like a punk.

Finally, after what felt like forever, Jasmine walked up. Recognizing the girls, her expression showed extreme concern about what was going on. Jasmine was dressed in a black Juicy Couture velour sweatsuit with all-black Diesel sneakers. She looked really cute, Charlene thought to herself, and she was dressed appropriately in case it went down. As she walked up, Charlene made sure to act very normal so that the girls watching and mumbling would see she wasn't stressing them.

"Hey, girl," she said as Jasmine approached.

"What's up?" Jasmine replied as her hello.

Shareena said, "Oh, she called her little friend."

"These girls are a joke," Charlene said to Jasmine. "You ready?" she continued.

Charlene took a step toward the main part of the mall, letting Jasmine know it was time to go about their business. Jasmine, still a little confused and having heard the girls make mention of her presence, was already in defensive mode. So as she slowly took a step she was staring in the girls' direction. Jasmine was straight from 14th Street and White Plains Road, and was Mount Vernon to the heart. She wasn't even about to just let these girls feel big-hearted. So she had to make it very clear that they didn't want it with her, and not to let her cuteness fool them. Jasmine shot them all looks of death as she slowly followed behind Charlene.

"Whatever, I want to see if y'all so tough back around the way," Takesha said.

"Bitch, you been locked up—your hometown is Upstate; Mount Vernon ain't around *your* way," Jasmine shouted back.

Charlene looked back. "Come on here, Jasmine, ignore them. They ain't even worth it."

She pulled Jasmine slightly by her arm. Of course the three girls were all yelling stuff like, "Watch yourself" and "I'll see you back home" and other random comments. Charlene was determined not to let them ruin her evening any more than they had. Hell, she was at a mall, one of her favorite places to be. After the distance between them grew, the smart comments trailed off and they were no longer within hearing range. As soon as they were far enough way, Charlene started laughing.

"Girl, you crazy," Charlene said.

Laughing back Jasmine said, "I hate fake fighters."

"Oh, yeah, I forgot about that one. Them girls who faking like they want to fight," Charlene said, laughing.

"Yeah, they knew damn well if they wanted something they could of stepped."

"Well, you know Takesha and Shareena ain't all talk, I'm surprised they didn't, actually."

"I'm not. Takesha on probation, she ain't trying to go back. She only been out a year. She wasn't that damn tough in there."

Charlene just laughed. She thought about how Takesha was once her friend. Shareena, like Jasmine, was just being a loyal friend, the beef was really between Charlene and Takesha. Back in the day Charlene and Takesha used to roll together. At one point a guy that Takesha was going out with, Kenny, tried to get with Charlene. Initially Charlene told him no thank you, and at the time it was because she wasn't interested. Charlene didn't know how much Takesha and he were dealing. Kenny was a hustler, he was flashy and handsome, just Charlene's type back then. She would have actually indulged when he first tried if she hadn't been dealing with a hustler of her own, one who was bigger in the game and she was more fond of. However, the more Charlene saw Kenny around the way, and the less she was dealing with the guy she had been messing with at the time, the more tempting Kenny looked. So it wasn't long before she started messing with him.

Charlene knew at that point that Takesha had been seeing Kenny, but she didn't find herself too concerned with that. Not that it made it right, but she didn't think Takesha had any real feelings for Kenny, anyway. Charlene assumed that Takesha was like her, and wasn't in it for love, she thought Takesha was a "I'll do you, pay me" girl. Apparently she guessed wrong, because when Takesha got that Charlene was sleeping with Kenny she promptly stepped to Charlene. Words turned into curses, and before long they were fighting in the street. Nobody around jumped in or stopped it, and both Jasmine and Shareena were there at the time. It was a fair fight, and although Charlene was the slimmer of the two, she was handling her own; her days in the street had taught her how to use her hands well.

Nobody else from the neighborhood broke up the fight, either, but the cops eventually did. When they pulled the two girls apart and pinned them against the cars, they patted them both down. Unbeknownst to Charlene, Takesha had been doing some trafficking for Kenny and she had a stash of his drugs on her. Takesha got arrested that day and did some time. As dumb as it was to have the stash on her, rumor had it that Takesha blamed Charlene for her arrest, Charlene had felt guilty for quite some time, mostly because she was messing with Kenny to begin with, which wasn't something a good friend would have done, regardless. She never felt the blame for Takesha being locked up, though. Of course. if Charlene hadn't been messing with Kenny, Takesha and she never would have been fighting, and then the cops wouldn't have come, and she wouldn't have gotten arrested. As far as Charlene was concerned nobody told Takesha to step to her, and nobody told Takesha to have drugs on her person.

As Charlene and Jasmine walked through the mall, Charlene told Jasmine how that whole scene had started, and they had some laughs about the old days. Still, all these years later, seeing Takesha did make Charlene reflect back and feel a tad guilty because she did know what she had done was wrong. However, it didn't help that Takesha was still acting like they were in high school and trying to start a fight. Although it made Charlene happy that she no longer lived in that neighborhood and she no longer lived that life, she realized that the street instincts are not something you always grow out of, and some people never change. Charlene had to admit, she was happy that Jasmine still had her bark in her. Having Jas stand up for her made her realize that there were some folks that would always have her back, whether everyone else thought she was scandalous or not.

Chapter 17

The funny thing was, a part of her told her it was too good to be true. That conversation with Isaac the other night went entirely too smoothly. He was so consoling and sweet and understanding, and after it all, perfectly sexual. That was far from how she expected it to go, even with the left-out information. She thought he would be devastated by the thought of anything causing a hindrance. Shockingly, Isaac was a champ about it, and he actually left Charlene feeling lucky. Unfortunately, after he had time to think about it he didn't find it so small after all.

He had called on her cell phone first, and she told him she was just getting home and that she would call him back. She put down her purse and work bag, kicked off her heels and went to the bathroom. Isaac had given her no more than five minutes before he called her right back on her house phone. She answered with a gut feeling that he was calling for more than just to say hello and see how her day went.

"Hey, Isaac, where are you?"

"On my way home from work," he answered.

"Oh, OK. You got out pretty early today," she replied.

"Charlene, I'm a little confused about what you told me the other night."

"It seemed Isaac wanted to get right to it.

"About what?" she asked, feeling the butterflies come swooping right back into her stomach.

"About the difficulty you may have getting pregnant."

"OK, what are you confused about?"

"Well, you told me initially the doctor said everything was OK, and then you tell me later that she told you it wasn't. Did you forget that part?"

"No, she called me back a few days later with that information."

"Why?"

"I don't know, I guess she got that information after she called me the first time."

"Oh . . . OK," Isaac said, as if he was trying to add it up to see if it made sense.

Charlene, eager to change the topic, added, "Is that what you called me about?"

"Yeah, I just was remembering that you told me when you got back that everything was fine . . . And then I was wondering, why didn't you tell me when she first told you?"

"Oh, I got ya . . . Yeah; well, she called me back after and told me about it . . . I guess it was found from a separate test or something."

"Oh, OK . . . Well, what you doing tonight?"

"Just relaxing for the most part . . . I have to wash my hair but then I'm relaxing."

"OK, call me when you get settled."

"OK, baby."

"All right, honey, talk to you later."

"Good-bye," Charlene said.

All she could think about as she hung up is how she was digging herself deeper into this lie. She felt like it was déjà vu, when she first met Isaac and she had to tell so many mistruths and she constantly had to struggle to keep her story straight. Despite all the practice, there was never a guarantee that he wouldn't catch on to something out of place. After all these years she'd hoped that all this would be behind her. Charlene knew firsthand the truth about what they say: that one lie just turns into more and more lies. She definitely didn't like this investigating that Isaac was doing. She didn't know why he couldn't just leave things as they were.

After Charlene hung up she went into her bedroom and started changing her clothes and getting comfortable. She pinned up her hair off her neck and threw on some lounge pants and a T-shirt. She slipped into her fluffy slippers and sat down on her couch. She turned on her television and started checking her mail before she started to channel surf. She had been home maybe twenty minutes when a knock came at her door. She rose up from the couch without having a clue who it could be. She thought maybe it was a neighbor or a deliveryman, because she wasn't expecting anybody. When she got to the door, she went ahead and peeped through the peephole and found it was Paige. Charlene opened the door with a look of confusion, surprised to see her sister.

"What are you doing here?" Charlene asked.

"Just stopped by to say hey," Paige replied.

"Just stopped by?"

"Yeah."

"How'd you even know I was home yet?"

"I wasn't sure, but I figured I would take a chance," Paige said, finding humor in the interrogation.

"Without even calling my cell phone? . . . Paige, what are you up to?"

"Nothing, I can't come say hello to my sister?" Paige asked with a laugh.

"Of course you can, but when do you ever?"

"Ha, ha, ha," Paige said sarcastically. "I was in the neighborhood and figured I should stop by and visit," she continued.

"What were you doing around here?" Charlene asked as she headed back to the couch to sit in front of her television.

"I had to drop a friend off a few blocks away," Paige said as she followed.

"Oh, OK . . . Well, at least somebody got you to come this way."

"Whatever. You act like you be coming back around the way or something."

"Nope, not much . . . There's nothing there for me."

"How about your family?" Paige asked, slightly laughing.

"I see you guys, and I visit."

"Whatever," Paige said as she joined Charlene on the couch.

Charlene continued to sift through her mail while Paige was seeing what was on television.

"Oh, I love this video," Paige said as the new Ludacris video came on.

"Of course you would, with your little hoochie butt," Charlene replied with a laugh.

"Whatever, just 'cause you over here trying to pretend that you wasn't the ringleader of hoochies . . . Don't point no fingers," Paige replied, damn near cracking up.

Even Charlene had to laugh at that one, because she definitely knew there was truth to that. She almost forgot, she couldn't pretend with just everybody 'cause there were more than enough people who knew the real deal.

"Whatever, hooker. I just don't like that song."

"I love it," Paige replied.

They both sat in silence for a minute watching the half-naked girls shaking their butts and tatas all over the screen, while Ludacris just stood there getting groped and caressed by them.

"I would die for her body," Paige said as this one girl strutted across the screen wearing nothing but two strings.

"Yeah, she does have a nice body. But we both know that won't get you but so far."

"I know, but it definitely gets you further than most."

Once again, they both started laughing. It had been a while since the two of them had spent this type of time together. Neither of them rushing to be somewhere, no one else around, no purpose to their meeting, just the two of them hanging out chilling. Charlene needed this, and she was kind of happy that Paige did take her chances and stopped by.

There was a time—for several years, actually—that there was tension between Charlene and Paige. Charlene felt angry at Paige for not being there when she needed her most, and Paige felt guilty about abandoning Charlene. There was a point where Paige was embarrassed by Charlene and her reputation in the neighborhood, and she didn't hesitate to let Charlene know. It made it even worse that their strict mother turned them against each other so many times. As time went on, those issues settled. Still, it took years for them to mature to see that all of that was no reason to keep them from loving each other the way they should. So, year after year they got better and better at being good sisters to one another.

As Charlene and Paige sat sprawled out on the couches in Charlene's living room, they laughed and talked. They watched all their favorites, some *Flavor of Love* reruns and an MTV *Cribs* episode or two. They watched television so late that Charlene never did wash her hair and she never did call Isaac back.

Chapter 18

The night with Paige left Charlene feeling refreshed and positive the next morning. She had needed that night to get her mind off of everything. When Charlene showed up to work the next day she was just as jolly as she wanted to be. Of course, most people would think that she had gotten some good stuff the night before, but that was far from it. She had just gotten a dose of therapy.

Once she sat down at her desk, as usual she checked her messages and emails. She had a message from Isaac.

"Hey, this is Isaac . . . What happened to you last night? I ended up falling asleep pretty early, but I thought you would call me back. Call me when you get this, I had to ask you a question."

Oh, boy, Charlene thought to herself. *Another question.*

Charlene continued getting settled at work. As she moved some paperwork from one in-box to another she couldn't help but think about what it was Isaac wanted to ask her. As usual she didn't call him back right away, she wasn't that eager to find out. Whenever Charlene could get a chance to prepare herself for what she might need to say, she took advantage of it. Whether it was the time before they called one another back, or while she waited on hold because he got another call, or telling him to hold on so she could buy time—Charlene sometimes needed to think before she spoke. She learned the hard way that freestyling could lead to getting caught saying something contradictory.

Charlene had finally decided that whatever the question was, if it related to this pregnancy thing she was sticking to her story and saying she didn't know all of the medical facts behind it. She was hoping it wasn't anything else. She had no idea of what else it could be, unless Isaac had found out about the ride home with Rich the previous week after she had told him she hadn't seen Rich in months. She didn't know what it was, but from the sound of his tone on the message, it didn't sound like a frivolous question. After she gathered her thoughts, she went ahead and called her fiancé.

"Hello?" Isaac answered.

"Hey, babe, good morning," Charlene replied.

"Hey, sweetie. What happened to you last night?" he asked.

"Paige stopped by, and we were talking for hours . . . It got so late by the time she left I just went to sleep."

"I thought you were going to call me," he said.

"I was, babe, but I figured you were asleep because you didn't call me, either," she replied.

"All right . . . Well, no big deal . . . I was just making sure you were OK."

"I'm fine; I actually really enjoyed Paige last night."

"Did you tell her?"

"Tell her what?"

"About what the doctor told you," he asked.

"Yes, I had told her before. She came with me to the doctor, so I told her the results as I found out."

"Why did she come with you?"

"Just to come with me."

"That was nice, I guess, I never knew girls needed company to go to those doctors for regular checkups."

"I didn't need her to come, she just did."

"Mmm. OK . . . Anyway, speaking of the appointment, I wanted to ask you . . . Why did the doctor check to see if you are fertile?"

"What do you mean why?"

"Why? Did you request her to check that?"

"No . . . Why do you ask me that?"

"From what I understand, doctors don't just test that. You have to ask to be tested for that, and even then, they won't test you until you're trying and you've tried the other normal practices. The only way they will do it otherwise is if the patient has some unusual circumstances."

"I don't know about all of that. I just know she told me that," Charlene said with a slight attitude.

Charlene had been caught off guard. It seemed as if Isaac had been doing his research. She wanted to just say, "*well, that's not the way my doctor does it,*" but she wasn't sure where he got that information. What if Isaac called her doctor's office and got that straight from them? Of course it could have been just some general information he heard, but she didn't want to risk it. He was clearly in an investigative mode, trying to see if he could catch her in a lie. It was obvious, since he had a new question just that fast from last night and he was waiting for her answers before he would tell her why he was asking. Charlene was no fool; she wasn't going to fall into his trap that easily.

"So, she just told you . . . Did she even tell you she was testing for that?"

"She told me she was going to run some tests, and she was going to check everything out and make sure I was healthy."

"Mmm . . . That's interesting. They don't usually do that."

Charlene was annoyed by Isaac's little interrogation. Maybe

she was wrong to be, since she should have been feeling guilty about her lies. Why was he doing research? Checking to see if she was telling the truth? Charlene thought to herself. She wasn't feeling his research findings one bit.

Finally fed up with him acting like he knew everything, she asked, "How do you know?"

"I just do . . . Some people who know told me."

"Why are you going around asking people about my body?"

"I didn't. I only asked one person, because I was concerned about you . . . And then when I heard that I was even more concerned."

"I thought you said we would be fine."

"We will . . . I just wanted to make sure you would be fine."

"Well, no one else can tell you that information but me."

Isaac could tell that Charlene wasn't too happy with his questions.

Charlene meant what she said but she also knew it was a good way to turn things back in her favor.

"I'm sorry, baby. You're right. Only you and your doctor really know, anyway."

"It's OK."

"Well, I want you to hang up with me and call your doctor and make a follow-up appointment for as soon as possible, and I want to go with you."

"Why?"

"You need a follow-up anyway, and I want to ask her some questions."

"My follow-up is supposed to be in six months."

"OK, well then, call her on three-way, then, I can ask my questions over the phone."

Charlene couldn't tell if Isaac wanted her to know that there was something he didn't believe, or that he wasn't letting up on this.

"What do you have to ask her, Isaac?" Charlene asked, unable to hide the frustration in her voice.

"Just some stuff . . . Like what we need to do to be successful, is there anything we can do to fix the problem, what caused it, etc."

"I can ask her that stuff myself, and tell you what she said."

"No, I'd rather talk to her. This may be an ongoing issue we have and I would feel better feeling her out and building a relationship with the doctor that will have the fate of my family in her hands."

Damn, how was Charlene to argue with that? He had stumped her and now she didn't know what to say. She had to admit, Isaac did have some right to be involved with this if she was going to be his wife and hopefully mother of his children.

"OK, Isaac. I will call her today and set an earlier appointment."

They spoke a tad more and then he told her to call the doctor when they hung up.

Charlene sat there confused about to how to handle this. She didn't know if she should go through the motions of pretending to make the appointment, or find reasons to miss the appointment, or go ahead and try to stop the whole charade before it got any worse. She was trying her best to get back to her work, but she couldn't help thinking about what had just happened with Isaac. It played back in her head. " . . . *I would feel better feeling her out and building a relationship with the doctor that will have the fate of my family in her hands."* She felt like she was being punked, she couldn't believe he was really taking it there. She did know that the next time she spoke to Isaac he would ask about it, so she had better figure out a plan before that time came.

Chapter 19

She had just walked out of her office door and before she could even hit the pavement, she got her cell phone out of her bag. She had noticed right before she signed off her computer that she had missed a call from Paige, and she really wanted to talk to her. She was dying to ask her what she thought she should do about Isaac's request, but she had been so busy at work she hadn't gotten a chance to call her earlier in the day. She immediately dialed Paige's number and waited for her to answer. She continued down the block toward her car as Paige's phone rang and she waited to hear her perky voice on the other end. She was looking for her maroon Altima in the midst of all the cars parked in the lot.

Five rings later, there was her perky voice, but on a recording. Charlene left a quick but urgent-sounding message and hung up. By this point she had already reached her car, had keyed in and had put down her bags in the passenger seat. She sat there for a moment to put her hands-free earpiece in before she pulled off, and as she fumbled with it and the phone, her cell phone began to ring. She became excited because she was all ready to spend her drive home talking on the phone, getting some insight from Paige. When she turned to glance at the caller ID, it was Jasmine. She was a bit disappointed that it wasn't Paige, but then she realized that Jasmine was the next best thing. Jasmine might have been the best thing if she had known about the whole story with the abortion years ago, but there wasn't but so much Charlene could explain without sharing her secret with her, too, after all these years. Jasmine and Charlene had become friends about two years after it happened, and Charlene had never told her. Now, Jasmine knew that Charlene was no angel growing up; hell, Jasmine ran with her all through high school. Still, regardless of all she did know, which was a lot, she didn't know about this little secret, and that was what Charlene really needed some advice on. But Charlene figured she would just get creative, she needed to talk.

"Hey, girl," Charlene answered her phone.

"Hey, miss, what's up with you?"

"Just getting off work, what about you?"

"I was off today, had to run some errands and stuff."

"That's cool, I can use a day off myself."

"I feel you, this day went by so fast I need another one already," Jasmine said, laughing.

"Yeah, I can use one just to sit back relax, and clear all of my thoughts," Charlene replied.

"How's everything going? You started planning the wedding yet?"

"Slightly. By the way, you know you're in it, right?" Charlene asked playfully.

"I better be," Jasmine replied. "You need help with anything?" she continued.

"Well, for now, I can just use your help on how to stay engaged and then we can address the wedding," Charlene said.

Through her laughter, Jasmine responded, "What happened?"

"Well, let's just say he is asking a lot of questions, and they're questions I don't think if he knew the answers to he would be too happy."

"Why he asking questions all of a sudden?"

"I don't know, I guess he is just being curious, and I have kept certain sensitive information from him this long, I don't think this would be a good time to tell him."

"I would think not, too. Big arguments and revealing new information should be forbidden during engagements. These men don't need much of an excuse to back out of the commitment," Jasmine said with a chuckle.

"So you think I should continue to keep some things from him?"

"For now, you had a story, now stick to it."

"Yeah, but I'm afraid that as he asks questions, the more I try to keep up with the story the more he is going to dig, and the worst it might be in the end."

"How much can he dig? It's in your past, what is he going to do? Go interview people from your high school and neighborhood or something?" Jasmine asked, laughing at the thought of Isaac out around town like a detective.

"I guess you're right, all he has is my word," Charlene replied, not joining in on the laughter.

"That's right. Don't go ruining that now by letting him know that your word hasn't been that great all this time . . . Just ride it out, you'll be down the aisle soon."

As much as Charlene knew what Jasmine was saying was kind of foul, it did make sense. Of course, in a perfect world you should go into a marriage completely open and honest. The problem was, in the real world that same honesty can cause a couple not to go into marriage at all. It's like when a bride or groom go too far at the bachelor or bachelorette party, do you wake up the next morning and confess? Do you just walk up to your partner on the morning of your wedding and tell them that you have slept with some stripper or some random guy? If so, then that wedding might not take place, and if it does, it wouldn't be quite as romantic as planned. Then you have the option of keeping that secret to yourself. It was a mistake, and your partner knowing can't take it back even if he truly wanted to. It would only make the situation worse, not better. Without that information being shared, the wedding can go as planned and it can be the fairy-tale event everyone wanted.

So, the logical thing seems to be to keep those secrets to yourself. It's not always a sneaky or deceitful thing, sometimes it's in the best interest of the relationship. Jasmine had helped Charlene realize just what she meant, and Charlene knew that this was definitely one of those instances. She was only trying to keep Isaac in love with the woman she was, and not turned off by the woman she once was. Charlene knew it was best. Some people ask for honesty, but they are not really ready to handle the truth.

After Jasmine helped Charlene decide that she wasn't ready to risk her engagement, she went ahead and wrapped up the phone call. Before Charlene and Jasmine hung up the phone, they said one of them would call the other back after they got settled at home.

Charlene walked in and went straight for the kitchen. All day she had her mind on the Oreo cookies that were on top of her refrigerator. She grabbed them and opened the refrigerator door to get the milk. As she poured herself a tall glass to accompany her evening snack, she gazed at a picture of her and Isaac on her refrigerator. It made her smile and feel a sense of joy. The picture was from when they went to Ocean City, Maryland, for a little weekend getaway one summer. A man came around taking pictures on the beach and had them strike some really funny poses, and the cutest one she put up on the fridge. She continued looking at it with a smile on her face until she put the milk back and walked away from the kitchen.

Looking at the picture made her feel confused. On the one hand she was with a great man who most women would die for, but on the other she was with a man she was so afraid to expose her entire history to. She didn't even know who to blame for that anymore. All she knew was that it was a problem, and she didn't know if it was about to spiral out of control. One thing she was learning the hard way was that dishonesty can be a deadly disease. It can start out as a small infection, but slowly it spreads and spreads and before you know it there is no cure.

Just as she lay down on the couch Charlene's thoughts were interrupted by a phone call. She thought it might be Paige, so she hurried to the phone and answered.

"Hello," Charlene said in an upbeat voice.

"Slut," the female voice said.

"What?" Charlene responded.

Click. The person hung up.

Charlene was pissed for about ten seconds. She looked at the caller ID, the call had come from a blocked number. Charlene couldn't recognize the voice but it might have been Takesha. This wasn't the first time Charlene had to deal with stupidity like this, so it could have been any number of people. She always assumed it was a female from her past who had never gotten over that Charlene had taken their man. Still, she couldn't wait until there were no more remnants of those days, because the calling-and-hanging-up game was so high school.

Charlene decided to put the ignorant call out of her mind. She lay back down on the couch and started surfing the television channels. After she flicked through about three, the phone rang again. This time Charlene looked at the caller ID before picking up and saw it was a blocked number again. Charlene was tempted to answer and start breaking but instead she let it go to her answering machine. She wasn't in the mood today, not at all.

★ ★ ★

850 calories and five television programs later, Paige finally called back.

"What took you so long to return my call?" Charlene asked as she picked up. She had been watching television for over three hours, and she had had over fifteen Oreos and two glasses of milk.

"I went to the gym, and I'm leaving now."

"The gym? Since when you go to the gym?"

"A little over a month now."

"You should have told me, I need to go with you."

"Please, for what? You nothing but skin and bones."

"Please . . . I just ate one and a half rows of Oreo cookies."

"Lol . . . PMS?"

"I don't know, but I know I sat here and tore them things up," Charlene said, laughing.

"You a mess," Paige replied. "What's up, though? You sound like there was more drama on your message than Oreo eating," she continued.

"Yeah . . . Well, Isaac called me and started asking me questions about how I found out, and why the doctor would test me for something that major without me asking, and telling me how he heard they don't normally do that and all of this," Charlene blurted out.

"Damn, really? He is really concerned with all of that?"

"I'm telling you, when it comes to him and having his children, he don't skip a beat."

"That is crazy. You would never think a man would be that into that stuff."

"Not Isaac. He wants me to make an appointment so he can come with me."

"You're not even pregnant, why does he want to go?"

"To see why I will have trouble getting pregnant."

"You can't get pregnant, though, what doesn't he understand?"

"Remember, I didn't tell him everything . . . And I can get pregnant, it's just highly unlikely that I will be," Charlene said, defending herself.

"First of all, not highly unlikely, damn near impossible the doctor said . . . I was there. Second, you haven't told Isaac yet, Charlene?"

"I told him what I thought was enough. Who would think he would come back inquiring?"

"Leen, listen. This is your relationship, but I really think you need to explain everything to him so that he doesn't have to go through trying to get you pregnant and all that frustration. You know he wants to give his father a grandchild before he passes, why would you want to deceive him into thinking that's possible? That's just mean."

Charlene didn't even know what to say. She had to admit it was kind of heartless. Still, she knew that either way there was going to be disappointment, she didn't see how her volunteering extra information was going to make it better.

"I feel ya, Paige, but I just don't know how. Besides, once I have to retract all my other tales I've told he may flip out."

"Not if you explain why you didn't tell him. What else you going to do? Have him come to the doctor with you and ask the doctor to lie for you?"

"I was just going to tell him I made an appointment, and then when it came, miss it for some reason," Charlene replied.

"What's that going to do?"

"I'm not sure if he really wants to go to ask questions or to see if I'm being one hundred percent truthful."

"And you think by missing the appointment, he is going to go away? He will just expect to go on another, and don't you think the more you prolong it the more suspicious he will become?"

Charlene couldn't take much more of Paige's sense talking. Just the thought of breaking the news to Isaac was not only making her heart beat faster, it was the absolute last thing she wanted to do. She made an excuse to get off the phone with Paige. Not to be mean, but she just needed some time to think for herself. She had asked Paige and Jasmine their opinions, but she realized that eventually she was going to have to face herself. Charlene knew that Paige was morally right, but what Jasmine had advised sounded so much easier to handle.

Chapter 20

Charlene took the night off from thinking through her situation. She was tired of going back and forth with herself. She started to think that maybe she was making a bigger deal out of it than it was. She hadn't killed anybody or cheated, she didn't think she should have to beat herself up over this. So, once she hung up with Paige and pondered over it for a bit, she went right back to watching television and eating Oreo cookies.

The next day, it crossed her mind once or twice but not enough to call the doctor and make an appointment or to call Isaac and tell him she wasn't making one. It was Friday, and Charlene worked her little heart out all day to get everything done so she could get off nice and early. She just wanted to go home and relax. It had been a long and daunting week, and she was looking forward to the weekend.

She left the office at exactly a quarter to five. Her boss had left early for the day, so she left out a little earlier than she was supposed to. On the ride home, she felt great. She was listening to Golden Girl holding it down as a guest DJ on WBLS and jamming to the latest R&B. Good days didn't come often for

Charlene lately, but she was actually having one today. She hadn't spoken to Isaac yet, and she had breezed through her workday. She didn't want to let all the drama take over her entire life. She was a newly engaged woman, and hadn't even begun to get into the happy wedding planning. Charlene wanted to finally just move on, even if it meant she had to ignore Isaac's little inquisitive tantrum. She had come this far from her past; she wasn't ready to let it grab her back down now. So she told herself what she had said many times before: you have to fake it until you make it.

She got home, put down her things and went to the bathroom. She was sitting on the toilet when her phone rang in her purse in the living room. She thought about getting it, but she didn't feel like jumping up to get it, she was enjoying that feeling of just releasing on her home toilet. So she let the phone ring to voice mail. After the phone rang out, a few moments later her house phone rang. She was almost done by then, but still not ready to wrap up. She was still relaxing, and she decided she would call the person back. Then her answering machine turned on, and seconds later she heard the voice of Isaac coming through the speaker.

"Hey, it's me, Isaac. I'm on my way there, be there in about five to ten minutes."

Charlene quickly wrapped up what she was doing, pulled up her pants and rushed to her purse to get her cell phone. She instantly checked the caller ID and, as she had expected, it was Isaac who had called both phones. She called him back from her cellular. He answered pretty quickly.

"Hey, baby," Charlene said.

"Hey, darling . . . You home? I'll be at your place in about five minutes."

"Oh . . . Yeah, I'm here. How did you even know I was home?"

"I wasn't sure, but I figured you would be soon. Even if you weren't there yet, I would have used my key and just waited for you to get home."

"OK . . . You would have been waiting for me in some silk boxers?" she asked playfully.

"Maybe," he replied. "I'll see ya in a bit."

Charlene hung up, realizing there was no need to even try to change or straighten up. He left her no time at all to do anything. When she really thought about it, she shouldn't have to still put on a show when he came over, anyway.

About ten minutes later, Charlene heard keys fiddling at her door. She looked up and Isaac was walking in. He was dressed in black slacks, a tan and black button-up shirt and black shoes. He had a fresh haircut and a new nice-sized diamond in his ear. He was looking absolutely delicious, and Charlene was hoping she could get a taste before he left. As soon as Isaac walked in, he, too, headed to the bathroom. Charlene sat on the couch flicking through channels. She had taken off her socks and shoes and was happily wiggling her toes, excited to relax on this Friday night. Once he got out of the bathroom, he started making conversation. Normally, all Isaac wanted to do was watch television and sit mostly in quiet. Not today, though, he was in a conversational mood.

"How is work going?" he asked.

"It's going well. Sarah is finally leaving so it's going to be a little busy until they replace her."

"It's about time. Didn't she resign like over three months ago?" he asked.

"Yeah, but they begged her to give them more time. But she finally left. Today was her last day."

"That's cool. I'm sure you can handle it," he replied.

"I hope so and hopefully they bring someone else in quick."

"They probably will," he responded.

A few seconds passed, and the television seemed to have their attention. Isaac had taken the remote and was flicking through channels now; they both were waiting for something that interested them enough to catch their eyes so they could start to watch it.

"So did you call the doctor?" he asked.

He threw her off. For some reason she thought possibly he'd forgotten about it, especially since he hadn't called or brought it up.

"No, not yet."

"What do you mean, not yet?"

All of a sudden, Isaac seemed to change his mood. He wasn't as relaxed and he wasn't flicking through channels anymore.

"I didn't call yet, I had got so busy," she replied. She didn't look away from the television, and she had started fiddling with her fingers.

Isaac on the other hand was looking right at her and was very focused.

"I asked you to call as soon as you hung up, and you couldn't find a moment since then?"

"Not that day, it was busy. Then today it was busy and I forgot."

"Forgot? Really? How do you forget about something like this?"

"Sorry, Isaac . . . I have a lot on my mind."

"You? This is my life we are talking about, too, here."

"I know, I'm going to make the appointment."

"Forget it . . . I'll make it, because I don't want to wait on you to clear your schedule and remember."

"That's not necessary. I'll get to it."

"Charlene, there is something up with this whole situation . . . something you're not telling me."

Charlene's eyes dropped momentarily, and she felt her heart

racing. Isaac's tone and anger had made her uncomfortable and nervous. Now he was putting her on the spot. She hadn't even made up her mind completely about which route to take with this whole thing, and now here he was with the flashlight in her face. She knew she didn't want to tell him under these circumstances even if she was going to tell him.

"There is nothing I am not telling you, Isaac, I wish you would calm down about this."

"It's hard to be calm when I don't know what's going on."

"Just relax. We will work it out. I'll call the doctor and we can go one day to get some more information."

"OK, well, in the meantime help me be clear . . . The doctor just said that you did not have normal fertility?"

"Basically," she replied, not looking in his direction.

"But she says you will have kids, it just may take some monitoring of your period and when you're ovulating and stuff like that?"

"Something like that."

Charlene's body temperature had risen. Her hands and face were clammy, and she could feel anxiety running through her body. She was partially angry and partially nervous. She just wanted this to end. It was bad enough she wasn't used to Isaac getting angry and yelling, but she hated his line of questioning. Of course, though, this was out of her control.

"Something like that?" Isaac asked.

He put down the remote and turned toward Charlene. She slightly looked his way, but didn't look him in his face. He took her face in his hands.

"Look me in my eyes, and tell me you are telling me the truth."

Not expecting this, Charlene's eyes were roaming on and off his. Then before she could stop it, her eyes started to well up with tears. Her body was becoming overwhelmed with guilt, fear, anger, sadness and every other emotion in the book. She just couldn't hold strong anymore. The tears began to stream down her face, but Isaac still had her face in his hand. Her tears weren't fazing him one bit. He just sat there holding her face, waiting for her to speak.

"I can't have children," she mumbled through the tears.

Isaac let go. "What do you mean?"

"I have a ruptured uterus and it is close to impossible for me to bear children."

"Close to impossible?" Isaac asked in a soft and saddened tone.

"The chances are very, very slim, the doctor said, and if I do get pregnant it would be a high-risk pregnancy for both me and the child," Charlene continued.

Isaac sat there in silence for a few moments, taking it all in. Charlene sat a few inches away from him, with tears still rolling down her face, trying to muffle her sobs.

"Why didn't you tell me all of this, Charlene?" Isaac finally asked. "This is serious."

"I was, but I didn't know how."

"A ruptured uterus? What is that from?" Isaac asked. It was like he had just replayed what she said back in his head, and just realized he'd missed a major part.

Charlene paused, her sobs stopped for a moment. She looked over at Isaac and could see in his eyes that he wasn't up for any bull. He wanted to get to the bottom of this. She knew it made no sense for her to even try to bother and play the vague game.

"I had an abortion and it didn't go well. My uterus was ruptured, and a few other organs were slightly damaged. I was pretty delicate down there, but it's been a while so the doctor said a lot has healed. My uterus, on the other hand, was really bad off, so it's not where it should be."

"You had an abortion? When was this?" Isaac asked.

"Yes . . . Well, actually I did it myself. I was afraid to go to my mother and afraid to go to the doctor. That's how I damaged myself in there."

"You did it yourself? How old were you?"

"Yes, myself . . . or at least I tried myself . . . with a knitting needle. I ended up going to the hospital an hour or so later and they completed what I started and fixed me up."

"How old were you?" he asked again.

"I was thirteen when this happened."

Isaac looked away for a second, and then locked his eyes on the floor on the other side of the room. To Charlene, it felt like forever, but only about ten seconds went by before he spoke.

"Thirteen, Charlene? . . . I thought you didn't start having sex until your last year of high school."

Charlene didn't answer right away. At that point Charlene wished she hadn't said so much. She was starting to think clearly again through the emotions, and she realized that she had said a lot. She didn't have time to think of anything else.

"It was younger than that; I was a little dishonest about that when we met."

"A little dishonest?" Isaac's voice started to rise again. He wasn't sad for her or himself anymore. He was angry again.

"Let me guess, you had more than three partners, too . . . thirteen having an abortion . . . You must have been real loose," Isaac continued.

Charlene just sat there. She couldn't defend herself, because there was no defense. More denials, more lies, what was the point? She wasn't going to give him any more information to throw in her face, but she definitely wasn't going to add any lies.

"The worst part is not that you lied to me and told me you only had three partners and you really were a ho. Not even that you were going to try to have me do the impossible, and turn a ho into a housewife . . . But you were going to waltz around here like everything was all good. Knowing you couldn't have kids, having me be oblivious to that, and you know how much that means to me. I told you what it meant to me to give my father grandchildren, and you didn't even have the decency to let me in on your little secret . . . well, secrets. That's the worst part."

"I'm sorry, Isaac, I really am. I didn't want to lose you."

"Really? That's why you have been lying to me through our whole relationship because you didn't want to lose me?"

Even though she heard the sarcasm in his question, she still answered. "Yes."

"I doubt that, Charlene. The reason for that was because you're a lying bitch. That's the only reason."

Isaac had already stood up, and by this point he had his keys in his hand and he was walking toward the door. Charlene had her head low, blinded by the tears that had been continuously flowing from her eyes.

"And you don't have to worry about losing me. You never had me—whoever the real you is," Isaac added right before he walked out the door.

Men can be so evil. When they are hurt, they only know how to lash out and hurt right back. He said everything he could think of to make Charlene feel lower than low, and even worse than she already did. It definitely worked, too. As soon as Isaac shut the door, Charlene's heart just dropped inside her stomach. The pain ran so deep that her first major sob was silent. It was as if she was gasping for air. Finally she caught her breath and just let out a loud, screechy sob. She knew Isaac had a right to be upset. The reality was he had even made some true points. All except the one that she was just a lying bitch. Charlene knew it wasn't that, although that is how it seemed.

It was fear, fear he wouldn't accept her. She knew that was no excuse at this point and he probably wouldn't want to hear that. She also knew the curse of getting caught in lies is that nothing you say after that is credible. Even the truth is a lie after that.

Chapter 21

The next morning, Charlene woke up a complete mess. She had cried nonstop for hours, crying her soul out. It wasn't even just pain from the harsh things Isaac said; it was the pain from knowing he was right.

She staggered into the bathroom and slowly walked in front of the mirror. She was a sight to see, her face and eyes puffy from the rough night. Her mascara had run down her face, and her hair was wild all over her head. Although she was awake, she wasn't ready to face the world. She didn't want to be bothered with anybody or anything. She couldn't have been happier that it was a Saturday morning and she didn't have to go to work. If it had been a workday, she surely would have had to call in sick, she was in no mood or condition to work on anything in that office.

She hadn't spoken to Isaac since he left. She didn't even bother to call him, and of course he didn't call her. She washed her face with some Dove soap as she tried to think on her own what to do next. Through the night all she did was cry, she couldn't even begin to think of what she should or shouldn't do next. Now that she was done sobbing and a little more alive, she knew it was time to make some decisions. As Charlene washed her face with the washcloth, she watched her every movement in the mirror. She watched herself wash her face in a way that she never had before. She stared at herself in the mirror, straight into her own eyes. It was as if she was trying to find something within herself, she was trying to see the real Charlene.

Once she had shaken off some of her self-pity, she went ahead and called Paige. She would have called her last night but just couldn't pull herself together. She wanted to let her know that it had hit the fan, but she needed time to be able to tell the story clearly.

"Hey, why you sound like that?" Paige asked as soon as she heard Charlene's voice through the phone.

"Take a wild guess," Charlene replied.

"What? Isaac?" Paige asked.

"Yeah, let's just say I'm no longer his little princess, now I'm a lying, dirty ho."

"Did he say that to you?" Paige asked.

"Pretty much."

"What happened?"

"He was asking questions again, and then he started getting upset when I told him I didn't make the appointment . . . Before I knew it—I just told him everything."

"Everything?" Paige asked in shock.

"Everything . . . about the abortion . . . everything."

"Whoa . . . And he was mad?"

"Was he? He said that not only was I really a ho, but I was going to actually let him try to have kids with me knowing I couldn't and that was the worst part of it all."

"Aww, Charlene. I feel so bad for him. He is probably so hurt."

"For him!" Charlene blurted out. "What about for me?" she continued.

"You, too, but he probably really feels terrible and deceived. With everything with his father and now to find this out."

"Are you trying to make me feel better or worse, Paige?"

"I'm sorry, Leen. I don't know, though. We knew he was going to be upset initially, you should just give him time to calm down."

"I just hope that he does calm down, that's all."

"How did it end? Like when he left, what was the last note?"

"He said some nasty things and walked out. We haven't spoken since," Charlene said.

"It was probably just hurt and anger. You should call him and let him know you're sorry."

"I just don't know if that's enough."

"It's definitely a start, call me back when you're done talking to him."

"What if he doesn't forgive me?"

"He will, he would be a fool if he calls off the engagement over something that happened over a decade ago."

"He wouldn't be a fool, though, if he called it off over his inability to trust me now or the fact that I can't give him kids."

Paige didn't respond right away. They both knew that Isaac had every right to be as pissed off as he wanted to be. Even though Paige was trying to be nice, even she knew that Isaac would be far from a fool if he called off the engagement. He would actually be a bigger one if he went on like nothing had happened.

"Don't worry yourself about that, Charlene, he is probably just upset right now and is probably not even thinking that way," Paige finally said.

"Yeah, that's what I would wish."

"Either way, you have to be prepared for whatever ways he is going to express his anger, because you can understand he is right to feel this way."

"I know, I just wish I didn't open my big mouth."

"Charlene . . . It was bound to happen. I don't know why you just thought you could live a lie . . . and such a big one at that."

"Whatever, Paige . . . I don't need a lecture right now."

"I'm not lecturing you, I'm just saying—don't regret it. Be happy it's finally out, and you guys can move on from here."

"Yeah, I guess . . . Let me go. I have to fix something to eat. I haven't eaten since yesterday," Charlene said.

"OK, bye," Paige replied.

After hanging up the phone, Charlene didn't head toward the kitchen right away. She sat on the edge of her bed thinking about what Paige had said. This could actually be a good thing, she thought to herself. She could finally be herself and not have to feel afraid that anyone or anything could blow her up to Isaac. She could actually feel better marrying a man who knew the real her. Of course, if they could get past this.

Eventually, after she stopped daydreaming, she headed toward the kitchen. She looked in the refrigerator, and there was nothing simple to eat. She was in the mood for some bacon, was in no mood to cook. So she pulled out the milk, opened up her cabinet and got out some Fruity Pebbles. She went in the living room with her big bowl of cereal and sat in front of the television. Once she nestled into the couch cushions, and turned on the television she began to chow down on her cereal. After the second bite, she didn't want it anymore. She looked at it once or twice and tried to take one more bite. Then she headed back to the kitchen to make her bacon. She dumped the bowl of cereal, and started getting a pan out for the bacon and toast she was about to make instead.

Charlene realized about midway through preparing her new breakfast that she had been awake almost an hour, and hadn't cried or called Isaac. She wanted to call him, but she was beyond afraid. Charlene wasn't one to handle the truth well. Facing reality head on wasn't her forte. Still, she knew that she would have to address it at some point. She just hadn't had any time to consider what she was going to say, or if she wanted to address it sooner than later. So when Isaac called he threw her off once again. Her phone rang just as she was placing the bacon in the skillet. She was actually excited to see that he had called her, and she was hoping that he was calling to apologize and make up.

"Hey," she said in a low tone.

"Hey," he said in a not-so-low tone.

Charlene could tell from his voice that he was still upset.

"Hi," she said.

"You just waking up?" he asked.

"No . . . Isaac, I was gonna call you but—"

"Nah, don't worry about that . . . I just wanted to come by there . . . I forgot my ring last night."

Charlene froze. Her heart stopped and she just stood there with her mouth open for a second. Spatula in one hand, phone in the other, just still.

"Your ring?" she finally asked.

"Yeah, my ring . . . the one on your finger . . . and some other things I need to get as well."

Charlene didn't even know what to say. Of course she knew that the incident from the night before would be something that could cause a major problem for them, and she even knew that it was grounds for a breakup. Still, for some reason she hadn't prepared herself for it. Even through all the crying and fear of losing him the night before, she hadn't gotten her mind around the thought that he would actually do it. It was like one of those things you say, but you don't really mean. Except this wasn't her call to make, and she was so not ready to give in.

"Isaac, please don't do this," she said after a long pause.

"Don't do what?" he asked with an obvious attitude.

"Don't do this to us . . . I am sorry. I know I was wrong for not telling you, and—"

"Really, Charlene, I don't want to hear it."

"Can you just hear me out, Isaac?"

"No, I can't. I don't want to hear anything you have to say."

"Are you serious, Isaac?"

"Dead serious . . . Now, can you just gather my things for me, so I can come by and get them . . . ? And can you put the ring in the box it came in for me, please?"

"So, are you calling off our engagement Isaac . . . just like that?"

"Is that what it sounds like? If it walks like a duck, and quacks like—"

"Oh, you think this is funny, Isaac. Did you ever stop to consider how I feel?"

"I don't think it's funny, not one bit. That's why, no, I haven't stopped to consider what you feel . . ."

Charlene could tell she was fighting a brick wall. Isaac was mad, and there probably wasn't much she could say at this point to calm him down. She also knew she wasn't trying to take her ring off her finger.

"Isaac, we owe it to ourselves to at least talk about this."

"You can talk all you want, but I have nothing to say and don't want to hear you. So go talk to them niggas you were fucking . . . not me."

"Isaac, you act like I was cheating on you. This was all before I even knew you."

"Uh-huh . . . What about all your lies . . . ? That was all while you knew me."

"Isaac, I understand I should have been honest, but when I met you I didn't know that I would fall in love with you or be with you like that. I didn't know that you were going to ask me to marry you."

"So you built our whole relationship on lies, because you didn't know if I was just another notch on your belt?"

"It wasn't like that, Isaac . . . I'm not that proud of things I did when I was younger, and I just don't like—"

Just as Charlene thought she was about to be able to have the talk she had been wanting to have with Isaac for quite some time, he cut her off again.

"Please!" he blurted out. "Save all of that feelings and shame stuff. I'm not hearing it. You had years to tell me that, and I really don't want to hear it now that you're caught out."

"Why you trying to make me sound so terrible . . . ? I'm still the same woman you knew for all this time."

"I don't know you."

Charlene's heart fell when she heard that. It went through her like a knife, the pain that he could even say that to her. Here he was the man that she was supposed to marry, and he just said he didn't even know her. What could she say to that? She knew that this wasn't going to be something she could sweet talk her way out of. She also knew that he had finally realized what she had known all along. Charlene decided to stop even trying to argue with him. Regardless of whether he was right or not, he was being an asshole and she wasn't feeling his attitude one bit.

"Fine, Isaac, see you soon," she responded.

Chapter 22

The arrangement Isaac and Charlene made ended up being that he would come by in two hours and she would have the stuff all gathered for him to just grab and go. Charlene decided that she wasn't going to make it that easy. In the time she had, she contemplated whether she should let him go for now and let him cool down and see what he did, or forgo the risk and fight for him right then and there. She figured since she was the one to blame for them being in that crap, that she would go ahead and do the latter. She figured she should just put all her pride aside and go for it. She even thought to herself at one point that she understood how girls try to trap men with babies because she truly wished she was able to get pregnant so she could be pregnant and make him stay.

The table in the foyer was covered with mail that Charlene hadn't tended to just yet. There were two of her light jackets lying over the chair that was in the corner, and a glass and a plate on the coffee table. Charlene definitely could have used some tidying up but she had been so preoccupied with everything that was going on she hadn't found a chance. The curtains were drawn back, letting the sunlight inside her living room, but it had no effect on Charlene's mood. Charlene could hear the neighborhood kids having a good time outside, but inside her apartment she was sitting down sulking, trying to figure out exactly what she was going to do. Unfortunately, she didn't have enough time to figure that out.

When he walked in he didn't use his key, he rang the doorbell. She was expecting that he would, so she was in the bedroom waiting for him. When she heard the bell she had to go get the door, ruining her chance to lure him farther into the apartment. She had already freshened up and got as casually cute as possible. When she went to the door, she had no idea how she should greet him. Throughout their whole relationship, they had never faced such a big issue and she had no idea what she was in for. Still, she was wishfully thinking that his coming by to get his stuff so soon was an excuse, and that he really wanted to work things out and have great make-up sex. She opened the door and watched him walk in, right by her. She wasn't expecting a kiss or anything, but a hello would have been nice.

He walked past her and stood on the other side of the entryway. He didn't go to the living room or anything, he was making it very clear that he wasn't there to stay and he wanted his bag she was supposed to have for him.

"I got tied up and I wasn't able to get all of your things," she said as she noticed he wasn't budging.

"Come on, Charlene!" he said.

She knew it would frustrate him, but she figured she had nothing to lose at that point.

"What? I put these two shirts right here," she said as she pointed to the two shirts lying over a chair. "But I didn't get to finish," she continued.

"Fine, Charlene," he said as he walked off to get the rest of his stuff. Charlene had no master plan. She wished she could have bolted the door and never let him out. She knew she had to work a miracle to get Isaac to give her even an ounce of sympathy. He was in the living room getting some DVDs of his, and she went and sat on the edge of the couch closest to him.

"Isaac, is there a way we can talk for one second?"

"No . . . and I know that's why you didn't get my stuff together . . . You figured you would try to prolong my stay here so you could feed me more of your bullshit. Don't even try it because I'm not hearing anything you have to say."

Charlene couldn't believe that he was really acting like this. She never knew that Isaac had such a mean streak. She felt like he did, actually, like she didn't know this him either.

"So, you're going to walk out that door, and never talk to me again, is that your plan?" she asked.

Isaac didn't respond.

"Isaac? Is that your plan . . . just end it just like this?"

Still nothing came from Isaac. He walked across the living room and picked up items that belonged to him as he went. He took his DVDs that were lying on top of the entertainment center and one or two of his CDs that were close by. He went in the bedroom after he was done walking through the living room. Charlene followed him to the bedroom and watched him as he looked for his belongings. After he threw a few shirts on the bed, he headed back toward the doorway. Charlene was startled as he approached her and she subtly moved out of his way. She didn't know what he was doing but she was wishfully thinking that he would change his mind about getting his stuff.

Unfortunately, he headed right back with a plastic bag and took some clothes and some other items that he really didn't need. He was there to make the wound worse, or just for his ring. The whole show was making her angry. She knew she was wrong, but she felt she was entitled to at least a chance to explain herself. He was treating her like she was really some street prostitute he cared nothing about, and it hurt. The more she watched him ignore her, the more she hurt. Before she knew it, the floods came. Her eyes started welling up, and the tears began to fall. She was trying to be discreet, but she knew that Isaac had noticed. He just didn't care.

He had finally finished what he was doing and then he stood by the door. She looked up and saw that he was waiting.

"You're done?" she asked.

"Yeah," he replied.

"OK," she said as she walked toward the door to let him out.

"The ring . . ." he said before he even stepped another foot.

She actually had momentarily forgotten, even though she was sure it seemed as if she was hoping he would forget.

Charlene looked at him. She didn't say anything, and she didn't make any facial hints. She just gave him a blank stare. She was all out of thoughts, and she didn't have a clue about how to gain control of the situation.

"Isaac . . . ?" she began.

"Charlene!" he responded.

He made it very clear in every movement in his body and every note in his voice that he was not trying to hear it. The situation didn't cause for anything other than for Charlene to come to terms with it, and let it go. But for some reason, in the back of her mind she hoped this was still not forever. Her silent hopes didn't take away the pain, she just couldn't grasp that he could possibly mean all of this. She couldn't believe this was all so easy for him. Yet, the look in his eyes and his body language showed that it was. Defeated, Charlene had no choice in the matter, so she took off the ring. Of course, she could have put up a fight, but she knew she had already done more than enough. The second the ring hit his hand, he walked toward the door, opened it and walked out.

She didn't realize it—not until she recognized that familiar pain that she had felt so many times with guys she had liked but had been too easy with—that this was history repeating itself. At that very moment she realized that all those efforts were in vain, that regardless of how long she tried to suppress her blemished past, it had finally made its way to the present.

Chapter 23

Of course Paige tried to be optimistic and tried to make it seem as if Isaac needed time to calm down. Although that's what Charlene wanted to believe, too, something in her heart told her that this was probably not just a regular lover's quarrel.

It didn't make it any easier to deal with when she had to answer people's questions at work. She told most people the ring was getting cleaned and engraved, and a few that it was getting appraised. She wasn't quite ready to face the embarrassment of having to retract her engagement news, and return the engagement gifts. It seemed like people knew something was up anyway, though, despite her trying to cover it up. It was like Charlene had become the emperor in his new clothes; she thought she was all covered up but really she was naked. It made sense with Isaac, but even her coworkers seemed to be able to see through her all of a sudden. They knew she was down, and nobody really seemed to believe her ring story. Her heartbreak was that painful, unmistakably visible regardless of how much of an illusion she tried to portray.

Charlene had called Isaac a few times, even though each time she knew he wouldn't answer or return her call. One thing Charlene did know about Isaac was that he was a stubborn Virgo and he would stand his ground on something just to prove a point. She really wasn't expecting him to answer, because he had done this type of thing before. She was hoping that somebody would talk to him, and let him know that he should at least try to have an adult conversation about it. To call off the engagement was extreme, and that type of decision shouldn't be made in haste. Charlene knew she was in no position to tell Isaac that, so she was hoping that someone else would. Her calls were to remind him that she was still trying and still wanted a chance.

Isaac knew full well that he was driving Charlene mad. He knew she hated to be ignored, and he knew even more that her guilt would eat away at her more without knowing exactly what Isaac was thinking or doing. But that wasn't why he was doing this. Isaac truly felt like he couldn't marry a woman who had been so deceitful and dishonest with him. He wasn't feeling that from their conversation, she wasn't quite the lady he thought she was. It's enough for a man to accept the fact that his girl has slept with men before him. Of course to marry a virgin would be the ideal choice, but the fewer partners the better. Still, if you really love the woman, you can overlook some of her indiscretions and wrong decisions in the past. The problem for Isaac was that not only did he not know she had so many indiscretions to overlook, it was that she lied about them all and would have continued to lie. What was the most hurtful to Isaac was that he really thought he knew his fiancé, he thought they had something special. He never would have thought she would keep such secrets, especially one that would alter his life so much. Charlene was well aware of his strong desire to have children, and yet she kept her secret to herself, knowing it would shatter his dream. He found it selfish and literally unforgivable.

Although Charlene hadn't had a conversation with Isaac about this, she knew that he was feeling that way. Some of the comments he had made since he found out and the way that he had completely turned off his feelings toward her, it wasn't hard to tell. She didn't know if she should just accept it and attempt to move on with her life or throw everything she had into getting him back, pull out all the stops. The bigger question for her was whether it would even matter, if she had no stop or trick that would work this one out. Having to question that made her have to face herself in the mirror and what she had done to Isaac. She started to feel like she was being selfish. Regardless of how much she loved Isaac, she still would be unable to fulfill his needs because she couldn't give him the baby that he yearned for.

She called Paige for the second time that day.

"What now?" Paige asked when she answered.

"That's mean," Charlene replied.

"I'm only joking, Leen . . . But I'm asking because you're not being patient . . . not giving him time to think it all over and calm down—"

"That's the thing . . . I'm wondering if I should give him just that—time," Charlene said.

"That's what I've been saying all along."

"No, I mean all the time in the world. Just let him go."

"Where did this come from?"

"I realized that even if we work it out, will we ever really work it out? I can't give him a child and that's not going to change . . . What incentive does he have to forgive me . . . to marry me and live terribly ever after?" Charlene asked, trying to contain the lump that appeared in her throat.

"Don't say that, Charlene. You can give him all the love in the world, besides, Isaac isn't with you because of your womb . . . He loved you."

"Not anymore . . . As he put it, he loved the woman he thought he knew."

"Charlene, he is mad right now. He will come to his senses.

He doesn't want the embarrassment of calling off the engagement, either. Besides he will realize sooner than later that he isn't going to find a Goody Two-shoes out there, so he might as well stick with what he got."

"Is that supposed to make me feel better?" Charlene asked, managing to laugh.

Finding the humor in it, Paige laughed back.

"You know what I mean . . . Just be patient, he will be back."

Even though there wasn't much in Charlene that felt the same way, she preferred to adopt Paige's optimism for now.

Chapter 24

Charlene's optimism about her relationship with Isaac slowly disappeared after a few more days went by and she still hadn't heard from him. Her optimism really ceased when something totally unexpected happened. She came home one afternoon, about six days after she had last seen Isaac, and she noticed a box in front of her door. She walked up to it and read the label, it was addressed to Charlene and had been sent from Isaac. The door to her apartment swung open as Charlene nudged it with her shoulder, since her hands were full. Once she stepped back inside she used her foot to shut the door. Immediately the belongings in her hand were dropped on the little table in the foyer. Charlene had to use the bathroom but she was dying to know what the package Isaac had sent was about. Without even removing her jacket, she sat down on the couch with the box, oozing with curiosity.

Charlene had allowed her imagination to run wild since the moment she saw the box. Only seconds later she was praying that it was a teddy bear from FAO Schwarz saying sorry, or I love you; she thought maybe it could be a unique gift that only she could interpret. Charlene thought that Isaac was ready to make up and that he had thought of a unique and sweet way to do so. So, filled with expectation, Charlene tore through the tightly wrapped box to get to what was inside. Once she got the box open, the first thing she saw was one of her favorite tops. Then, as she shuffled through, she saw more items that belonged to her until she realized that they were items she had left at Isaac's place. She looked around for something more inside the box as if what she had seen so far was a cruel joke, and then she realized that it wasn't. For a couple of moments, while she was still psyched to have received some form of contact from Isaac, she didn't feel the insult of it. Then, after she had searched a bit longer for some hidden message in the box and didn't find one, she felt hurt by the gesture.

Charlene didn't know if Isaac was trying to hurt her feelings or if he was just handling business. Either way she was getting weaker and weaker by every reminder that Isaac was a free man. She didn't mind so much that she was a free woman, because she knew what she was doing with herself and that she still wanted to be with Isaac. The difficulty was not knowing what Isaac was doing or if he had truly made up his mind that he was done with their relationship. After driving herself crazy, Charlene changed out of her work clothes into a velour sweatsuit and some Nike sneakers. Without analyzing it at all, she grabbed her keys off the table and headed out the door.

Her keys jingled in her hands as she walked to her car. Within seconds she was stitting in the car, then she inserted the key in the ignition, backed up and shifted to the driving gear on her way down the street. About a mile down the road, Charlene began to feel around inside her purse. She found her wallet, some gum, a brush and makeup bag until her hand recognized the shape of her cell phone. She pulled out the phone, and speed-dialed Isaac. She waited for a few seconds before she confirmed that once again he wasn't picking up.

"Hi, you've reached Isaac . . ." the voice mail began.

Charlene immediately pressed 1 to cut short his outgoing message.

"Hi, Isaac, I am on my way to your place. I didn't want to come unexpected, but I think we need to talk. See you soon," Charlene said before hanging up.

Charlene drove straight to his house with no second thoughts. She didn't change her mind, even after considering the possibility that he might not get the message and could have a girl there. Charlene thought to herself that if that happened it wouldn't matter to her, anyway, because it would be Isaac's scene to deal with—she would just show up. So, determined to see Isaac and make some progress, she was pulling up in front of his condo in his oh-so-quiet neighborhood.

But once she got there she noticed that she didn't see his car. She looked farther down the street and still saw no sign of his vehicle. She stepped out the car wondering if maybe for some reason he didn't have his car or it was at the dealer getting some maintenance. She walked up to his door and began to knock and waited a few seconds. There was no answer. She knocked a few more times. Still there was no answer. Feeling a bit defeated, Charlene walked back to her car. She pulled out her cell phone and hit REDIAL on the phone.

It was like she was in denial, because deep down she knew damn well that he wasn't going to answer the phone. Still, she sat there and let it ring, but this time when the voice mail picked up she didn't leave a message. Charlene sat in her car in front of his house for a bit longer, trying to think of what she could do. She began to look out the window and watch his place to see if she saw any movements.

A black X5 slowly came driving into the complex and Charlene diverted her attention to it. It pulled up to a condo four doors down from Isaac's and parked. A tall man with a medium build stepped out of the car and closed the driver's side door behind him. He then opened the back door, grabbed his brief-case off the backseat and closed the back door. The man slowly walked out of the parking area and onto the walkway toward his home. As soon as he began to walk, the door he was in front of opened and standing there was a woman with a baby in her arms. The man lit up with a smile upon the sight of his welcoming committee, and the woman looked just as excited to see him. Charlene sat and watched as he approached her, planted a big kiss on her lips and the baby's forehead and pro-ceeded inside. As soon as their door closed behind him, Char-lene snapped back to it.

She looked again at the house that she was parked in front of and wondered if that would ever be her waiting for Isaac to get home from work. Then she began to wonder if Isaac had left when he got her message that she was on her way and if he wouldn't return home anytime soon. Charlene was about to lose her mind. She was even tempted to call Lacy to see if Lacy would reveal what was on Isaac's mind. She knew that was a desperate move, because that would show how weak she was and then she could probably never face Lacy with the same ego again.

Charlene finally started her car and put the gear in DRIVE. She rode down the street looking for Isaac's car to see if he was parked somewhere waiting for her to leave. She hoped that he wouldn't go to such drastic measures to avoid her, but she didn't know what to expect from him at this point. Once she exited his complex she stopped looking for clues and headed on to the highway.

It was a Thursday night and Charlene was back at her apartment on the phone with Jasmine trying to keep herself occupied. She barely ever sat quiet in her house unless she was welcoming a crying session to come on, because she knew that was all that it took for her emotions to get the best of her. So she tried to stay as busy and distracted as possible. This evening Jasmine was up. Paige was all Isaac'd out. Paige hadn't said it, but it seemed she had become kind of tired of the Isaac moping and patience talks.

"Charlene, Isaac ain't Lebron James or somebody. He may be a decent guy but he is not some baller that's fine as all hell or something. I doubt he has girls all over him. He will stop feeling himself soon, and if not there are other Isaacs out there."

"Yeah, and then I'll be right back here again one day," Charlene replied.

"No, you tell the next one up front."

"Yeah . . . OK . . . and see if I ever get engaged again."

"We don't even have to think that far ahead because Isaac will be back soon . . . He will be horny soon," Jasmine said, laughing.

"Yeah, if he isn't getting some from the 'always there for him' Ms. Lacy," Charlene said sarcastically.

"Who is that?"

"His friend, but back in the day it was a flirtatious thing but he claims it grew into a friendship since nothing ever happened."

"You think they are having sex?"

"I don't know, especially now . . . I'm sure she is trying to console him."

"Whatever, Charlene, that's your guilt. Give it a few more days, still no call, we will go to his job," Jasmine said, slightly laughing but clearly being serious.

"Then it will really be on . . . I'm going to mail him this letter I wrote and hope he reads it and feels it in his heart to at least talk to me."

"Try it."

"The way he is acting he may put Return to Sender on it and send it back unread."

They both chuckled. They took that chance to go ahead and get off the phone since they had been talking for quite a while.

Charlene sat on the couch watching television and eating some leftover pizza she had in the fridge. She had been eating like a pig lately, eating junk food and late in the evenings. She knew she was gaining some pounds, but she hoped that Isaac could make up with her soon and reduce her stress eating. In the meantime she enjoyed every bite.

She watched television for about another hour before her mind wandered back to Isaac. She hadn't spent so much time alone with herself in years. In the past she would have had another dude in the mix by now, somebody to cushion the pain and sex her back happy. This time she knew that that wasn't going to help; besides, she didn't want to add any more risks to making things worse with Isaac.

She tried to keep her attention on the television program, but it became harder and harder. Eventually she went to look on her phones as if she thought Isaac might have called. Once she saw that she had no missed calls, as she had figured, she went ahead and dialed his number. She wasn't even nervous as the phone rang, because she was so used to the feeling of anticipation and getting his answering machine. The phone rang once, Charlene picked up the remote control. It rang a second time; she went ahead and muted the television. It rang a third time and the phone stopped ringing.

"Hello," a female voice said from the other end.

Charlene froze. She looked in the phone to make sure the number was correct and saw Isaac's name in the phone identifying the number she had dialed.

"H-el-lo," Charlene slowly said back.

"Hi, are you looking for Isaac?" the female asked.

"Yes," Charlene replied.

She didn't know if she should have an attitude, if she was even in a position to. She didn't know who this person was and just how sly she could behave in order to find out.

"Oh, he just ran out. Do you want me to tell him you called?"

"Who is this?"

"Tyra, who is this?" the girl replied.

"This is Charlene, his fiancée."

"Fiancée? Really? He said he was no longer engaged," the girl responded.

Charlene had tried to piss off the girl, but she ended up getting pissed off herself.

"Did he? . . . Well, tell him I called."

"Sure," the girl replied.

"By the way, why are you answering his phone?"

"Excuse me?"

"Why are you answering his phone? You don't think you're out of place?"

"No, I don't. He stepped out and left it here with me by mistake . . . I don't have to explain this to you, Charlene . . . I'm sorry. I'll explain it to him if he asks."

Charlene didn't know what to say. She wanted to ask a million questions, like how long have you been around? Where are you guys right now? What did he tell you about our engagement? Where has he been? How is he doing? Of course, she couldn't stoop that low; this girl was already playing her and had the upper hand.

"No problem," she replied. "Just have him call me."

"OK."

"Bye."

Charlene hung up and felt absolutely numb. She didn't

know what to think or do with herself. All she knew was that that wasn't a part of the plan. She hadn't prepared herself in any form or fashion for that pain and embarrassment.

What made it worse was that she couldn't even break on him because she knew chances were he wouldn't call her back. That only added to the embarrassment, because whoever Tyra was, if she relayed the message it wasn't as if she would see him actually call Charlene. Deep down she hoped he would feel bad that she had to face that and call her back. She figured, though, that he probably didn't care and wouldn't, anyway. After she took it all in, she went ahead and called Jasmine back.

"You see, I told you," Charlene said.

"Dag . . . That is crazy," Jasmine replied.

"I was in shock . . . First I was in shock that the phone was answered, but then it was a chick."

"Yeah, I don't know . . . I would have broke," Jasmine said.

"I couldn't. She probably would have made me feel so stupid. I don't know who she is or what she knows . . . It was bad enough, trust me."

"I can imagine . . . Talk about awkward."

"Damn, it's really over . . ." Charlene said in a real serious tone. She had had an epiphany in the past few seconds: that only she was still holding on.

"That could just be some jump-off to get him through, that doesn't have to be anything."

Charlene was tired of the optimism. She had lost weeks of healing time with her high hopes that he would come back. Really, Paige and Jasmine were telling her what anybody would say when they are trying to make you feel better. They probably knew, too, by now that Isaac was truly gone, but couldn't bear to tell her.

"Jas . . . No . . . Isaac is really playing me. He isn't doing the relationship lesson break, it's really over."

"Charlene—"

"Na, Jas. It's cool. I have to prepare myself for this; I can't keep waiting on him."

"I feel ya, girl . . ."

Charlene had told Jasmine only part of the story—that Isaac knew about her multiple partners and wasn't feeling it. And Charlene didn't want to go much further. Jasmine knew Charlene would have difficulty getting pregnant, but Charlene had told her it was because of the fertility issue, like she had initially told Isaac.

They hung up the phone after that, since there wasn't much more consoling to do. Charlene was happy she had called Isaac, because it was during the call that she had seen the reality. The reality was that there was a strong chance that she would be out in the clubs real soon looking for a new man.

Chapter 25

Charlene had really thought she'd outgrown it. She'd thought she no longer needed to run to another man to fill the void, that she had changed and had learned why, for so many reasons, that that wasn't the solution. She wanted to believe she was a strong enough woman now that she could lean on herself. Apparently not.

Sure enough, after she thought long and hard about it, she called up Rich. At first she hung up after dialing the fourth digit of his number. Then, less than a minute later, she tried again. She got all the way to the sixth digit and hung up. She was debating with herself if she was making a mistake. Not because it wouldn't be right to do to Isaac, clearly he wasn't concerned about her or her feelings. She didn't want to go back into Rich's world of chaos. Even more, she knew going backward was in the rule book of things not to do. But Charlene figured this would be an exception to the rule. She was in an emergency emotional state and she didn't have any time to look forward, so backwards it was going to have to be. Besides, she only intended for it to be an innocent conversation for some much-needed attention.

She eventually mustered up the courage to complete dialing his number and on the third ring he answered.

"Hey, miss," he said, sounding as smooth and sexy as she had remembered last.

"Hi, Rich," she replied.

"Your man let you free for a second."

Funny he should ask that, she thought to herself.

"Yeah, I guess he has," she replied, trying to hint at but not completely discuss the turmoil at home.

"Well, is that good news or bad news?"

"Both," she said, trying to be as vague as possible.

"Well, does that mean I'm going to finally be able to spend some time with you?"

She hesitated at first, unsure of how far she was willing to take this.

"Yeah . . . What you have in mind?" she asked.

Charlene wasn't sure if Rich felt like a lucky guy that she still thought enough of him to keep a relationship, and if he valued their relationship for what it was. Or if he just thought it was the same old Charlene doing what she normally does—dibble and dabble. She desperately didn't want to portray the likes of the old Charlene, but the new Charlene was craving the same affirmation that the old one had. She wanted a man to let her know she was good enough, because, unfortunately, she still didn't know that for sure herself.

"Let's hang out and get a bite," he said.

"Sure, come get me . . . I'll be ready in an hour," she said.

"OK, see you then—and wear something sexy for me."

"Got ya. See you soon."

"Bye."

There was a part of Charlene's answer right there. Yeah, Rich was figuring that you can't teach old dogs new tricks. He just saw Charlene's phone call as a booty call. Although a week or two ago that would've been the last thing she would have wanted, she didn't even care. She didn't care a few years ago, and she was in no mood to care tonight. For the first time in a while Charlene reintroduced herself to her true self and didn't feel like pretending. So, Team Dream Charlene, a nickname the guys used to call her because she had been with the whole team, was back.

Rich took closer to two hours, and Charlene had almost changed her mind by then. She'd slowly changed into something sexy as Rich had asked and when she looked in the mirror was momentarily disgusted that this effort wasn't for her fiancé, or ex-fiancé. She put on some tight jeans and a low-cut shirt. She didn't go overboard, but she knew she was accentuating all of her assets for him.

Charlene was expecting him to call and say he was downstairs and she would have come down. Instead, as she was sitting on her couch awaiting that call, her doorbell rang. When she went to answer it, it was Rich on the other side with his hand hovering over his crotch.

"I got to pee," he said as he scooted past her and didn't wait for her approval to enter.

Charlene had only gotten a glimpse of him before he disappeared into her bathroom. That glimpse was enough, though, to give her a little tingle, 'cause as usual Rich was looking fine as wine. He looked like he had just stepped off the pages of GQ. Even doing the pee-pee dance and holding himself he looked irresistible.

Once he came out of the bathroom, he stood in the doorway for a second. Charlene was bent over on the couch putting on her boots.

"Mmmm," Rich said, being flirtatious.

Charlene giggled under her breath at the perfect opportunity she had given him to go there.

"Why don't we stay here and order in?" he continued.

Charlene sat up and looked at him.

"You say that now, after I done got all dressed up."

"So take it back off," he said.

Rich was on a roll, and she could tell that soon he was going to have them rolling around on some horizontal plane.

"Ha, ha, ha, Rich . . . Seriously, I could have stayed in my chill-out clothes."

"Take those clothes off, then," he said again with a flirtatious undertone.

Charlene looked at him for a second.

"I'm kidding, Leen . . . We can go . . . I thought since it's later and we already here, we chill here. But it's cool, let's go."

Charlene looked at him for a couple more seconds, trying to quickly assess the best option. She wasn't feeling all that energetic and up to going out, actually, but she knew that if they stayed in, there was more of a chance that this idea would go from her getting some attention to her getting some extraspecial attention.

After she weighed the options, she figured she would take the risk and stay in.

"Fine, let's stay here," she said after a couple moments of silence.

"You sure? We don't have to," he replied right away.

"No, it's cool . . . Did we know where we were going, anyway?" she asked, slightly laughing.

"Not really . . . City Island would have been cool for food but I don't know where other than that . . . We can order in delivery and watch a movie."

"Sure, call and order while I go change out of these uncomfortable-ass jeans. Can't be lounging on the couch in these."

"Just leave them off," he said.

Charlene headed back to her room, not sure how she felt about their sudden change of plans and all of Rich's comments. A piece of her knew that he had every right to think it was somewhat appropriate, especially since she hadn't told him otherwise yet. She didn't even know if she knew how to assert herself and tell him that it was disrespectful. It was Rich; he would probably laugh at her and ask who she was trying to fool. She decided she wouldn't make a big deal out of it. She knew she couldn't deny that she did want to leave her jeans off and call Mr. GQ in her bedroom. The problem was she hadn't decided if she wanted to go that far, she wasn't sure if she was ready to disrespect Isaac in such a way or even if it was disrespectful to him. Out of anger, she could easily decide that Isaac shouldn't mean anything at this point and that she was free to and should go ahead and bang Rich's brains out. Still, though, she did feel bad about sleeping with another man that wasn't Isaac, and she wondered if this was the very lack of self-respect that got her where she was.

She came back into the living room and he was skimming through the Yellow Pages.

"What do you want to eat?" he asked.

"I'm in the mood for pizza," she said.

"Dominoes, then, it is," he replied.

"No arguments or suggestions?"

"Nope . . . Your wish is my command," he said.

"Ooh. I like that," she said as she sat on the couch beside him.

She wasn't sure if she was helping to lead things by sitting next to him versus on the adjacent couch, but she did know that the vibe wasn't saying sit anywhere.

Rich ordered their pizza and then they decided on and ordered a movie. They chose *The Break-Up*, a movie with Jennifer Aniston that she had been dying to see. She thought it was also a good choice because it was a comedy and it would keep things on a friendly level with some jokes and laughter. Except she forgot what they say about laughter being the way to a girl's heart.

The pizza had come and gone, and they sat on the couch side by side chuckling, giggling and cracking up laughing. Charlene was more tickled than Rich was, but they were both clearly finding the movie humorous. There was one scene where they were both laughing at something silly Vince Vaughn had done and they somehow leaned in toward each other. Maybe it was the movie about relationships that instantly made her want to get closer to Rich, but either way she had. She had somehow propped herself up on his body, leaving the situation to go any which way. The fact that the movie was about a breakup, one would have thought it would make her break down crying, thinking about Isaac, but it didn't. In fact it seemed she chose to resurrect a breakup with ol' Richy boy. Before the next scene began she was kissing on Rich's neck and he wasn't making any attempt to stop her. She didn't know exactly what had come over her or changed her mind, but something had because all of a sudden she was going in.

She had started aggressively fondling Rich as she licked and kissed on his neck and chest, and it wasn't long before he joined in, exposing her breasts and stomach. They were like two animals, trying to get to each other first until finally Rich gave in and let Charlene run the show. Once he succumbed to her seduction, she continued kissing on his entire upper body, making small circles with her tongue. Once she had covered most of his upper body with her mouth, she began unbuckling his belt to cover more ground. While she continued to kiss and lick down his stomach, with one movement she unbuckled his pants and with another reached in and removed his pipe. She slowly made her way down farther, and began making small circles with her tongue until she started her next technique. The circles she made on his pipe to get it fully erect and moist got it bigger and bigger until she placed the entire thing in her mouth and proceeded to pleasure him.

Charlene looked up and saw that Rich was enjoying his treat, his head was leaned back and his eyes were closed. She was sure he was thinking about how he had missed her many talents. She didn't want to end it there and she knew if she kept going much longer it would, so she slowed down until she stopped. Then she slowly made her way up on top of him. As she lifted herself up, she removed her loose pajama pants. She had on some lace purple thongs underneath, and she kept her white wife beater on. Once she came eye to eye with Rich, she subtly whispered, "You ready for the ride?"

"Definitely so," he said back, slightly smirking.

"Keep your hands on the inside and buckle up," she replied with a giggle.

Although she was giggling, she became serious. She slowly lowered her body back down as she moved her thong over to clear the way, and pushed down to let Rich inside of her. Both of their faces lit up from the initial feeling. It wasn't that it had been too long for Charlene, it was that Rich packed quite a bit more than Isaac, so to feel that much inside of her was a pleasant reminder of the good old days. They both moaned some and groaned some, as Charlene went up and down like a merry-go-round with her breasts bouncing in his face. She went back and forth, up and down and in circles, making every motion possible so this ride would be memorable for the both of them.

Moments into it, as she started to realize that it could end soon because she knew she was rocking his world, she remembered they should have put on a condom. She was so used to not using one, and Rich was no stranger to her raw insides, either, so she hadn't thought of it at first.

"Sorry, babe, give me a second," Charlene said as she leaned over for Rich's wallet. She quickly removed a condom, which she knew would be there, placed it on his erect and eager penis and got right back on top. Rich couldn't do anything but laugh at what she had done, and how she just kept right going like it was nothing. That was his porn star, as he used to call her. Lucky she did that, because about fifteen strokes later, Rich clinched up and grabbed her body as he released his little men and they were all inside the rubber hat.

Chapter 26

Some time had passed, and Charlene hadn't even cried yet. She had no idea where she got the strength from, but she didn't break down, not once. Between the girl answering Isaac's phone and her indiscretion with Rich, she was reminded that her past was only a day or two behind her and never that far away. Emotional Charlene would have had to throw a pity party by now and invite her friends over for it. But not this time. She wondered if she had literally run out of tears in her tear ducts. She did stay up late on a few nights in deep thought, though, running over in her mind all the ways she'd gone wrong and how she could possibly live the rest of her life right.

The night before was one of those nights, but she eventually went to sleep and when she awoke she was in the very same state of mind. She woke up ready to face her new life. She had decided that she was no longer going to go on with high hopes, she couldn't take any more. It made the pain that much more unbearable because she hadn't yet tried to trick herself into thinking she didn't care.

She left the house fairly early and headed out to run some errands. She went to drop some clothes at the cleaners, get her hair done, pick up something for her mother, and then headed home to clean and do laundry. When she got home, she had lost most of her Saturday. She put down her bags, pressed the answering machine button and ran into the bathroom. She started to release her urine as she listened to the first message, which was from her mother thanking her for her help today. The next message was from one of her coworkers, letting her know that she had come in earlier and left some work on her desk. Charlene had started to wrap up in the bathroom when the third message came on. It was Isaac. She damn near flew out of the bathroom.

"Hey, Charlene, It's Isaac. I'm returning your call. I've been real busy, but I know you probably need some sort of closure, so I'll let you know that I did receive your letter and it's all cool. I'm not mad at you anymore; I know this is the best thing for me. I hope we both have the lives we deserve . . . I love you."

Charlene immediately started crying when she heard that. She could hear it in his voice that his feelings were really thought out and he was on to the next relationship.

Charlene took a few seconds to cry her tears out and then she went ahead and called him back. He didn't answer the phone. She left him a message as well, just asking for him to call her. She was too emotional to express much more; she didn't want to do that on an answering machine.

She did call Paige, though. She told her all about the girl answering the phone and the message Isaac had left. Even Paige felt Charlene's pain.

"Leen, however this turns out, you will be fine."

"I know, I feel so bad. How can I mess up such a good thing? I really did love him."

"I know. That's why you should have been honest with him. Love would have endured all."

"Why isn't it enduring this, then?"

"Because it's after the fact. He feels betrayed. After all of these years he finds out something about your past. Most men can't handle a female that has had too much experience . . . But I think with Isaac it has more to do with the baby part."

"He said before that we would try."

"That's before he knew that your chances were as slim as they were, and before he knew that it's not normal circumstances, that it's because of an abortion of some other man's child."

"It was years ago . . . It was a mistake," Charlene said through her tears. Although she had tried to stop, she had been crying since she heard the message.

"I know, Leen, that's why I really didn't think he would be so heartless. I really did think he would be more understanding and get over it since he loved you, but he probably blames you."

"I guess he didn't love me enough. I can't help but wonder if he would of even made me his girl if he knew in the beginning."

"Who knows, don't worry yourself about that. All you can know is that he wouldn't be calling off an engagement over it if it got this far," Paige said.

"Yeah . . . Well, let me go throw some water on my face and get myself together."

"OK. Want me to come over?"

"No, I'll be all right. Thanks, though."

"OK, Sis, talk to you later."

"Bye."

Charlene did just that, she went into the bathroom and threw some water on her face until she calmed down. Then she sat on the edge of her bed and let her mind wander.

After about ten minutes she got up and went into the kitchen and got some of the Oreo cookies she hadn't been able to get enough of lately. She went to turn on the television to find herself a good girlie movie to watch instead of cleaning up. After she couldn't find anything quite sappy enough, she decided to watch her *How Stella Got Her Groove Back* DVD. She popped it in and went into the kitchen. She didn't quite know what to make that would be quick and easy, but she did know she had her mind on a sausage. It was frozen and so was going to take some time to fix, but she started making it anyway because she was dying to have one. Once she put the pot of water on the stove to boil it, she headed back to watch the rest of the previews.

She debated about calling Isaac back again, but she wasn't sure if she would get Miss Tyra again or even if she was ready to have a mature "moving on" conversation that he appeared ready for. She decided she would call him later after she had gathered all of her thoughts. She knew that her aggressive apologetic approach wasn't working; Isaac was on a whole different plane. One that she had no part in whatsoever. It hurt her the most that he was able to move on so easily, or at least cut off his feelings so fast. She knew that he had a right to be angry, but she couldn't believe that he would take it this far. At first she thought it was one of those lessons, and he had to make a big deal out of it for the sake of his pride. At this point, though, with all the time that had gone by and the Tyra thing she could finally tell it was more than that. Taking back the ring could have been a hint, but she thought that he would love her at least enough to try to work it out. There was a part of her that figured Isaac was right, this was the best thing for them. If he didn't even love her enough to get over this, they probably never stood a chance at a lifelong marriage.

Charlene had finally settled down on her couch with her nice juicy sausage sandwich and one of her favorite movies. She was actually into the movie and distracted from all of her own personal problems, sitting back admiring Stella's life. She wished she could afford to live like Stella did without the help of a man, and she wished even more that she could have a child to love her for if and when she was lonely. Charlene watched movies about strong, independent women to enjoy them, but also to aspire to be more like those women. *Erin Brocovich* was the movie that had inspired her to go back to school. It didn't take much for Charlene to see another possibility in real life through something fictional.

Charlene was halfway through the marriage part of the movie and about twenty minutes into the digestion phase of that sausage when she suddenly jumped up and ran to the bathroom. Instinctively she lifted the toilet lid and threw her body over the ceramic bowl to hurl, and out came a bunch of brown chunks. Out of breath she stood there, confused from not knowing that that was coming. She rinsed out her mouth and gargled with mouthwash and then headed back to the kitchen to look at the sausage package to see if they were spoiled or something. She looked at it and they looked perfectly fine. She sat there trying to remember whether the last time she had had one of them they made her nauseous, but she couldn't recall.

She eventually let it go and went back to watching the movie, and as she sat there she noticed her stomach feeling a little nauseous. She held her hand against her stomach, trying to soothe her belly back to normalcy. She regretted making the sausage, and was upset that it wasn't agreeing with her stomach. She got up to drink a tall glass of water, but that didn't help. After a while she turned off the movie, it had been interrupted too much to try to enjoy the rest, so she went ahead and switched to cable television and called her sister.

"What you doing?" Charlene asked.

"Getting back from the mall," Paige replied.

"What you buy?"

"Just some shirts I needed for work and some flat shoes."

"I need to go buy some things myself."

"Yeah, you always shopping . . . You don't need anything."

"Well, now that I have to be looking for a new man, I may have to revamp my wardrobe . . . Step it up."

"Whatever, missy. You slow yourself down."

"I was fine, over here chilling. I was trying to watch *Stella Got Her Groove Back,* but I was being greedy and ate some sausage and it made me throw up."

"Throw up?"

"Yeah. I guess it didn't agree with my stomach. I was sitting there and all of a sudden I ran to the bathroom and threw up all of it."

"Charlene? You don't think that's a little strange?"

"What do you mean?"

"You don't throw up like that."

"No . . . But . . . Paige, don't even go there."

"What? I'm just saying."

"Why would you say that when you already know that's not possible?"

"It's not *impossible.* I would at least check it out. Not being funny I did notice the other day you gained some weight."

"No you didn't," Charlene said, laughing.

"No, seriously. I'm not trying to play you, but in your face and belly area. I didn't want to say anything but it all makes sense now."

"Whatever, Paige. I am not pregnant. The doctor told me my chances were like one in a million—and what would the odds of that be after being with Isaac all this time I get pregnant now when we break up?"

"Maybe it's fate."

"Whatever, Paige, I'm hanging up with you . . . You talking crazy."

"Aright, whatever. I said to at least check. It won't hurt. You said you're eating like crazy and now this."

"Whatever, bye, Paige."

"Bye, crazy."

They hung up the phone, both slightly laughing at the other. Once off the phone Charlene began to really think about what Paige was saying. She knew it made sense, it would answer a lot. Her recent overeating, her cravings, her weight gain and now this sudden sensitive stomach. She started trying to think when her last period was, but since it had never been regular her entire life she didn't know if that was a way to tell. The more she thought about it the more mixed her emotions became. She was excited at the thought for a moment, because it would mean she could have children. Then it was also scary because of her situation with Isaac, and she knew the doctor said it would be a high risk for her and the baby. Yet, as much as she tried to deny it, she couldn't help but think of the possibilities. She didn't want to admit it to herself, but the idea excited her most because maybe if she was pregnant she could get Isaac back.

After a few minutes of sitting in silence, she called Paige again.

"Can you come over and bring a home pregnancy test?"

Chapter 27

As soon as Paige walked in the door, they both burst out laughing. They felt like high school girls sneaking around with the pregnancy test in the brown paper bag. Charlene knew most adult women take these tests alone, but she couldn't bear to handle the pressure by herself. Besides, she didn't know what she wanted the test to say, and she didn't want to be alone when she found out.

"I'm mad you even put this in my head," Charlene said to Paige as she took the brown paper bag out of her hand.

"You said you weren't listening, don't blame me."

"Yeah, but I couldn't help but wonder after you said all of that. I was sitting here thinking about it."

"Well, look, don't get your hopes up. I was saying it is possible and you are having pregnancy symptoms."

"Yeah, but how could I turn out to be the *one* in one in a million?" Charlene asked, trying to keep herself lighthearted about it.

"I don't know, but if you are, you know that it's some sort of miracle."

Charlene was reading the directions on the box when Paige said that. She looked up at her sister and got a little serious for a second.

"What if Isaac doesn't want it, what should I do? I can't have an abortion; it may be my only chance of having a baby."

"Charlene, I can't tell you what to do, but I will say you also have to remember the doctor said that it was high risk and she didn't recommend you trying to carry a child."

"She didn't say I should abort it if I get pregnant," Charlene said.

"Yeah, but she did say she suggested you don't get pregnant, to use protection and stuff."

"Paige, I don't want to think that way. If I somehow am pregnant I should take that as a sign . . . a good one, don't you think?"

"How about we find out first? We are doing all this talk and we don't even know if you are."

"You're right," Charlene said as she started to take the test out of the box.

She took it out, and glanced at the directions that were on the inside as well before she decided it was self-explanatory. Then she looked over at Paige.

"I have something to tell you."

"What?"

"I slept with Rich a couple of weeks ago."

Paige damn near banged her head on the wall she jerked back so far.

"WHAT?" she cried.

"I know, I know," Charlene said, sounding pitiful.

"When? And how did you let that happen?"

"A couple of weeks ago. Here. When I first spoke to that girl, I had him over."

"Charlene, are you out of your mind?"

"I know . . . It was to make me feel better about Isaac, I guess . . . I don't know."

"Did you use protection?"

"Halfway through."

"Halfway? Are you saying this baby could be his?"

"No. I'm not even supposed to be able to get pregnant, remember?"

"Yeah, but if you are. Could it be his?"

"Well, he came inside the condom, so unless he had some spectacular precum I don't think so."

"Whatever, Charlene, we will talk about that later. Go take the test first," Paige said as she shook her head and placed her forehead in her hands.

Charlene knew what that look was, and she could only agree with her so she didn't say anything more. She headed to the bathroom to take it. Right before she stepped inside, Paige called her name.

"Leen?" Paige called.

"Yeah?"

"Just know, whatever the result is, is cool. You're still young, you have forever to figure this out," Paige said.

"I know, I'm cool either way. I mean it."

"Just don't want it because you're thinking about getting Isaac back."

It was like Paige was reading her mind. She didn't want to be so see-through, but as soon as Paige said that, Charlene started to cry. Her eyes filled up with tears and she started sniffling.

"Don't cry," Paige said. "I'm sorry."

"No, it's not that. I don't know what I want anymore . . . My life has changed so much so fast."

"Leen, it really hasn't, we just don't see it coming; but trust me, your life hasn't changed courses at all. God has all this planned out, we have to go with it," Paige said as she reached out and hugged her baby sister.

"I know," Charlene said, releasing into her sister's embrace.

After a few more seconds of the Lifetime movie scene, they

let go and Charlene proceeded to take the test. Paige waited on the other side of the door while Charlene urinated. As soon as she was done, she opened the door and set the little plastic stick on the bathroom sink. Charlene stepped out of the bathroom.

"You look at it," Charlene said to Paige.

"You sure?"

"I'm positive."

Paige went into the bathroom and couldn't see any symbol just yet. She waited a bit more and slowly began to see a line showing up. She looked over at Charlene and she was standing in the doorway looking absolutely eager. Paige looked back at the stick and saw more of the line, and then slowly another coming across the first. She picked up the box to see if her assumption about what the two lines meant was correct, and sure enough it was. She looked up at Charlene.

"You're pregnant, Leen," she said.

"What!" Charlene shouted, and burst into tears.

Paige grabbed Charlene up in her arms and let her cry it out on her shoulder. Paige didn't know if they were tears of joy or pain, she just knew for the time being she would let her release them. Little did she know, Charlene didn't know which they were either. She felt a burst of emotion. Excitement, anger, sadness, fear and many more. She was angry that Isaac wasn't there to find out with her but excited because maybe there was a chance now that he would be there moving forward with her. She was still fearful because of the slight chance it was Rich's, and still she had no idea how this could even be, and if she would be able to keep it.

"You OK?" Paige finally asked.

"I guess," Charlene said as she sniffled up her tears and snot and tried to gain her composure.

Charlene reached over to look at the test herself; she had to double-check it.

"What, you think I can't read?" Paige asked.

"No. I just can't believe this," Charlene replied.

"Well, believe it."

"What am I going to do?"

"I don't know. I think you need to make a doctor appointment first thing Monday morning, see how far along you are, and see what the doctor says your options are."

"Yeah, I know."

They both stood there for a couple of moments in silence. It seemed both of them were a bit surprised by the results.

"Should I tell Isaac first?" Charlene asked.

"That's up to you . . . You may not want to tell him until you know the information from the doctor."

"Yeah, but I would want him to at least know."

"And what if it's Rich's?"

"It's not . . . It can't be."

"Why? Because you don't want it to be?"

"No, because I was having these other symptoms over a month now. I was just with Rich two weeks ago."

"Yeah, I guess you're right."

"So then I should tell Isaac."

"I guess, but let's be honest. You want him to know that you are pregnant with his child so maybe that will make him change his mind."

"That, too, and I want him to see that I am able to get pregnant."

"Well, tell him. Just don't be hurt if he is nasty or gets mad if the doctor says you really shouldn't carry it."

"The doctor can't tell me that."

"No, but she did tell you already that even if you did get pregnant the risk to you and the baby is very high."

"She also said the likeliness of me getting pregnant is very high, too."

"Well, Charlene, you knew for years that was the case. The

doctor wasn't guessing. You probably beat the odds on this one, but I wouldn't ignore her advice altogether."

"I'll see what she says and decide from there. I can't think about all of this in one night."

"OK. I'm going to get out of here and get back home."

"Thanks for coming. I don't know if I could have done it without you."

"No problem. Just don't tell anyone yet until you see the doctor. You don't want anything to cloud your judgment."

"I know."

Charlene walked Paige to the door, gave her a kiss good-bye and closed the door behind her. She went back into the bedroom and lay across her bed. She just lay there for about twenty minutes letting all her thoughts run rampant through her head. She wasn't sure which one to grab and stick to, she just went back and forth with each emotion. She knew her sister was right; she had so many things to consider. She just hoped that Isaac would at least speak to her now.

Chapter 28

She sat looking in the mirror for over ten minutes fixing her hair and applying light makeup. She didn't want to look too made up, but she wanted to look attractive. Isaac was on his way over, and Charlene was more nervous than she had been on their first date. You never would have thought this was the man she was supposed to marry.

She had called him in the morning and told him the news, and he agreed to come over and talk. She hadn't expected him to be so willing to see her, but she was beyond ecstatic that he was. She told him that she took a home pregnancy test and that it came out positive. He asked her why she had taken a test when she wasn't able to get pregnant, and she told him about the cravings and nausea. It seemed at first that he thought she was lying, probably just to get his attention, but she told him that she knew he would think that and she swore that she was telling the truth. She also told him that she was unsure about what he would want her to do or what the doctor would say. He told her that he wouldn't tell her to abort it just because of their breakup, but still she thought it was best that they sit down and talk.

Once Isaac arrived, he stepped inside and went to the couch

as he normally would. She was a little surprised that he didn't give her a hug or kiss, but she figured that he still wasn't feeling her. She was thankful that he was at least willing to talk but upset that it took the circumstances at hand for him to do so.

"Thanks for coming by," she said once she had sat down on the couch.

"No problem," he said.

"Listen, Isaac, I know you have every reason to hate me, but I must admit that I'm a little hurt that you didn't love me enough to try."

"Charlene, I didn't come over to talk about that."

"I know, but in order for us to address this, we have to address that."

Isaac didn't reply.

"All I'm saying is, I thought you owed me at least to try."

"Try? I tried for years. I have caught you in little lies here and there, and I tried to trust you this entire time even when things didn't add up. I couldn't try anymore when you not only constantly lie to me, you have no heart or morals."

"Isaac, that wasn't easy for me, OK? I was afraid that you would do just what you did . . . walk away."

"Whatever, Charlene. I walked away 'cause you lied, not because of the truth."

Charlene paused. His response was well put and she took a second to think of a rebuttal.

"Isaac . . . Look, I don't know what's what anymore. You have obviously put me behind you faster than I thought you could. You got girls answering your phone, you have moved on—"

"Tyra is just a coworker. I was at work late that night."

Relieved to hear that, Charlene tried to keep her calm demeanor.

"Well, still, I don't know where we stand. If we have a shot at all, or what. I do know that I am pregnant with your child and I don't know if you want it or if I can even have it."

"I want it . . . and I hope you can have it."

Isaac's words were music to Charlene's ears. All of the pain and anger she felt toward him were gone, she felt like this was her chance to get her life back.

"Are you willing to work this out?"

"I can't make any promises, Charlene, but I will tell you that I will try. I won't leave you to raise this child alone, I can tell you that."

"If the doctor says I can keep it, can we continue where we left off?"

Isaac didn't respond right away, but he was able to see exactly how Charlene saw things. She figured since she was able to have the child he wanted so badly, he could put the situation behind them and move on.

"I'll try, Charlene. I realize that if I never knew, we would have been just fine right now, but the fact still remains you lied about a whole lot to me, and I have to see if I can trust you again."

"All I ask is that we try," Charlene said.

"See what the doctor says, and we will plan accordingly."

"Are you saying if the doctor says I can't keep this child, you won't work things out with me?"

"Charlene, I'm only sitting here because you're pregnant. Just yesterday there was nothing for us to discuss."

"That doesn't have to be the case, though, that's just you giving up on us."

"See what the doctor says, Charlene . . . We will talk about the rest after," Isaac said, scooting to the end of the couch.

"You're leaving?"

"Yeah, I have to go," he said as he stood up from the couch. "Let me know what happens," he continued.

She started to walk behind him toward the door. He turned around and gave her a hug. Isaac could never know fully how his hug felt to Charlene at that very moment. He didn't know just how badly she needed that hug from him, to feel loved and protected, even just for that moment. She could tell he was feeling the hug too because he didn't make it quick. He held on for quite some time before he let go and headed out the door. Charlene kept that feeling with her for as long as she could. She leaned up against the door trying to hold on to his essence in her place.

The scary part was that everything depended on what her doctor said.

Chapter 29

She had to wait for her appointment because Dr. Ginyard had none available for three days. She wouldn't have been able to see the doctor for weeks, but they squeezed her in after she pleaded and told them it was an urgent matter.

The wait felt like forever. She hadn't told anyone else about the pregnancy—not her parents, not Jasmine, or any of her co-workers. She wanted to tell Tanai, because she felt like she deserved to know that what they had done as children could finally stop haunting them. However, she wasn't sure if the doctor's medical advice would be good, or if being able to get pregnant was good news. She decided she would tell Tanai regardless, but she would tell her after she saw the doctor.

At work for those days Charlene acted normal and went on with her normal workday. She had a few minutes every now and then when she felt a little queasy and wanted to just sit still at her desk for a while, but for the most part it was business as usual. Paige called her about five times a day to see how she was doing. Charlene had told her she had told Isaac, and although Paige didn't agree at first, she understood. Paige did not, however, know how to feel about Isaac leaving things in the air, pending what the doctor said. She told Charlene it sounded as if he didn't love her, or why would the baby be the only factor in what their future would be? For the sake of not further stressing out Charlene she didn't dwell on how foul it was, but she no longer thought highly of Isaac. She believed he just wanted a woman to carry his kids; he didn't really want to marry Charlene out of love. At least, that was Paige's new point of view.

Charlene only spoke to Isaac one day between the day he came over and the doctor's appointment, and that was when she called to ask him if he wanted to come. At first he said yes he would love to come, but after they spoke some more he changed his mind. He said he wasn't ready to hear the doctor say anything negative, he would rather go the next time around after he was at least mentally prepared. Charlene told him she, too, wasn't emotionally stable enough for the appointment, and she would like him to be there with and for her. He told her in so many words that she made this bed, and she had to lie in it. Charlene was confused; she didn't know how she felt anymore. She didn't know how she felt about herself, her guilt, the pregnancy or Isaac; she was numb from all the emotions.

Paige took off work so she could go with Charlene to the appointment; she felt no woman should have to go through that alone. She didn't feel Charlene should suffer because Isaac was being so insensitive. They both had thought that the baby growing inside her stomach would turn him from the toad back to the prince he had been, but apparently it hadn't been enough. Charlene was strong, though. She had no time to cry or worry about Isaac and how he was feeling because she had some serious decisions to make either way.

When Charlene first got to the doctor's office she signed in and sat down in the waiting room. Paige wasn't there yet, but she was on her way. Charlene sat there looking at all the pregnant ladies waiting. They looked so happy and full of life—

except one of them, who looked miserable, but she looked like she was about nine months and ready to pop. Two of the ladies had their significant others with them, and the guys looked just as into it as they were—looking at magazines and the signs on the walls, it seemed like they hadn't been dragged to go. It made Charlene feel like an after-school special that she had to bring her sister. She felt like she had gotten knocked up by some high school jock who didn't want to claim it, not that she had made a love child.

Paige walked in just as the nurse called Charlene's name to see the doctor. They both walked back to the exam room together.

"How do you feel?" Paige asked.

"I'm OK, just want to get this over with."

Once they got into the room, the nurse asked her some questions and told her to wait a few moments, the doctor would be right in.

Dr. Ginyard walked in and greeted them both.

"What brings you back so soon?" the doctor asked.

"I took a home pregnancy test and it came out positive."

As the doctor listened, she shuffled through Charlene's file to look for her notes.

"Positive, huh? Were you using protection?"

"Not really. I didn't think I could get pregnant, anyway."

"But didn't I tell you to use protection, because you didn't want an unplanned pregnancy in your situation?"

"Yes . . ." Charlene said, not knowing exactly what the doctor wanted her to say. The last thing she wanted was a lecture.

"OK. Well, first we have to take another test and make sure that you're really pregnant, and then we will talk about your options."

"How long for the results?"

"It will just take a couple of minutes; I just need you to pee in a cup for me."

Charlene took the cup from the nurse, went into the bathroom and did the do. Then she went back to the exam room. Paige was still there but the doctor had stepped out for a second.

"That test could have been wrong, you know?"

"I know, I've heard that before."

"Yeah, well, this would have been a waste of emotions," Paige said, laughing.

"I know. I don't even know what I want it to be."

"Don't think it matters, you probably are. The throwing up and all that wasn't just random."

"Yeah, I guess you're right."

The doctor came back in on the tail end of their conversation.

"Well, Charlene, you are pregnant," the doctor told her.

"I figured," she replied.

The doctor proceeded to ask her questions about her last menstruation and symptoms, etc. She determined Charlene was about eight weeks' pregnant. Once all that was done Charlene started asking questions.

"What happens now?" Charlene asked.

"What do you mean?" Dr. Ginyard asked in her high-pitched voice.

"I mean, what are my options, can I carry the baby?"

"I'm not going to lie to you, Charlene, I wouldn't suggest that you do, but I can't tell you what to do. I can only tell you the dangers."

Charlene immediately looked down for a second, trying to brace herself for the rest of the conversation.

"What are the dangers?" she asked.

"Well, your uterus is damaged so it's no condition to carry a child. There are very high chances that you will lose the baby at some point along the way. Even if you remained on bed rest, your uterus can rupture while you're giving birth and cause excessive bleeding."

"Would you say that there is no way I can have a successful pregnancy?"

"Of course not. Of course it is possible, just very risky. You can always have a scheduled Cesarean. If you are extremely careful and follow every instruction there is a chance that both you and the baby will survive, but there are no guarantees."

"So what would you advise?" Paige interjected.

"I can't tell her that. That is up to her and the father of the child. I can't say I would recommend it. This may be her only chance to get pregnant so she may not want to abort it, I really don't know. I just give the facts, you make the decision."

Charlene was just sitting there. She didn't know what to think. The doctor told Charlene that she should make up her mind in the next couple of weeks, because if she decided to abort there would be different procedures involved depending on when she decided. After giving Charlene some vitamins to take in the meantime, the doctor sent her on her way.

Once in the car, Charlene broke down in tears. She couldn't believe that she had to make such a hard decision. She knew that nobody could tell her what was best, but she didn't know, either. She also knew that this child inside of her would mean the world to her and Isaac, but she didn't know if she was willing to risk her own life. She tried to think about what kind of mother wouldn't risk her life for her child, and decided that only a bad mother wouldn't. Besides, just the thought of aborting it made her sick, because she knew that the abortion she had had before was what had her here in the first place.

Paige didn't have much to say. She assured Charlene that everything would be all right and that she was there to support her no matter what decision she made. Paige also told her not to base her decision on Isaac, to base it on what she wanted to do. She tried to stress to Charlene that this wasn't a minor decision, not that Charlene didn't know that; but that it was literally life or death.

Charlene knew that Paige was right, that Isaac shouldn't be a major influence in the decision she made. Still, it was easy for Paige to say, Charlene thought. She hadn't lost her fiancé or spent the last month miserable and depressed. As much as Charlene disliked Isaac for the way he was treating her, she still felt at fault for his behavior and wanted more than anything to have him back. She didn't know exactly what to tell him about her doctor's visit, or whether she should make the decision before she told him or with him.

By the time she got home she couldn't wait another minute to call Isaac. Paige offered to come up with her, but Charlene told her no thanks. Charlene said she could use the time alone to try to figure out what she wanted to do and she would call her later. In reality Charlene wanted to use the time alone to call Isaac and see what would happen.

"Hey, Isaac," Charlene said when she got him on the phone.

It was weird how she appreciated him even answering the phone. After weeks of getting his voice mail, even the simplest respect made her feel good.

"Hey, Charlene. What happened?"

"Well, the doctor said I am pregnant."

"How far along are you?" Isaac asked. You could hear the excitement in his voice.

"I am eight weeks, but I would have to get a sonogram soon to double-check the accuracy of that."

"It is my baby, right?"

"Isaac!! Of course it's your baby. How could you ask me that?"

"Just asking. I don't know what to believe anymore. Besides, except for a few days ago, I haven't spoken to you in weeks."

"Well, we were speaking eight weeks ago; we were obviously doing more than just speaking."

Isaac laughed. It was music to Charlene's ears. Although it wasn't exactly the topic that she would have selected to break the ice, she was just happy that it was broken.

"Babe, I am sorry about everything. I can't express how hurt I was, and I still am."

"I'm sorry, too, Isaac. Really, I am."

"I want us to work through this; we are going to be a family."

Charlene almost forgot about the decision, and she figured Isaac got caught up in the excitement and forgot, too.

"Well, Isaac, that's what we have to decide. The doctor said that the pregnancy could be risky, and if I'm not careful I can lose the baby or my life."

"Well then, we will have to be extra careful."

"I would have to be on bed rest the majority of the pregnancy and would have to have a Cesarean, which she said would make my chances better."

"Well, if need be you will quit your job and move in with me, everything will be just fine."

Charlene wanted to cry. Not just because she was miraculously able to get pregnant, but because she had her Isaac back. Charlene was extremely excited that the two of them had a chance at the future that she had always wanted. She agreed with him that they would pray and get through it together. They hung up the phone after Isaac said he would be over after work.

She hung up and went in her bedroom to think. She knew she had to call Paige, and Jasmine and Tanai and eventually her parents. She couldn't just yet. She needed to sit and think for a bit.

Chapter 30

Charlene didn't have time to get much thinking done before Isaac arrived. She did speak to Paige for a bit, but didn't tell her that she had made a concrete decision. She called Tanai but didn't reach her, so she left a message. Jasmine said she would call her back because she couldn't make a scene at work about it like she wanted to.

She planned on calling her mother, but that's when she stopped to try to prepare her words and more of her thoughts. She knew that with each person she spoke to, she would have to be prepared for the questions and the good and the bad that they would have to say. For her mom, she needed the most preparation of all. Ann Tanner wasn't going to hold her tongue, not in the least bit. So whenever Charlene spoke to her she had to put on her toughest layer of skin. But before she got around to making that call, Isaac showed up.

They sat on the couch, kind of like old times, watching television, with Isaac holding Charlene in his arms.

But things felt a little strange between them. Charlene couldn't help but feel a little distant toward him. She wanted this more than anything, but it was going to take a little while for her to feel completely comfortable with him again. Especially since deep down she did feel betrayed by him. She knew she was wrong for lying, but she couldn't help but feel like he had turned his back on her when she needed him most. Even worse, she wasn't sure if he ever would have held her again if she hadn't been pregnant. Although she knew that he could have walked away from the baby, too, it made her doubt his true love for her as a person.

She didn't know if he was too embarrassed to discuss all the many things they needed to discuss, or if he really just felt back at home with everything. She sure didn't. After about an hour, Isaac turned to Charlene and looked her in her eyes.

"I know our relationship was just put to a major test, but God saw through that and we survived. He gave us a child to remind us of the big picture and I'm looking forward to building our lives together," he said as he pulled the ring out of his pocket.

Charlene didn't want to—it was probably because her hormones were all out of wack—but she started crying. She held out her hand as he placed the ring back on the finger that he had so recently demanded she remove it from. It didn't have the same sweet feeling like the first time around, but it did feel nice.

He pulled her closer to him and hugged her. She let her body rest up against his. She released all of her energy and emotion, and let all of the weight on her shoulders lean up against him. She wanted him to feel just how emotionally drained and heavy the stress was on her, but there was no way he could ever really know everything that she was feeling. A week ago this would have been something that Charlene could only dream about, having her fiancé back. Now, here it was a reality and she didn't know how she felt about it. Despite the questions in her head, she didn't think twice about accepting her position back. She reached up and gave him a kiss to let him know that she was still there with him and that he hadn't lost her yet, just in case he had any doubts. Charlene knew she still had some rebuilding of trust to do if she wanted this to be more than only about the baby.

After they finished their emotional lovemaking, Isaac sat up and looked dead at Charlene.

"So . . . How do you feel?" he asked.

"I feel fine," she responded.

"Good . . . How does your family feel?"

"Well, I haven't had a chance to tell my parents just yet, but Paige is excited."

"Yeah, I know. Everything happened so fast."

"Definitely did," Charlene said, realizing for the first time how crazy everything was. She had been having sex for years and years, since she was a little girl and was deemed basically incapable of having a child, and now, weeks after a doctor confirming that fact, she comes up pregnant. Charlene felt like it was definitely the doing of something bigger than her, as if Our Savior up above was trying to tell her something or test her.

"Well, I hope your mother isn't upset that you're pregnant before we are married."

"I know, I thought of that. I doubt she will be upset, she knows the wedding is being planned."

"You never told her . . ."

"No, I couldn't," she responded.

"How could you—"

"Isaac, please don't judge me. I couldn't break the news to her. I guess I was praying for a miracle."

"Well, I guess you got it," he said, reaching out and touching her stomach.

"I guess," she said.

"Well, maybe we should speed things up," Isaac said, sounding excited about his thought.

"What do you mean?" Charlene asked with a smile on her face.

"Ya know . . . Have a quick, small wedding in a few months or just elope."

"I don't want to elope. I want a wedding."

"OK, so plan something quick and close."

"I'll look into it," Charlene replied.

"Let me know what you need help with."

"I'm happy to see that you care so much about this, but where is this coming from?"

"What? I just don't want your mother to be upset and embarrassed by us . . . and I want my dad to make it to the wedding."

"OK, I'll look into it for sure," Charlene said, readjusting herself on the couch, seeking new comfort. "Did you tell your father yet?" she continued.

"Not yet. I didn't want to tell him until everything was cool."

"Cool?"

"Like that it was for sure, and cool between me and you."

"He is going to be excited?"

"Is he? This is his dream, and mine, too. I just hope it's a boy."

"Don't do that."

"I do . . . You know the carrying of my father's family name is very important to us."

"Well, what if it's a girl?"

"We can keep trying," Isaac said.

"I look like a baby factory?" Charlene asked, laughing.

"No," he replied. "I'm just saying I'll love the baby regardless of the gender."

"But you'll be happier if it's a boy?"

"Basically," he said, chuckling at himself.

Charlene laughed back. Even though she already knew why Isaac wanted a child, it felt nice planning their family together and discussing it as a reality.

"So you didn't tell anybody yet?"

"I told Lacy."

Immediately Charlene could feel herself getting upset. She looked at him in his eyes to see if he had an idea, to see if he had said it on purpose. It didn't look as if he knew, or at least he played it off very well.

"What?" he asked after looking back in her eyes.

"Nothing," she said, deciding to leave it alone.

"What, Lacy? I couldn't tell her?"

"You can tell whoever you want," she replied.

"But you would have preferred me not tell her . . ." he replied with slight sarcasm.

"Not at all, I don't know how I feel that she was the first person you told, but hey."

"She just happened to be who I spoke to, and I told you why I didn't tell my dad or anyone else yet," Isaac replied.

"That's cool. I know that's your friend."

"Do you really? Or do you think me and her have something going on?"

"I don't know what you had going on for the past month or so, but prior to that all I knew was that y'all were pretty unusual friends."

"How are we unusual?"

"She just seems too comfortable, like she has been everywhere with you before."

"She has, but not sexually. Not everything is about that. She and I have just been cool enough that we have done a lot together."

"Yeah, well . . . like I said, I know y'all are friends. It's cool."

"Whatever, Charlene," Isaac said, sounding a bit annoyed at the sudden transition in the mood.

"What? I'm just saying. I wasn't complaining."

"What are you saying?" he asked.

"She is like your ideal woman, and it makes me wonder sometimes."

"Makes you wonder what?" Isaac asked as he pulled Charlene to hold in his arms. "You are my ideal woman, Charlene . . . you and only you. She is my ideal friend," he continued.

"Yeah, OK," Charlene said, blushing. "Mrs. Perfect Lacy, unscathed, silver spoon in her mouth, perfect upbringing, nose always up in the air . . . little Mrs. Black Barbie."

Laughing, Isaac replied, "That's what you think, huh? You're obviously not her friend. She is far from perfect and she really isn't stuck up like that. She just knows how to act that way. She is pretty and her life is straight . . . but perfect, that's a stretch."

"Whatever, it doesn't matter. Just let me know when you tell your father," Charlene said to try to change the subject.

All that talk about Lacy's beauty and perfection was not her idea of good conversation. At least not the conversation she wanted to have on the night of her engagement, well, second engagement.

Chapter 31

"**H**ow am I supposed to hide it until the wedding?" Charlene asked.

"I don't know, but you shouldn't be waddling around letting the world know you been fornicating," Charlene's mother replied.

Charlene was expecting her mother to make some sort of comment about the premarital sex, but she hadn't expected her to go this far.

"Mommy, the wedding will be very soon and I'll have the baby as a married woman."

"I hope you can find a dress that doesn't show your belly," she replied.

"I'll be looking next week."

"OK, well, keep me posted."

"Ma?"

"What?"

"No excitement, no congratulations? Just advice on hiding it?"

Charlene knew that her mother was aware of the miracle it was that she was even pregnant. As much as her mother tried to deny and erase the incident, she was right there when the doctor told Charlene that she probably wouldn't be able to have children. Also, through the years even though the incident was one of the unspoken truths in the family, inferences were made about Charlene not being able to bear children, so she knew her mother knew. That's why it hurt Charlene so much that she was saying the things she was saying.

"I'm excited for you, baby," her mother said. "I just don't want people thinking you're fast."

"Mommy, I'm grown and I'm getting married. What can they possibly think?"

"All of my church folks and family—what can they think? They can think you weren't waiting until marriage."

Charlene knew she couldn't say what was on her mind, not to her old-fashioned Christian mother. But God heard every word of it, unfortunately. To prevent the conversation from getting any more unbearable, Charlene decided to cut it short. She told her mother to go ahead and tell her father, and that she would call her back later.

Once Charlene was off the phone she jumped in the shower and started getting dressed. She had taken the day off, and she and Isaac were meeting for lunch to officially celebrate. Charlene still felt a little awkward about everything. She wasn't sure how to just be her, she didn't know what to still downplay or what to always be honest about. She felt like a fish out of water, not quite knowing what to do with herself. She felt like she and Isaac were pretending, pretending to be something they were not. In the past that wouldn't have bothered her at all, she was a professional at pretending. However, for some reason now she didn't quite feel comfortable with it. It could have been because she didn't know what was behind Isaac's wall, or because she finally thought she could stop pretending and be real. But it seemed that this time around, she didn't have control over that.

She finished drying herself off in her bedroom and began to apply lotion to her body. Charlene had beautiful caramel skin all over her body, and she loved moisturizing it carefully. Her skin was the root of her self-esteem, not because it was beautiful but because it was light caramel. Around her way, her light skin was what made her hot. The guys loved the light-skinned girls, and along with her hazel eyes they thought she was damn near a goddess. As the years went by and Charlene got looser, the only thing that kept her close to what she was was the skin that she lived in. It kept the real Charlene hidden—her insecurities, her fears and her secrets. It was like people didn't see through her bright smile and skin to her dark side.

When she was done lotioning up, she began to get dressed. They weren't going anywhere too fancy, but Charlene knew Isaac liked his lady to always look dashing. Besides, it had been a while since the two of them had gone out and she wanted him to feel impressed that she was his wife to be. She threw on her blue Arden B silk button-up shirt with a hot new black pencil skirt she hadn't worn yet. She decided to wear blue pumps and a blue and black purse to accessorize the shirt. She kept her jewelry classy but simple, just some diamond studs, a tennis bracelet and a diamond drop necklace Isaac had gotten for her one Christmas. To finish up the look of perfection, she applied M•A•C blue eyeliner, mascara and lip gloss. She was feeling quite sexy for a pregnant woman.

Just as she was putting on the finishing touches, the phone rang. She thought it was Isaac calling to give his estimated time of arrival, so she quickly picked up the phone before it went to the answering machine.

"Hello," Charlene said.

"Can take the girl out the hood, but can't take the ho out the girl," the female on the other end said.

Startled, Charlene replied, "Who is this?"

"Takesha," the girl said.

"What do you want, Takesha?" Charlene asked with an attitude.

"I want to let you know that I am going to beat your ass if you see Rich one more time."

"I don't want Rich. I have a man. Now don't call my house with this shit no more, Takesha, that's my word," Charlene said and slammed down the phone.

Charlene was fuming. *How did these chicks get her number?* she wondered. *What if Isaac answered one of these random calls one day?* she thought to herself. Somehow she was going to have to put a stop to it. Charlene tried to regain her composure so that she would be back in the right mood for her afternoon out with Isaac. To help, she threw on her Robin Thicke CD and floated along to his sultry voice.

Isaac showed up about twenty minutes later. She'd had just enough time to get ready and relax for a bit. He was looking quite spiffy himself. He was wearing a black Gucci sweater with a gray and red stripe through it, black knit hat with the same colored stripes, black slacks and black leather Gucci loafers. When he removed his hat, Charlene saw his haircut was fresh—a low-cut caesar, just how she liked it. It wasn't unusual for Isaac to look his best, but still Charlene got the feeling that this was a special day for him, too. Maybe he noticed that he shouldn't have risked losing her after all, or maybe he was just happy to have her back. Charlene didn't know but she was feeling much better walking out the door with him than she had when he walked in.

★ ★ ★

Once they got to the restaurant it was as if nothing had changed. They were chatting and laughing at stuff as if their relationship was problem free. It was as if their emotional roller coaster of a breakup hadn't happened at all.

"So, how did your dad react?" Charlene asked him.

"Charlene, you should of saw the look on his face. It almost made me cry."

"Why? What did he say?"

"At first he said nothing. He was just so happy, he had this look of shock, but then he tried to fight off his tears. It was real emotional for him."

"I'm happy to hear he was so excited."

"I knew he would be. He doesn't know how much longer he has, every time he goes to the doctor they tell him different lengths of time, he was starting to give up hope. This gives him something to keep fighting for."

"That's good. I hope it's a boy, too, because I know how bad you want a junior."

"Yeah, me, too. That would be the biggest blessing."

"I know," she said, laughing.

"So, what did your parents say?" he asked.

"I haven't really spoken to my dad yet, but my mother was happy."

"Happy?"

"Well, of course she was a little concerned with the fornication and how it will look walking down the aisle with a belly—"

"I figured she would," he interrupted.

"Well, you figured right, but overall she was happy that I'm pregnant."

"Was she surprised?" he asked.

Charlene was surprised he chose to address that. She thought they had a silent understanding to leave that awkward conversation in the past.

"Not really, she was more concerned with the fornication, but she said in so many words that she was happy that the doctor made a mistake."

"So all these years your mother knew about this, but it didn't bother her if you couldn't have kids."

"It may have bothered her, but I don't know, really."

"Did your dad know?"

Charlene was not pleased that Isaac was asking so many questions, but she knew she couldn't afford to be evasive with him so she answered them.

"I'm sure he did but me and him never discussed it."

"Never?"

"Never!" Charlene snapped.

Isaac's expression showed that he was startled by her response.

"I'm sorry for snapping like that," she added. "It's just that it was kind of like a taboo conversation in my family so I'm not used to discussing it much."

"I understand," Isaac replied, although he looked confused.

Charlene knew that she shouldn't keep Isaac in the dark about anything if she could help it. She just hoped that from being with her for the time that he had, he knew enough about her parents to realize that he shouldn't try to understand them. If anything, it could help him understand Charlene and where she had learned to live in denial so well.

After they had completed the main course they were well into some great conversation. They talked about everything from possible baby names to what was going on at their jobs. Charlene had to admit, she hadn't seen Isaac quite so happy or talkative in a long while. Before this, they had hit the place in their relationship where there wasn't much to say. So, although it wasn't that special in the scheme of things, this pleasant little lunch had made Charlene's day, or rather month. It gave her hope that she and Isaac were meant to be after all, like she hadn't faked her way into his life and they had a real relationship.

Chapter 32

Charlene had finally gotten used to all the attention from people asking and congratulating her about the baby. In the beginning it made her uncomfortable, but as time went on she began to like the interest. Coworkers were constantly asking about the wedding plans and she got to show them her ideas and dress options. Before Charlene knew it she was in the world of make believe. It was like a fairy tale all around her, she was once again this perfect little princess planning her big ball. With none of her past in her way, everyone treating her like she was so special and deserved to be, it was almost surreal. Even her mother had become really involved with the pregnancy and wedding. Other than some morning sickness and back pains, Charlene really didn't have much to complain about, or so she thought.

One morning she was leaving for work and she couldn't find her gray blazer. The weather had started to be crisp and the brisk air no longer allowed for light jackets. Charlene had put on a black sweater with a gray stripe through it, her ever-so-stylish gray tweed slacks with black boots. Although the black waist-length leather jacket in her closet would have gone well, she was kind of set on wearing her gray blazer. She looked around for it a bit until she remembered that she had left it at Isaac's.

Although it seemed a little frivolous, she decided she would stop by Isaac's on the way to work to get it. It would only make her about fifteen minutes late, and she thought seeing her boo boo would be a great start to her day. Besides, since she was pregnant her boss probably assumed it was morning sickness that often held her up, because he never questioned her.

She left with just enough time to make it to Isaac's, get her jacket, give him a snuggle and be on her way before the flex-schedule staff made it in. She called Isaac once she got in the car to let him know she was coming and to maybe have the jacket pulled out, but there was no answer. She figured he was probably in the shower or still sleep with his lucky self. Because Isaac was such a big shot at his company, he pretty much started and ended his day when he got good and ready unless there was a meeting scheduled or it was a busy season. Not thinking twice she continued on her way over to Mr. Isaac Milton's condo by the river.

Once she got there his Mazzerati was parked out front, and half the block looked empty except for a few cars. She walked up to the front door and keyed in, and tried to enter quietly so she wouldn't startle or awaken Isaac. She stepped inside and saw dishes on the table from what looked like his dinner the night before. Isaac was a neat freak and it was unlike him not to put the dishes away, yet it wasn't something that he had never done before so she brushed it off and went ahead and took the dishes to the kitchen. As she was placing them in the sink, she realized there were too many plates for just Isaac. She couldn't see what meal he could have eaten that would have required two dinner plates and a dessert plate. She was eating for two and wasn't eating that much, and she couldn't help but wonder why Isaac would be cooking for two. Ready to inquire about what he was doing or who he had had over last night, she finished up in the kitchen. She had tried to be quiet, but there was the inevitable clatter from some of the dishes and she figured Isaac might have heard it.

She was halfway up the stairs to his bedroom when he appeared at the top of the stairs. She had her head down watching her steps—as a pregnant woman her worst fear was to fall, especially down some stairs. She looked up when she heard a sound, and it scared her because she wasn't expecting him. Isaac looked just as startled, because he clearly wasn't expecting her, either.

"Good morning, baby," she said as she continued on her way toward him. He took a step down, still looking surprised and confused.

"Hey, Charlene, what are you doing here?"

"I came to get my blazer I left here the other night. You going in late today?"

At this point Charlene was three-quarters of the way up the stairs, and Isaac had slowly taken a step or two downwards.

"Uh . . . Yeah, I was just waking up to get ready for work now . . . I'll grab your jacket for you," he said as he turned back around toward the bedroom.

"I'm already up here now, silly, I can get it," she said as she completed the flight of stairs.

Isaac stopped and turned back around. "Charlene," he said.

"Yes, baby?" she asked as she opened the bedroom door, brushing off his attempt to delay her. She still had to be at work, so she would stop and play on the way back out, she thought.

Charlene walked straight over to the chair that her blazer was on and picked it up. She shook it out some and then put it on. She knew she had made the right decision to come get it; it just went so well with her outfit.

"So what did you do after we spoke last night?" she asked Isaac as she walked over to the mirror to check herself out.

As she pulled and tugged at her blazer she confirmed that

she was ready to go. Just as she was turning away from the mirror she got a glimpse of Isaac's bed in the reflection and it didn't look empty. She spun around and couldn't believe her eyes. Lacy was sitting in the bed looking like she had seen a ghost. She immediately turned to the door and Isaac was standing in the doorway, looking crazy his damn self. Charlene froze for a second and no one said anything. Then Charlene started to laugh.

"Isn't this funny?" she finally said out loud.

From the looks on Lacy and Isaac's faces, they didn't know what to say but they both looked in fear of Charlene's looney reaction.

"Charlene, I swear it's not what you think," Isaac started.

"I bet it's not," Charlene replied.

"Babe . . . I mean it—" he replied.

"Lacy, what do you think I'm thinking?" she asked, interrupting Isaac.

"Leen, I can only imagine . . . But I'm sure it's not what the reality is."

"Lacy, please give me the reality."

Lacy looked over at Isaac as if she didn't know if she should or shouldn't speak.

"Oh, he runs this show, Lacy?" Charlene asked.

Her calmness was throwing Lacy for a loop; it came off crazy and capable-of-murder-type behavior. She knew Charlene was mad, and had every right to be from the looks of things, but her reaction was weird. Not that it wasn't obvious that Charlene was being sarcastic or cynical, but no yelling and no tears are not the expected reactions to this kind of early-morning sight.

"Charlene, Lacy was locked out last night so she crashed here, that's all," Isaac said.

"Really, is that what happened?" Charlene asked Lacy directly.

"Yes, Charlene, it is. I got here really late, ate something and we fell asleep watching a movie."

"Aww, isn't that nice. What did you guys eat?"

"Charlene, why won't you talk to me?" Isaac asked Charlene finally, getting frustrated with her invisible-Isaac game.

"Why should I? So you can say whatever I want to hear?" Charlene asked, finally losing her cool. She had held on to it for a record-breaking time, but listening to his attitude just brought all of hers right out.

"What's that mean?" he responded in a not-so-low tone.

"It means I come over and find you in bed with some other chick, what do you think I want to hear from you? . . . The typical—"it's not what you think" line? Be real!! You couldn't even come up with something better than that?" Charlene yelled. Before he could answer, she continued back in a calmer voice, "So, I figure I will talk to Lacy, she may have something better for me."

"Charlene, it's the truth—" Isaac said.

"I don't doubt it. I just wanted to hear it from Lacy's mouth."

"Nothing happened," Lacy said. "As you see I'm still in the clothes I wore here last night."

Charlene looked and Lacy was in a shirt and some jeans, and looked like she hadn't changed clothes. Still, she couldn't just fall for that evidence that easily, or at least they couldn't know that yet.

"I see. OK, well, you guys carry on. I have to go to work," Charlene said with a slight attitude as she exited the room.

Isaac followed behind her.

"Charlene, I really hope you don't think that we were doing something here last night."

"I believe you. If you give your word, I'll leave it at that."

"I give my word."

"OK, done."

Charlene's tone was hard to decipher. If she was sincere, angry or sarcastic, she was hiding it well and intentionally.

"I gotta run, talk to you later," she said as she reached over and gave him a kiss on the cheek.

Isaac just stood there watching her, still kind of surprised it would be ending so amicably. He walked her to the door and out she went. It was hard to tell who was more confused—Charlene, who didn't know what to believe, or Isaac, who barely knew what had just happened.

Chapter 33

Charlene wasn't sure if she should make a big deal out of the Lacy situation but she chose not to for now. She decided that it did sound believable, and if it wasn't for her jealousy of Lacy she probably wouldn't have been so consumed by the other possibility. Since she knew that she had no real proof of anything other than Isaac's suspicious behavior that morning and him not calling, she figured she would just save it for later. She knew the trump card had more value in her hand than out on the table. Not to mention she had a slipup of her own that she wasn't sharing, so her conscience told her to let it go for now.

They say when it rains it pours, and for some reason Charlene was having a hard time getting everything back on track like it was before the breakup. They had been trying their best to keep all their hidden feelings to themselves, and all the skeletons that had fallen out of their closets unmentioned and left where they fell. They just didn't realize that some of it they didn't have any control over. It was like she was Scrooge, and the Ghost of the Past was haunting her.

Charlene and Isaac were walking through Cross County mall to shop for some maternity clothes for Charlene because she was growing by the second. They had separated momentarily when a somewhat-familiar face approached her. She looked at him, trying to jog her memory, and before she could she felt a swat on her behind. She jumped and let out a little yelp. Everything happened so quickly. Just as she remembered him, it seemed Isaac was making his way over after seeing the incident. She saw Isaac coming, but the guy didn't.

"Whatsup, baby?" the guy asked Charlene.

Before she could answer, Isaac walked up.

"Did you just grab my girl's ass?" he asked.

As soon as they made eye contact, the guy responded.

"Oh, shit! Isaac?"

Isaac looked back at him. "Kareem?"

"Yeah, what's up?" Kareem asked, looking genuinely excited to see Isaac and oblivious to the uncomfortable situation he had just created.

"I'm good . . . but, yo, Reem . . . This is my fiancé, and you just smacked her behind."

"This is your fiancé?" he asked. "You wifed up Charlene, the Team Dream?"

Charlene couldn't believe Kareem was actually saying that to Isaac.

"The Team Dream?" Isaac asked.

"Yeah, the whole team, if you know what I mean . . . She was like our cheerleader, but she was giving us more than just an A," he said, laughing.

Charlene felt like she was dreaming, and in attempt to wake up she just walked off. Next thing she heard was a loud noise and a scuffle. Isaac had hauled off and hit the guy and they were on the ground fighting. Security rushed over and broke it up while Charlene just screamed and cried. She had tried to reach in and kick Kareem one good time, but with her pregnant belly and small frame she couldn't do much more than that. Isaac had the best of the guy, anyway, but she wanted that kick for herself.

Once the fight was broken up, they mumbled some words to each other.

"You mad 'cause you trying to make our ho into your housewife," Kareem yelled.

Isaac just ignored him and walked away. The guy was still saying stuff.

"She ain't your girl, she's all of ours. Any one of us can get that when we want."

A security guard was walking Kareem out and another was following behind Isaac.

"Hey, Charlene. Let me just get one quick blow job for the road," Kareem called out.

Charlene ran up behind Isaac and followed him to the car. Isaac had held his tongue and ignored Kareem's comments. She knew he was embarrassed, but she figured he couldn't have been more embarrassed than she was. They both got in and just sat in silence for a bit. Isaac checked out his face in the mirror.

"Are you OK?" she asked.

"Am I OK?" he asked back. "No, I'm not. I just had to fight somebody I know because my fiancé fucked him and his whole team. No, I'm not OK," he continued.

"His whole team? He wasn't no damn sports player. It's just his way of being funny."

"I know he wasn't a sports player, he means his whole crew, Charlene . . . all his boys."

"Well, including you, I guess, because you almost let him—"

"I almost let him what? Disrespect you? Is that what you were going to say?"

Charlene didn't reply.

"I didn't almost let him do anything, you disrespected yourself and then you let them disrespect you on top of it. *I* defended you."

Charlene didn't even bother to argue, because she knew that Isaac was right. She just sat back in her seat and remained quiet. Isaac drove them home in complete silence, no music or anything. He almost wanted Charlene to say something, because he was still mad and ready for round two. It was senseless for her. Her reputation superceded her and was well known, so no explanation would clear her name. What the guy said to Isaac would forever stick in his head and she couldn't have made it better. So she didn't try. She sat back and was thankful that he didn't start making her feel bad or asking any questions. As far as Isaac was concerned, he knew all he needed to know.

Chapter 34

Things weren't any better for the next few days. Isaac had a chip on his shoulder, and Charlene was feeling too low to try to mend things. One of her worst nightmares had come true, but she tried not to let it break her down. She couldn't blame Isaac for his attitude; it wasn't something a man's ego could take that easily. Then he had to go to work with a busted lip and scratch by his eye. All in all he wasn't just brushing it off, and Charlene wondered if he blamed her more than he did Kareem.

Charlene was just about tired of things unsaid so she decided to call him and try to have a real talk.

"Hey, baby," she said once he'd answered.

"Hey," he replied, not sounding all that happy to hear from her.

"Isaac, we made a decision to make this work and I feel like we are giving up."

"What are you talking about, Charlene?"

"I'm just saying, we don't talk about things and confront our problems."

"I can't talk about this right now."

"See, I'm not arguing. I just really think we need to air

some things out. We are going to be married soon and we can't live like this."

"What? What do we need to discuss, Charlene?"

"Us. Me. The mistakes we have made."

"They're done, we just have to move past them. No need crying over spilled milk."

"Well, we haven't wiped all the milk up yet. What happened at the mall Saturday, I'm sorry about—"

"It's over with, Charlene."

"Are you embarrassed by me?" she asked.

Isaac was obviously caught off guard. He didn't expect that question and wasn't sure what to answer.

"A little bit," he replied.

Charlene's heart dropped. She had asked the question but clearly wasn't ready for an honest answer.

"Oh . . . OK," she said. "Is it your friends?" she added.

"I haven't really told my friends, I guess because that's not something you go around telling."

"You haven't told any of your friends?" she asked.

"I told Trice; and of course he thought it was something to be concerned with."

"Concerned with?"

"Yeah, like if I could trust you and things like that."

"And do you?" she asked.

"I'm not sure."

Charlene didn't reply.

"Not like that Charlene . . . but I can't lie and say that what Kareem said didn't sting."

"But you know better than him," Charlene said.

"Was anything he said a lie?" Isaac asked, like he had been dying to know since it happened.

Charlene wanted to lie, but she kept telling herself she'd learned her lesson from that, and besides, she didn't even know how to deny it.

"I was cool with some of his friends, but of course he was exaggerating."

"Did you sleep with him before?"

"Yeah . . . Once or twice," she said in a low voice.

"Did you suck him off?" he asked.

Charlene didn't reply right away. She started to regret she'd wanted to have this conversation.

"Yes," she said with shame riddling her voice.

"Did they call you Charlene the Team Dream?"

"I don't know what stupid things they used to say."

"Have you ever heard that name before at any time?" Isaac asked with frustration in his voice.

"Yeah, I guess."

"OK . . . So what exactly did you want to talk about, Charlene?" Isaac asked, full of disgust.

Charlene had actually almost forgotten. The conversation had gone so left she forgot what she'd called for. After a few more moments, she remembered.

"I thought we should discuss this. If you can love me for the changed woman I have become or not."

"Of course I love you for who you are, I have so many doubts about who you were and if I really know who you are yet."

"Isaac, I understand. I just need you to trust me. I'm not proud of my ways when I was younger, but I was literally young and dumb. I've changed and I've grown, and I promise you know all there is to know about me . . . this me. Things I've done in the past I would prefer to leave there because I'm not proud of it."

There was silence for a second.

"I don't need to know everything you have done in the past, and I don't want to judge you because of it. You have to give me a bit of time to adjust to the new you."

"There is no new me," Charlene defended.

"Well, to me there is, because I'm learning new stuff out about you every time I turn around."

"Isaac, my heart can't take another breakup, so let me know if you can handle it."

There was an uncomfortable silence.

"I'm still asking myself that question, so you're going to have to give me a little bit of time to get back to you."

"That's fair," she said, trying to keep her cool.

Charlene figured if she wanted to separate who she was today from who she was in the past, she had to try to portray a mature, strong young woman.

Once he agreed that there was no more to discuss, they hung up the phone. Charlene proceeded about her day. There were only a few weeks left before she would have to spend the rest of her pregnancy on bed rest, so she was hoping to have one last night out with Paige and Jasmine. She completed all of her errands and everything else she had to do so that she could meet them at this new hot spot that had opened in Rochester.

They all arrived at about a quarter to eight and they all looked quite amazing. Jasmine was dressed in a teal sweater dress with a big green belt, green and black boots and matching accessories. Her hair was swept up with some drop curls hanging low and she had light makeup on. Paige was dressed as stylish as ever, and looked absolutely flawless. Her pretty brown skin was accented with gold bronzer and a light gold eye shadow. She wore a brown fitted half sweater to accent her full breasts, with a tan tank underneath. Her jeans fit her just right, enough to show off her apple bottom. The tan boots she wore came up to the knee and tied at the top. They both looked like they had the perfect happy life. Charlene looked nice herself, except with her huge belly and pouty expression she didn't look as perfect and happy. She wore a black baby doll shirt with wide-leg jeans and ballet shoes. Her hair was in a ponytail, and she had applied the right amount of makeup. Charlene looked naturally pretty and the pregnancy made her look cuter.

They sat down and chatted for a while as they waited for their drinks to come. Charlene had ordered a Shirley Temple and the other ladies some fruity alcoholic beverages. They were excited to get out and get together, because it had been a while for all of them. They checked out the cuties and bopped their heads to the music, and for the first time in a while Charlene felt young again. She still had her whole life ahead of her, but she had almost forgotten that, what with all her recent drama in trying to keep the man that she for some reason thought was her last hope for happiness. Being out with her sister and friend reminded her that there was no last hope for her, not now and no time soon. She'd asked Isaac how he viewed her, but she should have been asking herself, she realized. Embarrassed by her old ways, she imagined that her life was over, and if Isaac couldn't see beyond her past, then she couldn't, and no other man would, either. But then she realized that was false and that other than the baby growing inside of her, there was nothing about the life she led that she couldn't do over.

As the night got later, the girls got looser. They were cracking up at each other's stories and jokes, and they were conversing with all the guys that stopped by to flirt. All of a sudden, Charlene looked up and saw Rich coming toward the table. Her facial expression changed.

"Hey, ladies," he said as he approached.

They all greeted him back.

"So, I thought it was a rumor, but it's true, you are pregnant," he said.

"Yes, I am," she replied.

"Who is the father?" he asked.

Everyone kind of looked at him in shock, not sure if he was being insulting or serious.

"My fiancé, Isaac," Charlene replied.

"Oh . . . OK," he said giving, her an awkward look. "I just thought you would have told me."

"Things have been kind of hectic, but I planned on contacting you."

At this point Paige and Jasmine were looking back and forth between Charlene and Rick like they were watching a television program. They both knew what had happened between the two of them and were finding his subtle hints quite interesting.

"OK, well, before you head out of here I'd like to talk to you," he said, realizing that he couldn't continue on with his live audience.

"Sure, I'll come over there by you," Charlene replied.

Rich walked off, and Charlene made a face of irritation.

"I knew that was coming," she said.

"What?" Paige asked.

"Him wondering if the baby is his," Charlene replied.

"You would think he'd just be happy that you're not saying the baby is his," Jasmine added.

"Yeah, you would think," Charlene added.

They tried to resume their mood and tempo for the evening as if that hadn't happened, but it was taking a bit of effort. Rich had bust up the groove, definitely for Charlene. As she started to wonder if she was playing herself, calling Isaac her fiancé with such confidence, her phone rang. She looked at the caller ID and got all excited. She wondered if Isaac had an answer for her, and hoped that he didn't want to have some deep conversation right then when she wouldn't be able to have one. Still, she answered with anticipation, hoping that he had called to say he loved her.

"Hey, babe," she answered, kind of loud over the music.

"My father died," he replied.

Chapter 35

She was numb sitting there at the funeral. There were over two hundred and fifty people there, and although she was proud to be there as the fiancé of Isaac, she would have much rather not have been there.

People were crying and breaking down, and some were sitting there paying close attention to the preacher. Isaac's mother was a wreck, and his aunts and other family members weren't holding up too well, either. Charlene felt emotionally absent; she didn't know how to feel. Isaac was just quiet and still. He hadn't said a word all day, and even though he looked like he was crying there were no tears falling from his eyes. Charlene could only imagine what was going through his mind.

The preacher said some great things about Mr. Milton and every word of it true including what an honor it was to know him. The more he discussed what a great father and husband he was, the weaker Charlene got. Eventually she let go and the tears came. Charlene and Isaac's mother both had faces moist from tears and Isaac was still dry-eyed. Charlene was crying for him, too, though, for the pain she knew he felt. His father meant everything to him; he wanted to be just like him. Charlene silently prayed that this wouldn't prevent him from being the father and husband he wanted to be, and that even though his father didn't get to see the baby as planned it wouldn't change his heart about being a family man, now that there was nobody to show. It was a silent and selfish prayer, but Charlene did worry about it some.

After the funeral everybody gathered at Isaac's parents' house. Charlene sat in the corner with one of Isaac's younger cousins. Tatiana was seven and she was as cute as a doll baby. Charlene sat with her, hoping to avoid all the depressing faces scattered throughout the house including Isaac's. She knew he had every right to pout but she didn't know what to say or do. Some of his family members came up to her to rub her belly and tell her how excited they were. Some of them asked about the sex, and if male was she going to name him Isaac Junior. She told them she thought that's what Isaac wanted, and if so then, yes, she would. She was happy that the baby inside of her was causing a more positive conversation, one about life and not death. She wished that Isaac could even for a second think that way. She could only hope that even if he didn't then, that he would at some point soon. What she was afraid of was that he wouldn't, or not for a long time. She knew it was hard, the death of his father was literally his worst nightmare come true. He loved his father so much; it would take more than the birth of his child to erase the pain from the death of his father.

Chapter 36

The next couple of weeks were definitely tumultuous for Isaac and Charlene. Charlene had only two weeks left before she had to go on maternity leave and remain bedridden. Isaac took only a week off before he returned back to work full time, and to most people it didn't appear as if he'd had a sufficient amount of time to mourn his loss. As much as it was his fear to lose his father, the one man on Earth that he treasured and looked up to, he hadn't prepared himself mentally or emotionally for that day. Then again, he knew, we are never quite prepared.

It had crossed Charlene's mind that Isaac might feel differently about marrying her now that his father was no longer around to see it. She was saddened by his death as well, but she also couldn't help but worry about her future and the future of the life growing inside of her. Charlene had grown a lot over the past few months. She had not only learned about herself, but also about other people. For the first time in her life, she was happy that she had had the past that she did, because she realized that otherwise she wouldn't be the person she was today. She wouldn't be aware of the good and the bad in the world; she wouldn't know what a lack of self-esteem can do to a person, and how easy it is to mistake sex for love and acceptance.

Charlene knew that she probably wouldn't get an answer from Isaac anytime soon, because the timing was wrong. Still, she couldn't help but wonder what his answer was to her question, about whether he could handle it now that he knew about her past. She was dying to know but never had a chance to bring it back up, and no time ever felt right. She hoped that he wouldn't bring it up one day and tell her he decided that he couldn't. That was one of the reasons she went ahead and set the date for their wedding. She figured she would make it that much harder for him to back out. The day she told him, she thought he could use a happy conversation. He did seem excited and agreed upon the date, so she figured that he was all for things moving forward.

A couple of days later he called and asked what the wedding colors were, and that took Charlene by surprise. She didn't know why he asked because he didn't say before he rushed off the phone, she was happy that his mind was on the wedding and not constantly harping on his father's death. She got the feeling he was telling somebody or doing something with the information, because he asked the question and said he would call her right back. The girls were wearing fuchsia, black and white and the guys a blush pink, black and white. Initially she wanted a destination wedding, but she decided against it because she would be too far along to travel.

The wedding plans were the only thing that kept Charlene in a great mood. She was able to drift off to her fairy-tale land, and just plan for and imagine her fairy-tale wedding. Her parents were paying for most of it, but Isaac already told her whatever they didn't agree to pay for he would cover, so she was in heaven. She was having it at Palisades Palace, and the ceremony was to be held outside in their beautiful chapel. She'd ordered a dozen doves and a dove trainer to release the doves upon the announcement of man and wife. The reception hall was one of the most exquisite in New York. It had three sections of tables, raised at different heights. It was ideal for the ballerina she'd always dreamed of having at her wedding. She wanted a ballerina dressed in all white to do a nice ballet dance, and she had finally hired someone she really liked. Things were coming together. Soon she would have to do everything over the phone from home, so she tried to do a lot in advance.

She was in the middle of looking at the new *Brides* magazine when her phone rang. She answered and it was Rich.

"What happened to you that night?" he asked.

"I'm sorry. Isaac's father passed away and I rushed out."

"Oh, you guys are back together."

"Yeah, we worked most of it out."

"No wonder you said it's not my baby."

"No, Rich, I said that because it's not."

"I think we need to sit and talk," he said.

"I don't think it's a good idea for you to come over."

"Meet me at Sammy's restaurant," he said.

"When?"

"In an hour . . . We need to have this covered so that it doesn't come back up later."

"It won't," she said.

"Yeah, OK. You say that until the *Maury Show* is calling me."

"Fine, Rich, I will come for a second. I can't stay, though."

Charlene felt a little uneasy about going to meet Rich, but for some reason she was always a little weak for him. She wasn't sure if it was because of all the guys she'd dealt with before Isaac he treated her the best, for what that was worth, or just that he was so damn fine. Either way, she knew that it would be one more secret from Isaac. After some thought, she figured she would rather get it out of the way, than risk it becoming a rumor or some misunderstanding that got back to Isaac.

Once she got to the restaurant, it was crowded, and she immediately wanted to back out. Just as she was contemplating getting back in her car and calling Rich to clear it up she felt a tap on her shoulder. She turned and it was Rich. He was dressed in a tan sweater with saggy jeans and his constructions, with a Padres baseball cap. He had two huge diamonds, one in each ear and a dangling diamond chain with a cross at the end. It looked like he'd just gotten there himself, because he had the keys to his Benz still dangling in his hand. As usual his beautiful complexion and big brown eyes turned her into mush as soon as she looked at him.

"Hey, I was thinking what a bad choice of location," she said.

"I know. Well, you said you weren't staying long, so let's sit and chat over there for a second," he said, pointing at an almost-empty corner of the place.

They started to head across the floor, asking people to excuse them and trying to make room for her to waddle through. She passed one large group of people, and she heard a voice that was too familiar.

"Charlene?"

Charlene looked up and it was Isaac. She almost fainted. She felt like this was one more thing to add to the big mess her life had become. There was a point when she practically had a second identity, and now she couldn't seem to sneak and do one damn thing without getting caught.

"Hey, Isaac," she replied with a nervous twitch in her voice that was a new problem she'd acquired.

"What are you doing here?" he asked.

Charlene knew that he'd already seen Rich, because he looked right at him when he called her name. Luckily, Rich was smart enough to keep walking, but that also made her look guiltier.

"I stopped by to get some of those shrimp, I was craving them."

She wanted to disappear. What was she to say? To lie or not to lie, at this point what was the difference?

"Oh, OK. Go ahead. Your friend is waiting for you," Isaac said and turned back around and started chatting back with the guy that he was sitting with.

Charlene looked at the back of his head for about five seconds. Then she glanced over at the corner and saw Rich sitting there looking in a different direction trying to look normal. Charlene heaved her oversized purse over her shoulder and walked right out the exit.

Chapter 37

She ended up at Paige's house that night.

She cried on the way there, and by the time she got there she was ready to try to face the fact that maybe happiness wasn't for her. Maybe she couldn't change who she was, no matter how hard she tried. Maybe we are who we are, and although we can grow into better people maybe we can't erase the innate creature that we are. What bothered Charlene the most was that she had had so many bad vibes about going to meet Rich and still she went. Trying to be slick, trying to do wrong and think she could hide it away and look right.

The part that hurt so much was that she knew Isaac would have no reason to believe anything that she said about it. She wasn't even going there to see Rich with bad intentions, but still there was no explanation. She couldn't tell Isaac that the only reason she went was to assure Rich that the baby was not his. She drove erratically down the highway, oblivious to all the other cars surrounding her. Her mind was filled with a million thoughts including replays of what had happened.

Just as she exited off the highway, her cell phone rang. She looked on the caller ID and it was Rich. She was hesitant to answer, but she realized she owed him an explanation and she was curious if he and Isaac had had any sort of conversation after she escaped.

"Are you OK?" he asked.

"I'm fine," she said.

"I'm really sorry about that . . . That was Isaac, right?"

"Yeah, it was. I have some kind of luck these days."

Rich slightly laughed. "Listen, I wanted to talk to you to let you know if the baby was mine I would be there, and I wanted to tell you that face-to-face."

"I appreciate that, Rich. You are such a sweetheart," she said as her emotions got the best of her and tears started forming in her eyes.

"I mean that."

"I almost wish it was. But from the date the doctor gave me I was already pregnant that night I saw you."

"Wow, OK."

"But if something changes, you'll be the first I let know."

"All right, baby, take care."

Charlene drove the rest of the way to Paige's in deep thought. She found herself in that place quite often lately.

Once she got there, before she even took off her coat she was telling Paige the story, detail by detail.

"You are sure that Rich is not the father, right?" Paige asked.

"Yes, it was only one time and according to how many weeks I am, I was already pregnant."

"Well, you need to make sure things are smoothed out with Isaac, because I'm sure him seeing you with another man doesn't help his doubts."

"If it was another man, that wouldn't be as bad as it being Rich," Charlene replied.

"That's true."

"It's a waste trying to explain myself, it's just going to sound like one big lie or excuse."

"So you think it's best you ignore the elephant in the room? I know you can't be saying that, because you and him are supposed to be getting married this year. That's not a healthy relationship."

"I will say something. Besides, I'm sure if I didn't, he will, and we will have a huge fight or he will call off the engagement again," Charlene said.

"Well, do something, Charlene. You and Isaac need to be able to let go of the past, and look forward to your future with your baby and making your marriage work."

"It all sounds so easy, but yet it isn't that simple," Charlene said after thinking over what Paige said.

"Life isn't simple, sweetie," Paige responded.

Charlene was frustrated and confused. She knew Paige was right, and certainly her life hadn't been easy. She knew in her heart that she was blessed, but she felt like the deceit from her life had become a curse. What was stressing her most was that she didn't know how to read Isaac's reaction. She had called him on the phone and he still acted calm and as if he wasn't even upset, but she knew that he had to be. At Sammy's he had said to her that her friend was waiting, and she was certain he had looked dead at Rich, so she didn't quite get why he wasn't asking any questions or flipping out. She didn't know if it was his version of what she had done when she found Lacy in his bed that morning, or that he had given up. She wanted to believe that he didn't want to upset her while she was pregnant, but she couldn't imagine he would let that roll off his back.

Chapter 38

Charlene was grocery shopping to prepare for the many hours she would spend in her home until the baby was born. She wanted Isaac to come but he had said he had errands to run. Charlene had already figured the real reason was that he was in no mood to be around her. They had been having some generic conversations since they saw each other in Sammy's, and she finally offered the information one day on the phone.

"Just in case you were wondering, me and Rich met that day to put some things to an end."

"OK," Isaac replied.

"Seriously, Isaac, it was nothing like that."

"OK. I believe you."

"I know you probably don't have a reason to, but you have to know that I am not the young dumb girl I was back then. I am not up to no good. I was meeting Rich to make sure some things were clear and over."

"OK, that was much needed, I'm sure."

Charlene gave up. She couldn't decipher his comments and didn't feel like a fight so she let it go. If he wanted to be so cool and let it go, so would she. She still had to go shopping by herself, though, this afternoon. She got all the snacks and drinks she wanted, food to cook and easy food to microwave. She felt like she was getting ready to hibernate for the winter.

Just as she was almost done with her food shopping, she turned down an aisle and instantly became a little uncomfortable with what she saw. There was a young girl about sixteen years old, and she was with a guy that looked about four years her senior. They caught her attention because he was touching on her in inappropriate places and kissing on her, and the girl was giggling away. She was about 5'5", 125 pounds with a pretty, curvaceous shape. She was medium brown with light brown slanted eyes, pouty full lips and a pair of adorable dimples. She was gorgeous and looked full of life. She was dressed in a tight shirt, which showed too much of her boobs, and infectious jeans—that's what Charlene called jeans that were so tight they could cause a yeast infection. The guy was dressed like a typical urban young male in a music video, with saggy jeans and a fitted hat. They were looking for whipping cream in the refrigerated section, and Charlene could overhear them making reference to their plans for it when they got home.

Charlene continued to watch the young girl and guy, intrigued and almost mesmerized by their mannerisms and behavior. Once Charlene realized how rude she was by staring at them, she looked away. She looked back one more time when she heard the girl giggle again; he had put his hand in her back pocket to cup her behind. Charlene looked the girl dead in her face and she realized that she knew the young lady. She knew her very well. She was Charlene when she was younger. She could tell from the looks on the girl's face that she welcomed every bit of the attention and actually felt quite special that this young man was spending time with her. She knew that this girl couldn't tell that all the groping and fondling this guy was doing to her in the store wasn't only an inability to control his attraction to her, but also his lack of respect for her. She was just a piece of ass to him, and didn't care whether anyone around knew that. She, on the other hand, was on cloud nine; young and clueless. Charlene felt sorry for her, deeply sorry for her. The way she had felt for herself the day she finally got a clue. It's almost easier to live in the dark than to face reality when you're in those shoes. It's an embarrassing truth.

Charlene finally managed to pull herself away from the spectacle they were making of themselves and leave the aisle. In the back of her mind she was hoping this girl would figure out what she was doing wrong. Charlene wanted to tell her but knew that the young lady would say something rude and obscene in response, so Charlene decided to mind her business. As Charlene finished gathering her things she could hear the girl from time to time, giggling in some other aisle.

Approximately ten minutes later Charlene advanced to the checkout lane with about two hundred dollars' worth of groceries. She waited for the customer in front of her to begin to pay for her items before she started unloading her cart. Frozen dinners, milk, orange juice, butter . . . Charlene was placing each item on the counter, trying to make sure she didn't forget anything at the same time. The sound of laughter broke her concentration. She looked over her shoulder and the young Charlene and the guy were standing on line behind her. Not wanting to be rude and stare or look sympathetic, Charlene quickly turned back around to finish. She glanced back at the young lady once or twice as she waited for her groceries to be rung up and bagged.

Just as Charlene went to pull out her money, the young lady placed the whipping cream and some chocolate sauce on the counter. As the young grocery clerk bagged the last of her groceries, Charlene took a pen and wrote on the back of the receipt the cashier had just handed her. She waited for the boy to finish loading the cart, and before she left she folded the receipt and turned to hand the note to the girl.

While Charlene walked away the girl looked down at the

paper in her hand. Initially the girl looked confused, but she discreetly opened the paper and began to read it. The note read:

If you don't respect yourself, these boys never will. Take it from me.

Charlene looked back and saw the girl reading it. Just as the girl finished she looked up and saw Charlene watching her. Charlene gave her a slight smile and a nod, turned away and walked out the automatic doors of the supermarket.

Once Charlene reached her car, she was happy that she had done that. She felt like the young Charlene really did comprehend what it was that she was saying, and even if she didn't change right away Charlene hoped she would get it together quickly enough to become a different older Charlene.

Chapter 39

She had spent some time with Isaac over the following week, but not enough to gauge if things were totally back to normal. They ran a few errands together one day, and he picked her up for work once or twice. Today he had stopped by to bring her some things that she needed and he seemed to be in an emotional place. He came up to her and hugged her for about two minutes straight. Charlene didn't know if it stemmed from his father, her, the baby or something else. When she asked all he said was that it was nothing.

Charlene knew that even after all they had been through, she still loved Isaac and still wanted to marry him. She prayed that his feelings weren't too different. She was happy that she and Isaac had decided that she would do her bed rest at his apartment. She took that as a good sign, but wasn't sure if it bode well for the future. For all she knew Isaac would request a paternity test the minute the baby was born. But she understood that she had to take things day by day.

"I know I was supposed to give you an answer to something and I never did," he said out of nowhere.

Charlene was surprised he remembered, since she asked the question right before his father's death. She got a little nervous when he brought it up.

"I did think about it and, honestly, it is a lot to swallow. I can probably admit that if I knew when we met, we probably wouldn't have made it anywhere," he continued.

Charlene looked at him and then turned away, looking down. It didn't sound like he was saying what she wanted to hear, but still she knew that it was all real talk, and something she kind of already knew. She didn't respond.

"Still, now that we have all this history and a baby on the way it makes you look at things kind of different. I won't lie, I felt hoodwinked and bamboozled but I can't change that," he continued.

"Isaac, I'm sorry for that, and I really do love you," she finally interjected.

"I know you love me, and I love you, too. The thing is it's just not that easy," he replied.

There was silence for a second. Charlene could feel herself getting jittery and nervous about what was to follow.

"I don't want my daughter being teased, being called Jump-off Junior. It's like we have to move from this area altogether to leave the past here," Isaac continued.

"Maybe we can start over," she said.

"Maybe we can. We do have a wedding set and a baby on the way, if there is a reason to move on we have one," Isaac said. Then he paused, he seemed to be really thinking. "I don't think I've been saying it the right way. I thought about the question, and I can handle it. Maybe not as well as I should, and I will probably always be a little bothered by some of it, but I can handle it," he continued.

"Are you sure?" she asked, feeling beyond relieved to hear him say that.

"I'm sure. Nobody's perfect. We all have different flaws. I tried to live my life for my father and now that he is gone, I feel lost. No one has all the answers. I can believe that these were mistakes in your past and you have only been with me since we met."

For a second Charlene felt her heart skip a beat. She felt guilty knowing that in fact she had been with Rich a few months ago. She couldn't afford to worry or look guilty at this point, though, so she shook it off.

"I'm sure your father was very proud of you, as am I. I know I'm a better person because of you. I hope that you know that you're the only man I want. I'll never forget when you proposed to me and all the things you said, and how much I felt the same way. I knew that day that you were all I needed and if I could erase my past to make today better with you, I would."

"Well, let's just try to erase it as we go forward," he said, not appearing very touched by her speech.

Charlene felt great being able to clear the air with Isaac, or as much as they could at this moment. She felt blessed to have another chance at happiness. The rest would have to mend over time, and she hoped that it would. Between the incident with Lacy and the run-in with Rich, it would seem that neither of them had their relationship as first priority. They both were going to have to put in some extra effort to get back to where they were. All she wanted was to have the life he had promised her that day by the pond when he gave her the ring. It wasn't impossible, and she was willing to do what she could to get it there.

Chapter 40

The clock read 1:52 PM and Charlene was staring off into space as she swung her legs in impatience. Her nails tapped the table and the room's silence absorbed the tapping sound. Finally a vibration added to the tapping noise. Charlene's cell phone, which was sitting on the table, started to vibrate as it rang. She looked at the display screen and pressed TALK.

"Yeah?" she said into the phone.

"I'm outside," the voice said through the phone.

"Be right out," she said.

Charlene jumped off the seat, grabbed her stuff and headed toward the door. She had been waiting on Isaac for an hour or so and she was ready to go. Not only was she starved, she was looking forward to a day out. Charlene waddled down the hall, slowly stepped down the stairs and continued to waddle out the door. Isaac was sitting inside his car directly in front of her building. As soon as he looked up in her direction, he began to smile. Charlene was a sight to see. She looked absolutely gorgeous as she made her way to the car. She was dressed in a turquoise baby doll top that hugged her swollen breasts and lay over her round, pregnant belly. She wore fitted jeans with turquoise beaded thong sandals. Her hair lay in curls on her shoulders, and hovered over her glowing, flawless face.

Isaac had stepped out of the car as she got closer. He met her at the sidewalk and leaned in and gave her a soft kiss on her lips.

"Hey, babe," she said.

He took her by her arm and walked her to the passenger side of the car. He opened her door and helped her sit inside. Once she was all the way in, he closed the door beside her and walked back over to the driver's side.

As soon as he sat down and closed his door, Charlene joked, "I feel like an old lady."

Isaac laughed. "No, you're just getting older."

"Oooh, I don't like how that sounds."

"You still look good, baby," Isaac said.

"Thanks, baby, even though I know you're trying to make me feel better."

"No, never that," he said, chuckling as he pulled out onto the street.

There wasn't too much traffic, but the cars ahead were causing Isaac to drive a steady 35 miles per hour. It was a sunny, clear day, and New Yorkers always tried to cruise in their cars to take pleasure in the nice weather because they never knew when it would be gone for good. That was the same reason why Charlene didn't mind the not-so-fast speed. She was starving, but she, too, was enjoying the day. She had her head leaned back against the headrest and she was, tapping her thigh to the soft music in Isaac's car. That was, until she reached over and turned up the radio when she heard her song by Robin Thicke get introduced by the radio jock, Shaila. Charlene immediately started swaying side to side and humming.

"You and that dang song," Isaac said.

"Yeah, the same way you are with the Young Lloyd song," Charlene said as she snapped her fingers and swayed to Mr. Thicke's crooning.

As soon as she started to sing some, Isaac started laughing and reached out and turned down the volume.

"For real, babe, where do you want to go eat?"

"I thought you said we were going to Sea Shore," she replied.

"Just wanted to make sure you didn't change your mind, you know how funny you have been with your food."

"No, I can go for some shrimp, I'm starving since you took so long."

"Sorry, my mother needed me to move something at the house, so I stopped on my way to you."

"No problem," Charlene said as she turned the volume back up slightly.

She sat and swayed to the R&B music the rest of the ride as she enjoyed the scenery.

Twenty minutes later they were sitting inside Sea Shore. There was a decent crowd but it wasn't congested in the restaurant at all, like Charlene and Isaac liked it. The waiter had been by to take their order and had already given them their water and bread to start with. In the section next to Charlene and Isaac sat a large party of eleven, it looked as if they were celebrating. There was a Latin couple sitting two tables away and an old man sitting alone about four tables in the other direction. Light jazz music played overhead, and the sound of forks and plates clanking together filled the area. Charlene looked around at the other patrons and wait staff.

"You look so happy," Isaac said to Charlene as she chomped down on her bread.

"I'm hungry," Charlene said with a smile and a mouth full of bread.

"No, not that . . . That makes you look greedy."

"Ha, ha, ha," Charlene said sarcastically. "So what you mean, then?" she asked.

"I mean you just seem in a really good mood."

"I am. Why wouldn't I be? I am at one of my favorite restaurants, with one of my most favorite people on a beautiful day."

"That's good. I'm happy to see you're happy."

"Thanks, babe," Charlene said as she delved into her freshly buttered bread.

Charlene took a few bites and then went over his last response.

"Why, are you not happy?" she asked.

"Very much so."

"Good . . . What are you so happy about?"

"I'm happy to be spending forever with you. I'm happy that I'm with a woman that I love and that I can be proud of. I'm happy you're carrying my child inside of you and that we are going to make a wonderful family."

Charlene was speechless. She had not expected him to say such sweet things, and definitely never thought she would hear him say he was proud of her when she thought she was an embarrassment.

"Thank you, babe," she managed to say without breaking down.

"You don't have to thank me . . . Thank you. Thanks for choosing me."

"Izzy, you're going to make me cry . . . Stop it.

"I mean it. When I saw you walking toward the car today, I was mesmerized by how beautiful you were and how lucky I am to have you."

"Thank you, baby, I feel just as lucky. That's why I look so happy," Charlene said, giving him a big cheese smile.

At that moment the waiter brought over their salads with ranch dressing.

As soon as he walked away Isaac looked straight back into Charlene's eyes.

"I wanted you to start getting your stuff together to move in with me, so we are settled by the time the baby gets here."

"Oh, I thought we were waiting until after the wedding," Charlene responded, sounding a bit confused.

"Yeah, but we might as well get started this weekend, there's no real reason to wait. Besides, I don't want any more time to go by where I can't be with you."

"This weekend it is, then. I will call a U-Haul truck and arrange it."

"Great," Isaac said as he dived into his salad.

Charlene had no idea where this excess of emotion was coming from with Isaac, but she wasn't complaining. She didn't know how to react, really, so she tried to act as if it was normal.

However, maybe Isaac was reading her mind, because he added, "It's like I fell in love with you all over again."

"What, you had fallen out of love?" Charlene asked.

"Not at all. We all fall in love with our partners more than one time. It can be ten times throughout a long relationship. This is probably my second or third," he answered.

Charlene took a second and then said, "Second or third?"

"Yeah, I think right before I proposed to you may have been the second time. I didn't put my finger on it that time, but this time I know."

"Where did this come from?" she asked.

"I'm not sure. Maybe just thinking about how great our future is going to be together, or maybe seeing you waddle to my car today," Isaac said with a giggle.

"Cute," Charlene said with a hint of sarcasm.

"I feel like I'm in heaven with you right now," Isaac added.

"Well, I am very flattered, and I am just as happy with you

by my side. I love you so much already that I feel the way you do about us on a regular basis."

"Well, I'm sure when you finally move in and we are always together, the novelty will wear off," Isaac said, chuckling.

"Probably so," Charlene said, laughing back.

A steamy plate of shrimp scampi and yellow rice was placed on the table in front of Charlene by the waiter. Then he placed lobster tails in front of Isaac. Charlene didn't even wait for the waiter to leave before she took her fork and stabbed at one of the pink critters on her plate. Isaac giggled at the sight of Charlene's hunger taking over before he even picked up his fork. The two of them sat there enjoying their meal and enjoying each other. Isaac was right about one thing, Charlene was so very happy.

Chapter 41

The sun was about setting, and the winds were picking up. The weather called for a light jacket, but Charlene wouldn't know because she was indoors, as she had been for several days now. She was on the Web looking up information about mentoring young girls. Ever since that day in the supermarket she felt like she'd found her calling. She'd always wanted to do more with herself, and now she'd finally found something. Charlene realized that she would feel better if she could help young girls that are misguided and use her own experiences as a guiding tool. Charlene knew that having access to someone like her when she was growing up would have been a huge help. Charlene had been too afraid and ashamed to talk to her mother or sister, and her friends made what she was doing seem like the hip thing to do. She knew that those friends had influenced a lot of her decisions, and not having a positive role model to consult with didn't help. Her sister was out doing her own thing, and although her mother tried to keep her on the right track, Charlene always had seen that as just one more way her mother was strict and annoying.

She found a few sites, including the Big Brother and Big Sister programs, and she was looking for which one worked primarily with ill-advised young girls. For the first time in her life she felt passionate about something that didn't deal with herself. The more Charlene thought about it, the more she really was excited about it. She even hoped that she could somehow make it a new career. She knew that she could make a difference by sharing with these girls her stories of being loved and left, and of mistaking sexual attention for anything more than what it is. She wanted them to know that what they needed to do was learn how to love themselves—that that was the key to being a self-confident young lady and a well-rounded adult. It's easy for females to rely on males to solidify their worth, Charlene thought, but if we left it solely to them we would never know how great we are. Charlene only wished that when she was younger she had known what she knew now.

She was printing out some information when she felt this sudden pain in her side. She took a deep breath and tried to wait out the pain. After a few inhales and exhales, she still felt the pain. She continued to breathe in and out heavily until the pain subsided. She went ahead and started grabbing some of the documents off the printer to make sure it was printing the right stuff and correctly. After she reached over to get the second sheet, she felt the pain again. This time it was close to excruciating and she shrieked with pain. She remained still until the pain passed, and then as soon as the relief set in she burst out in tears. She instantly panicked and called Isaac. The phone rang five times and then went to voice mail. Charlene quickly hung up and called Paige.

"What's wrong?" Paige asked as soon as she heard her sister sobbing on the phone.

"I don't know. I am having pains and they hurt really badly," she said.

"Where?"

"On my side."

"The side of your stomach?"

"Yes, and it's really sharp."

"Maybe it's contractions, I'll be right over."

"Hurry," Charlene said through her tears.

Charlene patiently waited for her sister to arrive, as well as another pain. She lay flat on her back holding her stomach with both of her hands, praying that she wouldn't feel another one. For another ten minutes, she was pain free and almost relaxed when she felt another one. This one wasn't as severe but enough to make her hold her breath for a second. When the pain let up, more tears came down. She was so afraid and worried about the pains and where they were coming from. Last checkup she had, all was going well with the pregnancy, and her bed rest wasn't to begin for a few days so she didn't quite understand what she had done wrong. Her scheduled Cesarean was over two months away, and these pains represented warning signs to her. She tried to think of all the things she'd eaten, and if she had overworked herself at all that day. All she'd had to eat was some Polly-O cheese strips, and she had been cleaning up before she started research on the computer, but nothing strenuous that she could recall to trigger the pain she was feeling.

Paige arrived soon after and immediately grabbed some of Charlene's things to get ready to head to the emergency room. Once she had Charlene ready to go, they started to walk out together. Paige was holding Charlene's arm in case another pain started and overwhelmed her. They hadn't said too much to each other, and Paige seemed as worried as Charlene was. They both knew that this could be a bad situation, so they didn't want to say too much about it. They remained fairly silent until they got in the car.

"You're feeling OK?" Paige asked.

"Scared, but a little better . . . I haven't had any pains since you came."

"That's good, then. What did Isaac say?"

"I called him twice, I can't get him, I think he's still stuck in a meeting for work."

"We will keep trying him. He'll probably be pissed off if we don't try hard enough to get him. Leave him a message and tell him we are going to Lawrence Hospital."

Charlene reached in the backseat to get her phone out of her purse, and suddenly let out a loud groan as she felt another sharp pain in her side. She immediately sat forward and tried to brace herself through it. Paige looked at her frantically and with sympathy. After a few seconds, Charlene released her clenched hands from the seat and started breathing heavily. Her eyes began to well up with tears again.

"They're probably contractions, Leen," Paige said in a low tone.

"Yeah, I know."

They left the obvious unsaid: that if they were contractions, she would be having the baby prematurely. Neither of them wanted to discuss the possibility of losing the baby, or of it being too undeveloped to make it outside of Charlene.

Paige handed Charlene her phone and reminded her to call Isaac. Charlene took the phone and dialed his number. As much as Charlene was yearning to speak to Isaac she didn't want to talk with him about how this could mean losing the baby. She didn't want to hear the fear in his voice, or put the thought in his head that they may not have this child. She prayed that she would leave the hospital today with some medicine or information, and everything would be fine. In the back of Charlene's mind she also didn't want this to be a reminder of why she was having such a fragile pregnancy to begin with. She was hoping that this was just a scare and that it would all be over with soon. Despite all her fears, she wanted Isaac by her side more than anything right now. She dialed the number and waited for his voice mail to leave a message.

"Hey, Charlene," he said when he answered the phone, obviously having looked at his caller ID.

"Isaac?" she asked, surprised he'd answered.

"Yeah," he said matter-of-factly.

"Where are you?" she asked.

Isaac could hear it in her voice.

"What's wrong?" he asked, sounding alarmed.

"I am having some pains and I'm on my way to Lawrence Hospital with Paige."

"Are you OK?" he asked.

"I'm not sure," she replied, trying to sound optimistic.

"I'm leaving now, I'll meet you there."

"OK, we will probably be there in a few minutes."

Charlene hung up the phone and sat quietly beside Paige. A million thoughts ran through her mind. She was worried, afraid and optimistic all at the same time. She kept telling herself she hadn't come this far to lose the baby. She loved this little person inside of her, and it would crush her and Isaac both.

"What did Isaac say?" Paige asked, breaking Charlene's train of thought.

"He is going to meet us there," she responded.

"Good, he needs to be there, Charlene. Regardless of its big or small, he should be there."

"I know," Charlene mumbled back, in no mood to talk.

Then, suddenly, the sharp pain returned. This time it caused Charlene to lift out her seat in search for a comfortable position to endure it. With her upper body suspended halfway out the seat, Charlene breathed her way through it. Just when she thought that the pain was going to subside, it started back. She once again started breathing as heavily as she could and clutched the seat. She continued to do this for a few minutes until she realized there was going to be no relief this time. Paige kept looking over at her, rubbing her leg as she drove as fast as she could.

They eventually reached the hospital. Paige jumped up and went around to Charlene's side of the car. Charlene was still clenched up in pain as Paige's helped her out. They managed to make their way through the hospital doors and up to the nurse's station.

"She is pregnant, and it looks like she is in labor very early," Paige said in a crackly voice.

It must have finally hit Paige, all the emotions and fear she had felt for her sister, because she began to cry. She wished she could remain calm and optimistic for Charlene, but she lost it.

The nurse, seeing the look of pain on Charlene's face and Paige's emotion, picked up on the sense of urgency and hopped out of her seat to assist Charlene into a wheelchair. Then she wheeled Charlene down the hallway into a Labor and Delivery room and placed her next to the table. Charlene tried to ask questions along the way, but she could barely respond. She'd had no relief from the pain since it had started in the car. She couldn't even cry, she couldn't release that energy because she needed it all to bear the pain. Paige answered most of the questions about the timing of the pains, and Charlene tried to describe what it was like.

A few moments later, another nurse arrived and with the help of both nurses, Charlene was up on the delivery table with a fetal monitor attached to her. They were taking vitals and all other information when the first nurse said to the other nurse, "She is bleeding some."

"Where?"

"Her panties have blood in them."

Charlene looked up to see what the second nurse's expression conveyed but it was too late, she had run out to get a doctor. Charlene then glanced at Paige—she was standing in the corner with her hand over her mouth, sobbing. Everything had gone so bad, so quickly that she had completely lost all her composure. Charlene started crying as well, and she reached out her hand to her sister. Paige hurried over and held it.

"It's going to be okay," Paige said.

Both of their faces drenched from tears, it was obvious that neither one of them thought this was going to turn out okay, but it was the right thing to say. Paige rubbed Charlene's hand as they held on as tightly as they could.

Soon the doctor walked in. He immediately checked the fetal monitor. He then sat down at the foot of the bed, put on his gloves, lifted the cloth over her waist and began to examine her.

He told the nurse to connect an IV, they didn't have much time.

"You are fully dilated, you are about to have this baby."

"I'm supposed to have a Cesarean," Charlene managed to get out.

"Miss, this baby is heading out, its head is too low to wait. If I prep you for a C-section by the time I go in there to get it, the baby will already have come out and there would be nothing to get," the doctor said.

"Can you call my doctor, Dr. Ginyard?" Charlene asked.

"You do not understand, there is no time for all of that."

As soon as he made that point, Charlene shrieked with pain from another sharp contraction.

The doctor and nurses then started all that other medical preparation that they do. Paige stood over Charlene, looking like a mess. Her eyes were bloodshot, and her nose and eyes were running. Charlene was trying to see what was going on around her, and yet remain as calm as she could to endure the pain.

There was so much noise and chaos, she could barely comprehend any one thing.

"I'm breaking your water," the doctor informed Charlene.

Charlene could feel the large gush of moisture release from her body.

Then the doctor told to her push. Charlene hadn't taken any Lamaze classes, but she had seen childbirth portrayed enough on television to know what she was supposed to do. She began to push, and the pain was so overbearing, she let out a loud yell and stopped. The doctor began saying something to a nurse, and she came and injected something into the IV. The machine attached to Charlene was beeping and blinking, and the doctor and nurses kept watching it. Along with the machines in the room, nobody seemed to be calm. Everyone— from the nurses, to the doctor and Paige—looked frantic and focused on what was going on. Poor Charlene was the only one oblivious to what everyone else saw, but if it looked down there anything like it felt to her she could understand the panic.

"Doctor, please bring my baby out alive," she said with tears streaming down her face.

The doctor and the nurses looked back at her with looks of sympathy, none of them responding right away.

"OK, I'm going to need you to push for me."

Charlene tried to push once again for as long as she could before the pain forced her to release.

"She is hemorrhaging, we have to try something else," the doctor said to a nurse as he gestured for her to get something.

Charlene could still hear the machines beeping and could see one of the nurse's sad facial expressions. Charlene held out her hand again, and Paige walked over and held it tight. They both cried and held hands while the doctors and nurses worked around them. After a moment went by, Charlene was completely calm and oblivious to her surroundings. She had her sister's hand in hers, and she could feel the love and support right in her fingertips, telling her that it was going to be all right.

Chapter 42

Isaac walked in, and the first person he saw in the waiting room was Jasmine. Paige had called her when she was sent out of the room for a few moments. He went up to the nurse behind the table and asked for Charlene Tanner.

After a few moments of pacing, a doctor walked out and greeted him.

"Are you the father?" the doctor asked.

"Yes, I am," Isaac answered.

"Come with me."

The doctor walked Isaac down a long hallway. The farther they got, the more Isaac could hear baby cries and noises. He felt a flutter in his stomach from the excitement and the fear that he was feeling. The doctor passed a few rooms with families and nursing mothers in them, and Isaac peeked in each one looking for a sign of Charlene or their baby.

Finally the doctor stopped. Isaac looked to his left and there was a window looking into a room of babies.

"It's a girl," the doctor said, pointing to one of them.

Isaac looked in and saw the little bin, with the tiny body wrapped in a pink blanket with the last name Tanner on it. He immediately began to tear up. He tried to wipe his tears, but the emotion was taking over.

"She is premature, but she is breathing on her own and it looks like she will be just fine."

"That is so great, thank you, doctor," Isaac said, trying to gain his composure.

"You can hold her very shortly."

Isaac couldn't break his stare from the little lady inside the plastic bin. She was gorgeous.

Just as he turned to ask to see Charlene, he saw Paige walking up the hall with the phone to her ear.

"Can I see Charlene?" he asked.

The doctor gave him a look, one that Isaac wasn't prepared to see or understand.

"What?" Isaac asked.

As he saw Paige getting closer, from the look on her face he could tell that the doctor's expression was self-explanatory.

"Where is Charlene?" Isaac asked in a panicked tone.

"I am so sorry, but she didn't make it," the doctor replied.

Isaac jerked his head and neck back in disbelief about what he had heard. It was almost as if he was going to shake himself back to reality. He took a few steps backward to sit in the seat beside him. He put his face in his hands and shook his head several times as the doctor tried to explain.

"Giving birth is strenuous on the body. Her uterus ruptured during labor, and she was hemorrhaging really badly and her pressure began to fall. We managed to save the baby, but we couldn't control the bleeding. Despite all of our efforts, it wasn't successful. I'm so sorry."

Just at that point, Paige reached the area where Isaac and the doctor were standing.

"I was holding her hand, I felt her let go," Paige said as she burst out in tears.

Paige was completely hysterical. She looked like she had been through hell and back. Her eyes were bloodshot; her face was flustered and blotchy. She stood there with tears rolling down her face, sobbing uncontrollably. Isaac was numb, and at first didn't react to the sight of Paige's pain. After a few seconds of watching Paige, he stood up to hold her.

The doctor took this as a sign to walk away. There was nothing more he could say at this point.

The more Paige shook in his arms, the more he began to feel the pain in her heart and his own. Then his own numbness began to wear off, and the tears began to roll down his face. Charlene's angelic face was all he could see. He mumbled some things to himself as his tears got bigger and his shakes heavier.

"Why? Why?" he mumbled.

He was speaking to himself or God.

He was saying a lot through his tears, some that couldn't be understood. He was in pain. The joy from the birth of his child was completely smothered by the pain from the death of his fiancée. First his father, now Charlene. Isaac felt like his world was crashing down right before his eyes.

Paige and Isaac stood there, just holding on tightly to each other, trying to squeeze out the pain. A few people walked by them, and one even stopped to look through the window at the babies not too many steps away. Still, they didn't move. Isaac was hoping that it wasn't real, that the doctor was going to come back and say something different. The longer he stood there, the more it set in. This was one time Isaac didn't want to hear the truth.

Chapter 43

Four months had gone by, and Isaac was carrying his daughter, Charese Tanner Milton, into her grandmother's house. It was unusually warm for a fall night and Isaac thought it would be a great chance to make good on the visit he had promised Mrs. Tanner for two weeks already. The door opened and Ann Tanner was standing on the other side with a big smile on her face. She stepped out the way as Isaac eased by with Charese in his arms. Once he was inside, he turned back to give Mrs. Tanner a kiss on the cheek.

"Hi, Isaac," she said as she leaned her cheek outward to receive his kiss.

As Isaac walked toward the living room he unraveled the blanket that little Charese was covered in. When he reached the couch, he placed the blanket on an arm and pulled off Charese's little baby beanie hat. By that time Mrs. Tanner was standing beside him with her arms extended to take Charese off his hands. Isaac carefully placed the baby in her arms. As soon as Charese was pressed close against Mrs. Tanner's chest, just like most grandmothers, she lit up with joy.

"Hey there, angel face," Mrs. Tanner sang in Charese's face.

Charese cooed and kicked her feet as her grandmother wiggled her finger by her side. Isaac sat by and watched the loving fun they were sharing. Isaac had been by at least four times since the baby was born, and Mrs. Tanner had been by his condo quite often as well. Still, it was never easy to see his daughter in the arms of the mother of his lost love. Not only did Mrs. Tanner look so much like Charlene it made it hard for him not to think of her, it was a reminder that Mrs. Tanner would be the closest that Charese would ever get to her mother in the flesh. The look in Isaac's eyes showed both his pain and pleasure at the sight of them together. He often felt thankful that Charlene had given him such a beautiful gift, but he also was wracked with guilt for wanting to have this child, knowing it was a risk. He'd been filled with mixed emotions since Charlene's death. Only time would make these visits easier to deal with, so meanwhile Isaac carried himself the best he could.

"She looks just like her mother," Mrs. Tanner said.

"I know. Everyone says that," Isaac replied.

"As she gets more of her features, I can see she has your eyes, but when I look in her face I see Charlene."

"I know. I'm happy about that but I will admit it doesn't make it easy to look at her sometimes."

"Amen. That's OK, that's why this is my little angel face."

The room fell silent for a second, as Mrs. Tanner rocked Charese and gazed into her eyes.

"I'm really happy you put Tanner in her name as well so she can grow up and never forget her mother."

"I wouldn't let that happen," Isaac said.

Isaac's eyes began to moisten, and his voice began to crack and he knew at that point he couldn't take much more of the emotional moment. He walked toward the couch to take a seat, hoping to break the momentum.

"Isaac, I never mentioned it before, but I heard about all what you and Charlene went through during her pregnancy, and I wanted to make sure I told you that I'm happy to see you guys were strong enough to get through it."

"Thanks," Isaac said, trying to keep it short. He really had no desire to have a conversation about Charlene right now. With both his father and fiancée passing months apart, Isaac had been an emotional wreck. He had been doing his very best to remain strong for his daughter, but it didn't take much to weaken his spirit so he didn't want to take the risk.

"It was my fault she was that way. I was so strict on her," Mrs. Tanner continued. "I never trusted her to do the right thing, so she didn't trust herself. I know that now. I wish I had the chance to tell her that."

"If we all had one more chance to tell her some things, I'm sure we would all take it."

Footsteps began to approach the living room doorway and after a few moments Webster Tanner was standing in the living room.

"Is that my little angel?" Mr. Tanner asked as he walked toward his wife and swooped Charese out of her arms.

"This is all he talks about these days, Isaac," Ann said to Isaac. He is driving me crazy . . . Charese this, Charese that."

Mr. Tanner took a break from cuddling with Charese to extend his hand to shake Isaac's hand.

"Hey, Mr. Tanner," Isaac finally said.

"Hi, Isaac. My apologies, I been looking forward to seeing her. Excuse my manners."

"I understand, she is the new addition to the family, she excites everyone," Isaac said.

Ann stood up after the room fell silent.

"Would you like anything to drink?" she asked Isaac.

"No, I'm OK for now," he replied.

"I'll take a glass of water, Ann," Mr. Tanner said.

Isaac and Mr. Tanner sat in the room alone for a few moments. Isaac pulling himself together from the intense talk he'd just had with Mrs. Tanner, hoping that was the end of it. Mr. Tanner was never very talkative, and today was no different. He sat and played with Charese in his arms and was in his own little world. Mrs. Tanner returned with the glass of water and sat down beside her husband.

As the four of them sat there in the room, Charlene's presence was felt. There was a picture of her sitting on the end table taken when she graduated from junior high school. She looked absolutely gorgeous, holding a rose, wearing a blue gown, with a huge smile on her face. As Isaac sat there he smiled at the picture sitting across from him and at Charlene's daughter. And with Charlene's parents in their happiest state, it was as if Charlene was telling him, *"Izzy, everything is going to be just fine."*

SHE'S NO ANGEL

Janine A. Morris

The following questions are intended to enhance your group's discussion of this book.

DISCUSSION QUESTIONS

1. Why do women lie to guys they date about how many men they have slept with and how sexually experienced they are?

2. Why is it so hard for men, unlike women, to overlook a woman's indiscretions?

3. The usual stereotype is promiscuous girls usually come from a home without a father figure. What is the explanation for the girl that does have a father figure but is still just as sexual?

4. Is a woman's inability to have children a valid reason for a man who strongly desires children to leave her?

5. Is "honesty's the best policy" a realistic motto to live up to in a relationship? Is the truth about "mistakes" and indiscretions better kept a secret?

6. Do you think it's intimidating to be with or marry a successful black man due to the image that they're the "cream of the crop" so as their woman you'd have to always feel "good enough for them" or risk them "upgrading"?

7. How do you judge a woman's worth? Through her character, career, beauty, or other traits? And do her indiscretions lessen her worth?

8. Are most people just a product of their environment? Charlene grew up in a neighborhood where people

didn't have high expectations or standards and the females didn't carry themselves with the highest regard. So were Charlene's actions inevitable?

9. At what age can you no longer use the "I was young and dumb" excuse? What age is it that you become too old to do certain immoral and scandalous things?

10. Do you think Charlene should have chosen to carry her child despite the fact that it was such a risk to her own life?